The Last Word

The Last
Word

A DEADLY DEADLINES
MYSTERY

Gerri Lewis

**CROOKED
LANE**

NEW YORK

Copyright © 2024 by Gerri Lewis INK

All rights reserved.

Published in the United States by Crooked Lane Books, an imprint of The Quick Brown Fox & Company LLC.

Crooked Lane Books and its logo are trademarks of The Quick Brown Fox & Company LLC.

Library of Congress Catalog-in-Publication data available upon request.

ISBN (hardcover): 978-1-63910-631-8
ISBN (ebook): 978-1-63910-632-5

Cover illustration by Rob Fiore

Printed in the United States.

www.crookedlanebooks.com

Crooked Lane Books
34 West 27th St., 10th Floor
New York, NY 10001

First Edition: February 2024

10 9 8 7 6 5 4 3 2 1

To my husband Bob
and my son Christian
No explanations needed!

Chapter One

N o sooner had I slid into one of the coveted sidewalk tables outside Tazza when I sensed my mistake. Looking up, I saw the
Nosy Parkers at the next table over. Gabby's back was to me, though
her sister and I were nearly face-to-face. I sighed inwardly. With the
gossipy Parker sisters within breathing distance, all thoughts of orga-
nizing my day with a quiet cup of chamomile faded.

"Look who's here," Abby said, clapping her hands in delight—or
was she rubbing them in anticipation? "Winter Snow, obituary writer
extraordinaire."

Gabby—a sturdy counterweight to her wiry sister—turned,
smiled, and leaned toward me conspiratorially.

"Who died?" she asked, making it sound like a crime.

In fact, the people I would be writing about today had lived fascinating lives, and I couldn't wait to memorialize them the way they
deserved. Instead, I resigned myself and smiled back. Any perceived
lack of cordiality on my part and I'd be grist for the rumor mill.

"Ladies, how nice to see you," I said. "What brings you out so
early?"

Clear summer mornings in Ridgefield, Connecticut, are always brimming with walkers pushing strollers, trotting alongside dogs, or power-hiking up Main Street. Looping around the village is one of my favorite ways to start the day, especially when I end up in one of the charming coffee shops that substitutes for my nonexistent office. I noted that the Nosy Parkers, donned in matching flip-flop sandals, weren't dressed for walking.

"People-watching is always the best in the mornings," said Gabby in a breathless giggle. "You get the juiciest stories by just sitting here with your coffee."

And eavesdropping, I added mentally.

"Everyone who's anyone is out early in this town," said Abby.

"Not everyone," corrected her sister. "The Flower Lady doesn't always get started as early as she should, if you want my opinion."

"This from a woman who could kill a plant by looking at it," said Abby with a smirk.

I looked toward the brilliant blues and yellows dripping over the sides of the hanging baskets affixed to the lampposts lining Main Street. The flowers flourished all summer long thanks to Spencer, who rode around in a John Deere Gator with heavy watering equipment loaded in the back and a furry friend named Biscuit panting on the passenger seat. The vision always made me smile.

"Looks to me like she's doing all right," I said.

Failing to stir the flowerpot, Gabby shrugged, ready for something more scandalous. The "whisper campaign," as I called it, could be lightning fast in our small community. It could also linger on, morphing as it went, as in the telephone game. And the Nosy Parkers did much to fuel that change—though they always preserved kernels of truth. As much as townies might cross the street to stay out of the narrative, they would also pull up a chair to hear it.

"Save my seat," I said, getting up to head inside the coffee shop, where I'd decided on a visit to the unisex bathroom for a welcome break.

A minute later, leaning against the wall and waiting for the door to open, I reviewed my project list. Priority number one was an artist who'd hit his stride later in life. After a brief illness that even the doctors couldn't put a finger on, he'd left a mourning family and a stunning collection of mixed-media paintings prominently hung on the walls of homes and businesses all over the country. This celebration of his life was an obituary I would enjoy writing.

Priority number two was a woman who'd died at age ninety-three. She had no living kin, so I'd been asked by the funeral home to write her up. Her many friends talked of her light-up-the-room smile, love of all things knickknack, and unmatchable green thumb. She'd been very active in beautifying the grounds of Ballard Green, the charming, affordable cottages just steps from our town park. Donating time for this woman would be my pleasure.

Looming over my head were obituaries for four young men whose remains had been unearthed in the gravel basement of a nineteenth century addition to an eighteenth-century house on Main Street. What started as renovation had quickly turned into excavation after it was determined that they were likely fallen soldiers from the Revolutionary War. While not a major part of the war, the 1777 Battle of Ridgefield was the only inland battle to have been fought in the state of Connecticut, and the town celebrated the anniversary every five years. Our first selectman—a quaint New England term for mayor—had asked me to write up the soldiers for the town's reenactment brochures. The problem for me was that state archeologists were still unsure if the bones belonged to the British soldiers, or colonists. Talk about tombs for unknown soldiers.

Suddenly the eerie ringtone I'd downloaded last Halloween erupted from my satchel, and all eyes in the café turned on me. I was grateful the Nosy Parkers were outside.

"Winter Snow?"

The stern authoritarian voice reminded me uncomfortably of my sixth-grade history teacher.

"Speaking," I said, turning my back to the patrons. I hoped the flushing sound on the other side of the bathroom door didn't reach the phone.

"Would you prefer to call me back?" the woman asked.

"No, it's fine. Who's calling?"

I inched past the tank-topped sun worshiper emerging from the bathroom and closed the door behind me. Sans permanent office, this was not my first conference a la cafe commode.

"This is Mrs. Roth Arlington," said the voice on the other end of the line.

That stopped me short. Mrs. Arlington was a well-known philanthropist in my hometown, and her name was on most thank-you plaques adorning the local walls, from the library to the playhouse, the Aldrich Museum to Founders Hall.

"I need an obituary right away," she said brusquely.

This sort of urgency was normal in my business.

"I'm sorry for your loss," I said. "Who is it for?"

"No loss," she replied. "At least not yet. It's for me, and I will need it by Friday."

Occasionally I get a pragmatic client who wants to prearrange everything as part of their estate planning. However, those requests are rarely urgent.

Mrs. Arlington now had my full attention.

Despite the fact that all sorts of things can go wrong if you attempt too many obits at once, I was not letting a business booster like Mrs. Arlington slip from my grasp. We settled on three o'clock, and she gave me her address.

"Ms. Snow," she added before clicking off. "If you can't write it by Friday, don't bother coming."

* * *

Back at the table, the gossipers were leaning conspiratorially together. They looked at each other, communicating in that way siblings can do without words, and I could tell they were debating whether to let me in on their latest secret. I sipped my tea, lost in thought over my odd phone call from Mrs. Arlington.

"Winter," Abby finally said, her voice hushed for state secrets. "There are twice as many New York cars in town. We don't think they're visitors from North or South Salem either. They live here."

No news there. Since the pandemic, people had been trading the confines of New York City apartments for more spacious homes in the suburbs—especially families with young children. The schools were good here, the air was cleaner, and the newly popular hybrid work models had aptly offset the hour-and-fifteen-minute commute to the city. For two meddlesome women who thrived on infidelity and divorce, out-of-state license plates seemed rather benign.

"Don't you get it?" asked Abby. "They haven't registered their cars. It means Ridgefield is not getting all that tax revenue." She crossed her arms over her slight frame and harrumphed.

Gabby pulled a sheet of paper from her purse and waved it toward me proudly. "We're writing down all the plate numbers so we can turn them in to the tax assessor."

I glanced at the list she thrust in front of my face—ten or so plates. "How much do you think we're talking about?" I asked.

"Well," said Abby, as if savoring a bite of lemon meringue, "you see what's on the roads here—BMWs, Audis, Lexuses. Not to mention all the Benzes, Porsches, and high-end Teslas. At the Mobil station yesterday, I even saw a hot-pink Taycan with vanity plates that read SNOB. Anyway, the point is, this next gen is not humble when it comes to cars, especially the New Yorkers moving in."

While Abby was leaving out a significant cross-section of more affordable sedans and midsize SUVs, not to mention my '98 Subaru not long for this world, she was right about the wealthier set.

"Let's say," Abby continued, "conservatively, the average car in town is fifty thousand, with an assessed value of thirty-five K. Ridgefield taxes are at twenty-eight forty-three, so the lost revenue on that car would be nearly a thousand bucks a year. Follow?"

"So far," I said, surprised as much by how much some folks shelled out in car taxes as by Abby's grasp of the local mill rate.

"So, if these ten cars are unregistered," Gabby chimed in, waving her list again, "that's about ten grand the town is losing this year."

"Something to honk at," I agreed.

"This will flame your cute little Irish face," said Abby, pausing for drama. "We've seen ten cars with New York plates in *just the last hour.*"

Gabby nodded, a prosecutor resting her case, utterly certain of conviction.

"You two are a credit to our community," I said, glancing at my phone. "All right, then." I took a last long gulp of tea, pocketed the shortbread cookie I hadn't even bitten into, and rose to go.

"What's the rush?" asked Gabby, looking a little miffed by my lackluster response.

"Deadlines," I explained.

"It's weird," Abby said, "You'd never guess by looking at you that you write about dead people. It gives me the creeps."

She shuddered and leaned away, as if being near a blue-eyed, fair-haired woman with freckles was akin to sitting next to the devil.

My obit business is still in its infancy, and while I love what I do, I find myself constantly justifying it by pointing out that obituaries aren't just end-of-life notifications and tributes. They facilitate acceptance for the grief-stricken. They immortalize a person for their earthly accomplishments. They are a piece of history that will live in genealogy research and community memory. In that sense, I am a keeper of the collective conscience.

I smiled, retreated from the table with a wave, and said, "It's a living."

* * *

The tone and tenor of Main Street felt different today as I made my way toward the library. Still bustling, it was edgier, with people darting in and out of stores, horns blowing at jaywalkers, cars jockeying for parking spots. It didn't dawn on me that everyone was in preparation mode for Tropical Storm Holden until I saw a man walking with a triple pack of flashlights in one hand and a propane tank in the other. The town alert text that had startled me awake this morning now came back to me: *High wind, flash flood advisory. Expect to shelter in place for at least three days.* I could picture the shelves of the town's single supermarket already picked clean as desert bones.

None of this worried me. I had a generator at my well-stocked cottage on Mamanasco Lake. I'd have company, as I knew my uncle Richard would join me there tonight to ride out the storm. We'd cook and catch up. The lights would flicker. The generator would start to whine. As in storms past, Richard and our elderly neighbor Horace would sip Maker's Mark at the large window overlooking the water, watching the rippling black mirror spasm with light.

I put these thoughts aside. Save for the wind kicking up, it was still sunny and warm, and I had deadlines to meet.

At Prospect and Main, I entered the architectural anomaly that was the Ridgefield Library. The 120-year-old redbrick building had sprouted contemporary wings in the last decade, thanks to a twenty-two-million-dollar expansion that included automated checkouts, a conveyor-belt book return, and movable shelving to allow for multi-use space. I settled into the same small room with the window facing Prospect Street that I always reserved.

Three hours later, I had working drafts for the mixed-media master and nonagenarian gardener. Both would get final reads before deadline tomorrow.

The darkening sky didn't look nearly as ominous through the window as it did when I stepped outside. The wind had whipped up, and no amount of swiping could keep the hair from my face. I crossed Prospect and cut through the parking lot to Big Shop Lane. The sky opened up before I reached my car, making dry clothes the new imperative.

Ridgefield Alerts texted again, this time demanding people stay off the roads. Back at home, I changed out of my wet clothes, raked a comb through my shoulder-length tangle of knots, and was back in my clunker twenty minutes later. The town might flood in the lowlands, but not where I was going.

Chapter Two

Between the waterfall West Mountain Road had become, the madly swaying trees, and my overwhelmed windshield wipers, I was starting to wonder about the wisdom of this errand.

Winter Snow, 29, died after being crushed by a fallen oak when she ignored tropical storm warnings to write about dead people . . .

While the lure of a big client had gotten me into the car, it was my curiosity about Mrs. Arlington's sudden need to write her death notice that kept my foot on the gas. From the occasional write-up about her in the *Ridgefield Press*, I knew only that she was a reclusive philanthropist and widow of the late Roth Arlington. I figured she was terminal, or maybe even suicidal.

West Mountain didn't have great cell service on a good day, so I jumped when my ringtone shattered the white noise of the rain. It was Scoop. I put him on speaker.

"You sound like you're in a wind tunnel," he squawked. "Tell me you're not driving."

Aka Kevin Blake, Scoop was a reporter for the *Ridgefield Press*, our weekly newspaper.

"It's more like boating," I said.

"Are you crazy? A tornado just tore through Branchville. Where are you going?"

"The estate area."

"A job?"

Scoop had earned his nickname as a cub reporter when he literally scooped up a litter of kittens abandoned in a fruit stand parking lot. After preventing vehicular feline-slaughter, he had tracked down the culprits and reported it, bringing police interest and eventually fines for animal cruelty. The clincher was that the court ordered the original owners to give up the mama cat too. She now lived comfortably in Scoop's apartment in town above the funeral home.

I recapped the unexpected call from Mrs. Arlington, omitting the Friday deadline. While Scoop and I weren't related, we shared the curiosity gene. He let out a low whistle.

"She's an odd duck," he said.

"What do you know about her?"

"Not much," he admitted. "I've tried to interview her a few times for various charity causes, and she always declines. The main thing I wonder about is Henry Harmless."

"Henry who?"

"Harmless," he repeated. "He lived with them for years when Roth was still alive. There were different rumors about them, probably none of them true—you know this town."

While I wanted to hear them all, this wasn't the time. "I'm going to need to pick your brain later," I said. "Were you calling about something in particular?"

"Right," said Scoop, his voice bottoming out. "I need an obituary."

"Not your mom!" I nearly shouted to be heard over the chaos outside.

She was his only family and resided in the Memory Care unit at Meadow Ridge in Redding. I couldn't count how many offers from bigger papers he'd turned down over the years to stay close to her.

"No," Scoop said quickly. "Mom's still ticking away—though she has no idea who I am anymore. It's for Croak."

"What happened?" I asked, and picturing the headline, I kept my smile to myself—*Beloved Frog Croak, Croaked*. "Did Heady or Topper get to him?"

His two rescue cats were named for his favorite beer. In fact, at any given time, Scoop might be fostering a half dozen cats until he could find them homes. He was best friends with the folks at ROAR, our animal rescue shelter.

"They know better," he said, sighing. "No, I let him go. Now I'm worried he won't survive."

"Better to be with his amphibian friends than in captivity."

"True," he said. "I just wish there was a way to check on him— you know, to make sure the other frogs accept him back."

Scoop would ban flyswatters if he could.

"I think until we know otherwise, we should assume the best," I said. "Anyway, let's talk about it tonight."

The turn to Mrs. Arlington's house had appeared through the spray.

"Be careful out there, Winter."

As I made my way down the driveway, I was relieved to see there were no overhead wires—likely the utility lines were buried for many of the homes tucked away in the estate area. A quarter of a mile and many muddy ruts later, a stately fieldstone mansion materialized like an oasis. As I rounded the crescent of cobblestone before the front door, I heard a loud crack and looked back in time to see a long mass of leafy tentacles crash down across the driveway. The oak from which it had fallen looked oddly disfigured as it swayed in the wind. Apparently I'd be staying a while.

Chapter Three

The front door whined open before I could ring the bell. A girl somewhere between her late teens and early twenties jumped back in surprise. Her childish hand clapped over the "oh" forming on her lips.

"I'm here to see Mrs. Roth Arlington," I said.

The wind carried the rain sideways. Despite the porte cochere and my attempt to pull the car as close to the door as possible, my breezy white top looked as if I had entered a wet T-shirt contest. I tugged my canvas satchel forward to shield my body, an effort more symbolic than effective.

"The damn driveway alarm won't shut up," the girl snapped. "I wasn't expecting anyone."

Her slick dark hair was cut bluntly to her chin on one side, cropped short on the other, revealing studs and loops in her ear from lobe to top. She had pale creamy skin, shocked by large brown eyes under thick sprays of enviable lashes. Tattoos like dead vines snaked up one arm, jeans and a tucked black tee accentuated her slight frame, and her burgundy boots that buckled across the ankle were out of sync with the warm August weather.

"There's a big branch down," I said, thumbing backward into the deluge. "Maybe that's the problem."

"Effing fantastic."

"Anyway, I'm Winter Snow, the obituary writer. She's expecting me."

Her eyes were saucers as she stepped aside to let me into the refrigerated foyer.

"Can't you turn the alarm off from inside?" A rhythmic dingdong repeated itself from elsewhere in the house.

She glanced uncertainly down the hall toward what I assumed was the location of the offending system.

"Would you mind taking off your shoes, ma'am?" she asked as she refocused on me.

I kicked off Onex sandals and wiggled bare feet on white marble, recoiling at being called *ma'am* at the tender age of twenty-nine.

"You're a flood!" she erupted.

It was true. Water pooled around me.

"Then I'll need a towel," I replied evenly.

She jerked her head in annoyance and retreated down the hall.

I took in the two-story ceiling, ornate mahogany chairs, the shiny marble—shinier since my soggy entrance. Crystal sconces wept frozen teardrops. A chandelier straight out of *Phantom of the Opera* danced in the gray light. Next to the grand winding staircase, a gilded mirror reflected a hot wet mess: hair plastered in tangles against my skull, blond highlights like lightning bolts, raccoon eyes. The girl must have turned the alarm off from the inside as I suggested, because when she returned and tossed me a towel, I could no longer hear its annoying beep.

"Step back," she said, trying to reassert herself. With a second towel, she stooped and began wiping the floor.

"And the lady of the house?" I asked.

"I'll find her after I clean up your mess."

Phone in hand, I clicked the number Mrs. Arlington had called from earlier. I could hear ringing from deep in the house, followed by a patchy connection, which sounded like the woman thought I was canceling our appointment. The call dropped, so I texted that I was in her foyer, locking horns with a punk waif gatekeeper—phrased more nicely, of course.

A minute later, I got my first look at Mrs. Roth Arlington. She strode in, tall and large boned, with big hands and feet and a snowy head that reminded me of Bea Arthur from the *Golden Girls* reruns I sometimes binge on. Remnants of her former beauty were evident in high cheekbones and steel-gray eyes. Her no-nonsense looks were enhanced by a cane, which she wielded more like a scepter.

"Good God, Brittany, Ms. Snow is shivering," she chastened. "Warm up one of the guest room robes. And turn on the gas fireplace to dry those wet shoes."

As Brittany scurried wordlessly away, Mrs. Arlington turned to me and said, "The girl has no common sense."

"She seems capable in her way," I said.

Mrs. Arlington did a slow double take before replying icily, "Shall I expect fluff in my obituary as well?"

After that bumpy start, I was relieved when a short time later I was wrapped in dryer-warmed white terry cloth while my clothes spun in circles in another part of the house. We sat in a large sunroom, dim and dreary now under the onslaught of the storm. Further dampening the mood was too much furniture from a bygone era—dark and gaudy, heavily scrolled. Beyond the many windows, patio chairs tumbled down a large expanse of lawn, propelled by the wind toward a swimming pool.

"Again, I'm sorry about Brittany," Mrs. Arlington said from a tufted leather chair. I was perched on the edge of a high-backed mahogany chair, backed by a fluffy white pillow.

"Can't you find someone who better suits your needs?" I asked.

"Obviously, but . . ." She waved a hand in a *Why bother?* motion. "The truth is I feel sorry for the girl. She really doesn't have anyone except her boyfriend—who is nearly as useless. I give him handiwork, but his real value is keeping her company at the guesthouse."

"Maybe he can clear the branch blocking your driveway," I suggested.

I settled into the chair and froze as I felt something move against my lower back.

Mrs. Arlington chuckled. "I rescued her a few weeks ago from one of those puppy mills."

I turned in relief to find a tiny Great Pyrenees with big serious brown eyes staring back.

"Diva, come," Mrs. Arlington commanded.

Instead, the dog stretched languidly and stepped around to my lap, where she made herself comfortable. She looked up at me mournfully.

"I swear she talks with her eyes," Mrs. Arlington said fondly. "I think she sees a kindred spirit in your robe."

Diva was clean, soft, and warm. I let her stay.

"Excuse me a moment," Mrs. Arlington said, picking up a portable landline phone from a pile of devices on the marble-topped table next to her. The iPad and iPhone were in sharp contrast to their dated surroundings.

As my host delivered tree removal instructions into the portable phone, I watched the pool beyond the green expanse slosh like an angry sea. Miniature debris-strewn waves broke onto the decking and toward a pool house, which was ensconced in giant arborvitaes at the edge of the woods. The pool house door had blown open and now flopped haphazardly with the gusts. Diva shook in my lap with each rumble of thunder.

"Yes, as soon as the storm passes," Mrs. Arlington confirmed. "Thank you." She hung up and turned to me. "Now tell me how you got into this deadly business."

My clients often ask about my background. I suppose that sharing the intimate details of their own lives makes them feel entitled to know more about mine. I ran through my usual spiel: falling in love with the written word at a young age, studying journalism at UConn, returning home to work at the *Press* and realizing I had a knack for human interest stories—easily enabled by deep roots in a small town.

"I became the go-to person at the *Press* for obituaries," I said. "From there, it felt inev—"

"But there was something else," Mrs. Arlington cut in.

"Sorry?"

"Personal."

Diva shuddered against me as thunder clapped again, followed by a flash of light outside, flickering bulbs inside.

"Mrs. Arlington—"

"Call me Lottie."

"Lottie," I said. "I'm not sure I follow."

"More than eight decades on earth, Miss Snow, have taught me two certainties about people. One: there are no certainties. Two: we wear our sad stories with every word we speak."

For a moment we locked eyes.

"My father died when we . . . when I was young," I replied.

"And?"

"And I think it gives me empathy."

She studied my face a moment as if trying to eke out more. No way was I letting this interview become about me, I thought, and bored my blue eyes into hers. Finally, she nodded, mostly to herself. Rising, she strode imperiously across the room to a rolltop desk and pulled a manila folder from the top left drawer. She returned and handed it to me.

"You'll find next of kin, service arrangements, charities. Also, I followed the directions on your website to the letter, though I'm guessing you'll have questions. There's a thumb drive in there if you need it."

As I began to open the envelope, her left hand flew upward in a halting motion. "Later. Right now, let's talk."

The questions I asked about her—her marriage to Roth Arlington, how she'd gotten to Ridgefield—were met with clipped nonanswers. Instead, she circled back to me.

"I'd especially like to know why your parents were so fixated on seasons."

I shrugged. "Maybe you can ask my mother. She'll be visiting soon, and I know she'd love to meet you."

"Maybe," she said.

She then stared off, losing the bright curiosity her eyes had met me with earlier.

"Mrs. Arlington—"

"Lottie," she spoke abruptly, as if coming back to this world.

"If you don't mind my asking, why do you need this done so quickly? I mean, if you're feeling out of sorts or something . . ."

Up came the hand again.

"I am neither depressed nor suicidal, Miss Snow. But I *am* a realist. It is logical to think I might be next in line to die."

"Are you being threatened?"

She turned to look out at the doomsday view.

"A shame we didn't get a funnel," she said. "Just get the obituary finished by Friday."

Neither of us was surprised when a short time later the lights finally went out, leaving us with only gloomy landscape. I was surprised, however, that no generator kicked on in a house this grand. Mrs. Arlington switched on battery-powered lanterns positioned throughout the room, which did little to cheer the space.

"At least your clothes will be dry by now," she noted.

It reminded me that Brittany had waved goodbye about half an hour earlier.

"Who will stay with you until the power comes back on?" I asked. It often took days after a storm before Eversource line crews could untangle the snarl of wires from fallen branches.

"Why would anyone stay with me?"

"I thought because of your concern about . . . well . . ."

The hand again, conversation closed.

By five thirty, I was back in my dry clothes and hopeful that I could navigate down to Mamanasco, where I imagined my uncle's comfort foods cooking away, oldies blaring from the speakers, one of his special reds breathing on the sideboard. Mrs. Arlington's cane tapped on the marble floor of the foyer as she walked me out.

"Why don't you and Diva come stay with me while we wait for the power to come back?" I asked impulsively. "Knock wood, our generator has never failed."

For a split second, her face betrayed a hint of brightness, then closed. "No thank you, Miss Snow. I'll spend my last days at home."

Chapter Four

B ack at the cottage, leaning against the kitchen counter and sipping chilled Matanzas Creek Chardonnay, I relayed my episode to Uncle Richard and my neighbor Horace. As predicted, the place was an olfactory awakening and the Beatles crooned "Hey Jude" through a pair of Sonos portable speakers.

Richard's daily walking routine kept him trim, and the only giveaway that he had reached the sixty-year mark was that his once-blond dome was now silver. His bright-blue eyes crinkled into a smile as he handed a glass of Ruffino Cab to Horace. My cucumber-chopping neighbor, who was well into his eighties, wiggled his bushy Santa Claus brows and lifted his glass in a toast.

"How was the drive? Could we get her here for dinner?" my uncle asked.

"And a drink," Horace added. "Sounds like she needs one."

What should have been a ten-minute drive from her estate to the lake had taken over an hour as I skirted splintered trees, downed limbs, and swales of water. When I finally reached the cottage, relief came not only from getting there but also from the warm glow through the windows—rare among the corridor of houses along the water. Climbing into yoga pants and my well-worn UConn sweatshirt completed the effect.

"Now that I know the route, it wouldn't take any time at all."

"It'd be interesting to see the damage around town," said my uncle.

Richard was a CERT, a Community Emergency Response Team volunteer—always ready to assist the Office of Emergency Management with damage assessment.

"Not me," said Horace. "The farther I travel from home, the faster I age."

"Mrs. Arlington is stubborn," I said.

"Call her anyway," said Horace. "You'll feel better. Heck, we'll all feel better."

Mrs. Arlington picked up on the first ring. At least her landline was still working.

"Yes?" she inquired with an intake of breath that sounded like dread.

Odd—she had appeared so self-assured earlier. And she didn't seem aware that it was me calling either. With no power, her caller ID probably wasn't working.

"Lottie, it's Winter—from this afternoon."

Recovering some of her composure, she replied, "Winter. I didn't expect to hear from you so soon."

"Listen, my uncle made this fabulous lasagna, and he insists we bring you a warm meal."

The silence on the other end felt longer than it was.

"How nice of you," she said finally. "But really, there's no need. Diva and I already ate the leftovers, and I have plenty of battery-powered lanterns. Besides, I wouldn't want you out on the roads, such as they are."

"It's really no bother," I replied hopefully.

The sternness returned to her voice. "Actually, I'm heading upstairs now to finish my memoirs. Thank you anyway."

I knew conviction when I heard it, so I told her to call if she changed her mind. I repeated my invitation to have her stay with us until the power returned.

"Winter, the obituary you write will be the final version, so please do well by me," she replied. "There's more than you need in the envelope I gave you."

It occurred to me that this might be a woman who thrived on deadlines—her memoirs, her obituary. As a journalist, I could appreciate that. Maybe she had simply chosen to preplan her funeral and Friday was her self-imposed deadline.

And then her comments about being realistic and about spending her last days at home seeped back into my brain.

"I promise I won't let you down," I said. "Good night, Lottie."

"Goodbye, Winter Snow," she replied. "And thank you."

* * *

"What do you make of that?" I asked.

We were digging into cheesy lasagna out on the deck. The storm had trimmed the warm front, and branches bobbed on the water like tiny shipwrecks, leaves fanning out like lifeboats. No doubt the neighborhood would call for a lake cleanup day soon.

"She's clearly troubled," Richard replied.

Horace grimaced through a mouthful. "They say people often know when they're about to die," he said thoughtfully. "Maybe she had a premonition."

"Or a death threat," said Richard.

I looked at the lake and wondered if any bodies lay at the bottom. Shallow and nearly a mile long, Mamanasco was Ridgefield's largest natural lake. The shoreline still held a few last vestiges of

Ridgefield's more modest era, cottages with small docks and decks dangling over the water's edge. These had once been summer retreats for folks escaping the oppressive New York City heat. My uncle's cottage had been one of those before he bought the one next door and renovated, providing enough space for my sister, my mom, and me after our father died. It was now a two-story with a vintage exterior so as not to "fight with the landscape," as my uncle liked to put it. A small patch of green separated our house from the weathered shack losing the battle against time that Horace called home.

"Why would anyone threaten an old woman?" I asked.

"An old woman with a sizable fortune," Richard clarified. "Too bad you don't know who inherits."

After dinner, Horace promised not to light candles in his tinderbox of a home and said good night, his old-fashioned flashlight wobbling over the grass. My uncle retired to the guest space over the garage, where he still kept some of his things. He would return to Village Square in the morning when the roads were easier to navigate. I suspected his real motivation was to check on Horace again in the morning. His efforts to convince his old neighbor to sell his eyesore abode and move to the age-restricted community where Richard now lived had not been successful. Horace had been on the lake for sixty years and had no intention of leaving at a time when he appreciated the peacefulness the most.

I poured myself another glass of wine, snuggled into a cozy chair in the study, and opened the envelope Mrs. Arlington had given me.

A life well lived, I thought as I read. Born to hardworking parents—her dad a municipal worker, her mom a schoolteacher—Leocadia Wysocki Arlington was the oldest of three. She had a brother and a sister and was the first in her family to have gone to college. Her father had died shortly after she moved to New York City to start a job as a secretary, and two years later her mother followed.

I could find no evidence of her wedding to Roth Arlington and no mention of Henry Harmless, the mystery name Scoop had thrown out. Instead, she went into great detail about her career, noting how she had become one of the first to work with computers and that she eventually ran a department at a time when women were still undervalued.

Leocadia Arlington was currently eighty-one years old. *Eighty-one years young* was what sprang to my mind. She had been witty, sharp minded, and had a no-nonsense attitude during our visit. Although not overly tolerant of her assistant, she was protective of the girl, especially when I asked if she was thinking of replacing her.

From the computer printouts, I could see she had taken a stab at her own obit and had a real knack for storytelling. If only she wanted a job!

I pulled out my ever-present iPhone and checked the time. It was nine thirty, and I knew my night-owl buddy Scoop would still be awake. When he answered, though, he sounded groggy.

"Are you okay?" I asked.

He sighed audibly. "Just a little tired. After the storm, I went out to look for Croak."

"You're kidding, right?"

Croak's new home, a four-hundred and sixty-acre parcel the town had protected from high-density development by taking it by eminent domain, was called Bennett's Pond, though it could easily have been dubbed the second Battle of Ridgefield. The fight had taken place in the courts, with Ridgefield the ultimate victor. Loaded with great hiking trails and the pond for which it was named, it was a town treasure and presumably where Croak now enjoyed his new life. Looking for Croak in that environment would make looking for a needle in a haystack seem easy.

"I thought I might recognize him—you know he had that little mark on his back," said Scoop.

"And?"

"It was impossible. It was like a chorus of frogs, and not one of the little guys looked like Croak."

"You should assume that Croak is enjoying his newfound freedom."

"You're right." Scoop sighed again and then asked, "Did you call for a reason?"

"I wanted to pick your brain about Mrs. Arlington."

"What else can I tell you?"

"You mentioned something about rumors surrounding someone named Henry Harmless," I said. "Do you have any details?"

Scoop yawned loudly. "Look, the three of them lived up there together. Rumors fly around this town. If you want, I could do a little more homework for you, or we could just ask the Nosy Parkers."

"I'd prefer to leave them out of it. And whatever you find, I need it before Friday."

"What's so special about Friday?"

I stared at Lottie's photo and thought, *Good question.*

Chapter Five

M rs. Arlington's impending doom was a cloud I didn't need right now. I considered the small doorway at the opposite side of the study. Beyond was a twelve-by-twelve-foot space delegated to the HO scale train set my uncle had started for my sister and me after our dad died.

Three sides of the room held a horseshoe-shaped world of mountains, villages, pastures, and cityscapes we'd created over the years. By silent agreement, we all worked independently on our creations, and consequently there were often surprises awaiting in this safe haven. My sister, Summer, had preferred coiffed landscapes with neat rows of trees. My creations were more random spurts of imagination that kept a neighborhood or town from becoming too Stepford-like.

I rose, stretched, and stepped inside the room. Over the past few years our visits had tapered, and now the rails looked dusty, the mountains seemed smaller, the cities felt abandoned.

"That's odd," I said aloud, a habit I had acquired since living alone.

Off to one small corner lay something I had never seen before: a tiny graveyard. The backdrop, a large lake surrounded by rock formations and trees, was also new. A scene in progress.

Tiny tombstones with miniscule writing were lined in neat rows—someone had gone the extra mile to make it look authentic. One stone had a colorful spread of miniature flowers dotting the grass. It didn't take much imagination to realize that Uncle Richard had built a burial site he could visit.

Losing my dad and then, ten years later, my sister had taken its toll on all of us, especially on Richard. I'd had my schoolwork and later my job for distraction. My mom became Granny Nanny to my sister's babies in Florida.

Richard's step finally grew lighter after I graduated from college and began working at our local paper. Now his life was filled with his teaching job at the state university in next-door Danbury, his CERT work for the town, and his endless efforts to feed me and Horace. I hoped that his addition to the train room meant that he was finally ready to bury the dead.

I spent the next half hour dusting trains and tracks with the special brushes we kept for that purpose. I never allowed our sad story to interfere with the happy memories this room held—this was my escape place. With a satisfied appraisal, I finally turned out the lights and went to bed.

*   *   *

When I awoke the next morning, the day felt like a promise, with the sun warming my cheeks and glitter covering the lake outside my window. Framed in the view was a large outcropping of rocks simply known as The Cliffs. While they are no rival to the Hudson Palisades, in terms of scale, their command of the relatively small lake is undeniable.

As teens we used to wind down the trails of nearby Richardson Park, hang out on the warm stone, and dare each other to jump. I have no idea how we didn't kill ourselves when we hit the bottom of the shallow lake or one of the odds and ends that high schoolers were rumored to have thrown in there, ranging from school desks to cookware, stop signs to caskets—even an old car. Yet here I am, living testimony that even stupidity can sometimes outwit disaster.

I snatched my phone up on my way to the bathroom, noting from my alerts that thousands in town were without power. Residents on cul-de-sacs and dead-end lanes would be trapped for days before wire-tangled branches and debris could be cleared. Often soggy terrain caused trees to continue to uproot long after a storm had passed. I wondered if Brittany and her boyfriend had the sense to check on Mrs. Arlington.

I threw on last night's yoga pants and sweatshirt and headed downstairs, where I carried Mrs. Arlington's envelope, my computer, and a hot cup of chamomile to the living room and picked up where I had left off last night.

Mrs. Arlington had started out as a secretary before moving into the then-nascent field of computer programming, which had led to her running an entire department. Her boss, Roth Arlington, had become her mentor, and in Leocadia, he'd found an earnest learner.

Oddly, there was nothing in Lottie's notes to suggest she and Roth had married. In my experience, people always wanted to include how long they'd been married in their obituaries. But maybe Lottie had just lived with Roth all this time. Despite her dismissal yesterday, if I wanted this obituary to be accurate, I would need to talk to her again.

"Good morning," said my uncle as he moseyed into the room. "Making any progress?"

"More questions than answers," I said.

"There always are," he said cheerily. After disappearing into the kitchen, he called out, "Avocado toast will be ready in twenty."

Uncle Richard's avocado toast puts hipsters to shame: thick crusty toasted bread spread with homemade pesto, slivers of perfectly ripened avocado, and slices of fresh garden tomato topped with melted Brie.

Sometime later, the spell of Mrs. Arlington's life story was broken by what sounded like a drummer with a bad tempo—much more noise than avocado toast called for.

"What's going on?"

My stomach growled in response to the sumptuous platter on the kitchen table.

"I'm getting ready to simmer sauce. There will be a bunch of people in need of a meal tonight, including Horace."

Richard was the kind of neighbor who knew exactly which people from his old neighborhood did not have generators. He also knew that the last major storm had caused outages in some places for nearly two weeks, damage that stretched pocketbooks and spiked stress levels that were already higher than the Cliffs these days.

A moment later, Horace tapped on the kitchen sliders and slipped inside to join us for breakfast. Feeling the soothing tug of family, I sat back and enjoyed the banter between these two old buddies. If it weren't for them, I'd probably already be in New York City.

Obituary writing in Ridgefield, population twenty-five thousand, was surprisingly profitable, despite so many young families moving in as boomers retired to Florida to escape the state income tax. Yet for my business to survive in the long run, terrible as it was to admit, I would need to be near more dead people.

As if reading my mind, Horace asked, "Anything new with the apartment hunt?"

Richard grew quiet, and although neither ever said it, I knew they didn't want me to leave Ridgefield, even if my plan was to do so only on a part-time basis.

"Rents are sky-high. RT—that's the real estate broker—has a couple of leads," I said. "I do have a new client, though. He's a CEO with an unfortunate terminal diagnosis. He wants to meet with me to write his obituary so his family isn't burdened."

"Wow, talk about trying to stay in control," said Horace.

"I get that," said Richard. "A grieving family doesn't need one more thing to worry about."

Of course Richard would feel that way. He was the white knight who'd ridden to the rescue after my dad died.

"Actually," I said, "writing an obituary can be cathartic for those who are grieving."

"Your dad was my best friend, and I felt terrible pressure to get it right."

"And you did," Horace said. "It was a wonderful tribute. Maybe Winter gets her talent from you."

"It just wasn't enough," said Richard, slipping into one of his self-pummeling moods.

"Let's see, you introduced your best friend to your sister, and you were best man at their wedding. You planned his funeral, wrote his obituary because Winter was way too young for that. You executed his will, built a lake house, raised his family—did I leave anything out?"

Suddenly I knew exactly what cottage belonged in the train room next to the cemetery—it would be Horace's.

"Don't forget booting my mom out the door to go back to school for her nursing degree," I said. "You rescued this family."

Richard smiled at me. "I reaped all the benefits."

I patted my uncle's hand and gave him a cheek kiss. "On that light note, I'm going back to work."

* * *

Back in the living room, I slid open large sliders to the summer morning and reviewed my to-do list. Most clients whose family members had died asked me to take care of everything, including the submissions. Along with the *Ridgefield Press*, Mrs. Arlington wanted her obituary to run in the *New York Times*—a potentially pricey venture. I was glad to see she wasn't skimping on her last words. I was also to deliver a copy to her lawyer.

I checked the bars on my phone. Barely half, though still working, so I tapped in her number.

Nothing.

I tried her landline. It was hard to know if it was out of service or if she just wasn't picking up. It looked like I'd have to drive over there to get more details if I wanted to do this right.

I left Uncle Richard mumbling about running downtown for more tomatoes so he could provide his personal Meals on Wheels service, as he called it. He was referring to the town program run by volunteers who deliver food to the housebound. It's funded by generous contributions, and I'd bet my bottom dollar that Leocadia Arlington's name appeared on that donor list as well.

Chapter Six

An hour later, I was walking the loop around the village, surveying the damage. The steady buzz of chainsaws rippled through the town, and après-storm cleanup was already well underway. It always surprises me how quickly town folks manage to return their properties to normal after a storm. It was as if a pristine lawn could erase the memory of the inconvenience the storm had bestowed.

A severed limb from a large oak had already been neatly cut and stacked, its splinters swept and piled, and I imagined the collective sigh of relief: our historic Lounsbury House appeared completely unscathed. This beautiful mansion built in 1896 was modeled after a building the Connecticut governor saw at a world's fair in Chicago. Once his family home and now an event venue owned by the town, it is one of the most stunning buildings lining Ridgefield's magnificent Main Street.

With the Main Street power grid restored, no doubt prioritized in order to get necessary businesses up and running, I ended my walk at Tazza for tea. A short time later, juggling a chamomile for me and a Darjeeling for Mrs. Arlington, I was heading up West Mountain Road, hoping it wasn't too early for me to visit.

Clusters of workers removing downed branches that had not become entangled with any part of the power grid slowed the drive. Even if you sent a brigade of people willing to clear trees, without a line crew from Eversource who could make the area safe, the outages would be prolonged. As yet, I saw none.

I turned into the muddy drive of the Arlington estate, passing what I now knew was the cottage where Brittany and her boyfriend lived. No vehicles were in the driveway, though there could be one in the attached single-car garage. As I pushed the Subaru through water-filled potholes, I was relieved to see that no trees blocked the way.

Emerging through vegetation, I was suddenly startled by the massive size of the house. Yesterday, as I raced to get out of the storm, I had barely taken it in. Today, with the sun hovering overhead, the mica-flecked fieldstone mansion set on the backdrop of an expansive lawn looked like a castle shimmering with diamonds.

I parked under the portico, climbed out of the car, and was immediately affronted by Diva's loud puppy bark at the front door. There was no response to the ringing doorbell despite my nonstop thumb press. The barking grew more frenetic, and now the dog was scratching loudly.

The handle I jiggled was locked. The only sound came from Diva's yapping, which shifted to the window off to the right of the entry. Barely visible through the tangle of shrubs covering the lower part, the furry white ball leapt against the glass. When I moved toward her, she moved to another window, continuing the process, and I realized I was following breadcrumbs.

Diva finally ran out of windows, so I continued in the direction she had been pointing me. An unlocked side door opened into a large mudroom loaded with jackets on hooks, boots and shoes along the wall, a stepladder, and some buckets, as well as a stand holding several umbrellas. The room had built-in cubbies, plenty of additional hooks, and a long bench where one could sit to put on outdoor attire. At the opposite end was another locked door, this one with divided windowpanes, and that's where Diva had planted herself.

She panted heavily with pleading eyes. Her nose was Rudolph red.

I gagged at the blood, tugged my cell from my pocket, and punched in 911. No bars.

Diva was now heading back the way she'd come. She then stopped, returned, barked at me, and again headed back toward the entry hall.

I tapped the pane as I considered my options. The house was old, and this particular door looked like the original, including the glass. Not wanting to waste any more time in case Mrs. Arlington needed help, I grabbed a metal bucket, stuck my hand inside, gave a hefty thrust, and shattered one of the glass panes.

Diva, thank goodness, had the sense to stand back far enough that no shards reached her. I cleared the pane, picked out the spikes that could spear me, and reached in for the doorknob. It was one of those old-fashioned things that required a key to open it from the inside, and there was no key in sight. I kicked at the door in frustration.

I thought about the stepladder. Why was that out here unless . . .

I grabbed it, pulled it near the door, climbed up, and began running my hand along the top of the doorframe.

Diva watched me.

"I'm trying, girl," I said aloud.

No key. That would have been too easy. Turning toward the outer door, I repeated my efforts.

And there it was, an old-fashioned skeleton key waiting on top of the doorframe like an invitation. When I climbed down and inserted it into the lock, it turned, and I was suddenly in the kitchen with Diva pulling at the bottom of my jeans, trying to lead me to a place I was pretty sure I didn't want to go.

Scraping the major glass pieces to the side with my foot, I moved cautiously forward.

The house was crypt quiet save for the clicking of Diva's nails as she traveled across hardwood and marble. I shadowed her from the kitchen to a long wide hallway, which I assumed would lead to the foyer and the squeaky front door I had entered yesterday. Along the way, a dining room large enough to hold a banquet emerged, and I noted the long windows where my furry white friend had appeared as she tried to direct me to the back door of the house.

Clever dog, I thought, realizing what a meandering path she had taken around heavy furniture to find perches low enough to climb so that I could see her.

My steps must have slowed as I took all this in, because suddenly Diva was at my feet, nudging me. Again I listened and heard nothing, unless you could count the panting dog and my pounding heart.

I passed a large living room on the right. It was laden with more heavy furnishings, ornate Oriental carpets, a grand piano, two separate seating areas, and a fireplace so large I would barely have to stoop if I were to step inside. A picture window framed by pooling drapes overlooked the wide lawn rolling toward the pool.

At this point, my hope was to find Mrs. Roth Arlington curled up on her sofa under one of the throws that draped the furniture, eyes closed to the world after going peacefully in her sleep. An easy obituary to write. Hope was at odds with my gut, though, and the blood on Diva's nose was hard to ignore.

Ahead of me was the front-to-back foyer with its grand sweeping staircase and myriad rooms spreading out like fingers from a hand, and it was there that Diva had planted herself in a fit of heartbreaking whimpers.

Chapter Seven

The fear of leaping from the Cliffs was nothing compared to what I felt as I approached the woman sprawled at the bottom of the staircase, her head in a halo of red.

With shaky fingers, I pulled my phone from my pocket and opted for text. With the New York State line so close, I had hoped I'd get a Connecticut tower. And if not, I prayed New York would have 911 text response, as our state did.

I then knelt and searched for a pulse in her neck—I felt nothing. I went for her wrist. Still warm, with a faint thread of a beat. Warm was a relief, as was the slight rise and fall of her chest.

Diva vanished and returned with a mud-crusted sneaker I assumed must be Brittany's, because it looked too small for the woman sprawled on the marble. The dog's wagging tale suggested it was now her new toy and she wanted to play.

"Not that smart," I muttered to the dog, stepping outside in search of better cell service because I had not received a reply to my text.

Diva dropped the shoe and rushed past me into the yard. Obviously, taking care of business trumped her game of fetch.

Suddenly I was connected, though it was a Westchester operator.

"I need help in Ridgefield, Connecticut," I said.

The phone cut out.

Frustration rose like a flash flood when I raced back inside to the sunroom and found the portable Mrs. Arlington had used yesterday—dead. Logic said there had to be a hardwired landline somewhere. I ran back to the kitchen. My shoes crunched on broken glass as I crossed the room to a long counter running to the left of the door I had broken through. Several keys dangled from a hook on the wall, and one in particular caught my eye. It was a skeleton key—the one that would have opened the kitchen door if it had been in the lock. Next to that was an old-fashioned wall phone.

With relief, I heard the dial tone.

* * *

Diva was nosing Mrs. Arlington's unconscious face when I returned. I tugged the long blue robe she had been wearing gently down to cover her legs. A slipper matching the one still on her foot was perched on one of the upper treads of the staircase. The only first aid I thought wise was to cover her with a throw I had dragged from the living room. Aside from the blood-caked hair, the blanketed woman looked like she was only napping.

Mrs. Arlington had been right when she said Diva could talk with her eyes, because right now she stared at me, sad and soulful. I gently rubbed her head. I would take care of the blood on her nose after the paramedics got here, which from the sounds coming from West Mountain was just moments away.

Two cops burst onto the scene with a siren blaring and the ambulance following. The officer emerging from the passenger side was of medium height, with a sculpted build that suggested he spent a lot of time at the gym. He scanned the landscape warily with eyes so dark they looked like empty sockets in his pale face. His blond buzz cut was sprinkled with gray, and he looked to be in his late forties or early fifties. I remembered him with distaste from my reporter days. Tom Bellini. He was the kind of guy who could kick your #MeToo ire into gear with just one leering look. Swallowing my revulsion, I called out.

Tom's body language relaxed when he recognized me. The other cop emerging from the driver's side remained rigid. Paramedics pushed past me, and I stepped forward.

Tom did the introductions and made a point of letting me know that Kip Michaels was a new hire in training. Kip was tall, good-looking in a brooding way, with dark wavy hair and a trim fit body. Cool gray eyes locked onto mine, and I had an impulse to wipe my mouth in case I was drooling.

"Winter Snow, what's the story?" asked Tom.

Kip didn't hide his open appraisal of me as I stammered through my explanation. *Here come the freckles*, I thought. The EMTs had now brought Mrs. Arlington out on a gurney and were lifting her into the back of the ambulance. Diva was doing a little dance around their feet, and one of them waved at me to call her.

"Your dog looks agitated," said Kip, his voice as cool and distant as his demeanor.

"She's not mine."

Tom whistled and bent to pat his knee in a *come* motion. As if contemplating another stint at being an orphan, the white ball of fluff stood her ground. Her head swiveled back and forth between us and the paramedics as if she were watching a tennis match. When they closed the doors, she whined.

"Come on, Diva, let's go inside and clean off your nose," I said, mimicking Tom's knee patting.

The dog still looked uncertain, so I turned and headed toward the house. She made her decision, and the next thing I knew, she was dashing ahead.

"Reverse psychology," I said over my shoulder.

It worked for the cops as well, because we were soon standing in the foyer as I relayed the path I had taken to find Mrs. Arlington. I mentioned Brittany, who I hoped would look after things until her employer returned.

Tom and Kip checked the house while I waited downstairs. They returned within ten minutes and ushered me back to the foyer. Nothing appeared disturbed, they said, and it seemed Mrs. Arlington had been alone when the accident happened. Aside from the rear door I'd destroyed—Kip's words, not mine—all the exterior doors were locked, and there were no open windows low enough to climb into. Kip opened the front door to lead us out and declared it to be an accident.

"She must be psychic, then. If she dies before Friday, she will have been spot on," I said.

"What do you mean?" Kip asked, suddenly interested.

I explained about the odd request for an obituary by week's end.

"She's old—probably just putting her life in order," said Tom.

Kip was eyeing me in a way that suggested it might have been me who gave her a shove down the stairs.

"I just think it's strange to ask for an obituary so urgently," I said. "It's not like she was going off to war or anything, and she looked pretty healthy. Maybe someone had a key and got inside. She was definitely afraid of something."

"A shove down the stairs is a pretty unreliable way to commit murder," said Kip.

"True," I said, feeling my face flush. "And ignoring inconvenient facts isn't a reliable way to do police work either."

Kip frowned and looked ready to say something when Tom interrupted.

"You won't need 911 in the future," he said.

His hand lingered as he pressed his card into mine with his cell scribbled on the back. I realized that while I had been sizing up his partner, Tom had been doing some calculations of his own.

Kip turned away and headed back toward the cruiser, from which I could hear the radio squawking. I stuck the card in my pocket.

"What about things here?" I asked as Kip waved at Tom and pointed to the radio.

"We need to go, and so should you," he said. "We'll be back after this call to check on the house."

I did a mini salute as they climbed in their SUV and set their lights flashing. A spray of gravel chased them out.

* * *

The toilet tank was as good a place as any to get fresh water, given that without electricity, the water pump wouldn't work. I did a respectable cleanup of the floor where Mrs. Arlington's head wound had bled. I used my skeleton key to open a back door and then carried two buckets from the mudroom over soggy grass to the pool.

The pool house, set back in the trees, looked spine-chilling. Dark windows and branches draped over it made it look like a gothic interpretation of a thatched hut. I shuddered. Appendages from three patio chairs and a partially sunk umbrella stuck out like someone's version of a doomsday sculpture.

Back at the house, toilet tank refilled and water now sloshing in the sink, I cleaned Diva's nose. Mrs. Arlington had an ample supply of bottled water in the walk-in pantry, where I also found a bag of puppy food. I filled two bowls, and Diva ate and drank like it was her last supper.

With no power, vacuuming all the fine slivers of glass was out of the question. I did a reasonable sweep with the broom I found in the large walk-in pantry. With the pane broken and the house less secure, I would have to lock the outer door I had originally entered. I tapped the skeleton key in my pocket.

All the housekeeping finally done, I plopped down on a kitchen chair and assessed the situation.

I had no idea if Mrs. Arlington would live, so I had to figure out what to do with Diva. If she died, I would take Diva to ROAR, because they were highly successful when it came to placing pets. Right now, however, with the woman hovering between life and death, I couldn't give away her dog. Instead, I packed up the dog bowl and food. I looked around for a leash, though with this large property, she might never have needed one.

Diva seemed to know I was in the process of deciding her fate, because she rested her head on her front paws and stared at me bleakly.

"Don't worry," I sighed. "I won't let anything happen to you."

Just then her head bolted up, and she sprang from her resting spot. She approached the back staircase that ascended from the kitchen with her ears twitching and a low growl rumbling in her throat.

The chair I nearly rocketed from fell over with a loud crash. How thoroughly had the police investigated the upstairs? I strained to listen and thought I heard movement.

It's just that overactive imagination your family is always teasing you about, I told myself as I forced out the breath I had been holding.

The Last Word

An open window upstairs was probably blowing something in the breeze. Diva let out a loud bark. My heart pounded in response.

I was about to tiptoe to the second floor when loud thumping came from the front staircase, followed by the unmistakable sound of the front door squeaking open and then slamming shut.

Chapter Eight

I punched in 911 on the wall phone again. After answering multiple questions about the intruder, I was instructed to stay in a safe spot until help arrived.

"Come," I whispered to Diva, who for once obliged. I took the key from my pocket and locked the outer door after closing both softly behind me. At least I wouldn't have to watch my back if the intruder had only pretended to exit. That is, unless the intruder had a skeleton key of their own.

Tuned in to my vibe, Diva stuck close. I paused at the edge of the house and poked my head around the corner. The Subaru looked just as I'd left it.

I listened. No crunch of gravel. No sound of someone running away in another direction—nothing. Just Diva's panting and my breathing, which was beginning to mirror hers.

I scooped her up in my arms. Darn, she was heavy for such a little thing. I made a run for my car, scooted her across into the passenger seat, and hopped in, slamming the door and hitting the power lock behind me. I retrieved Tom's card from my pocket and texted him—*Intruder in house. I called 911.*

His reply was immediate. *On our way.*

Why had someone been hiding upstairs unless they were up to no good? Maybe Mrs. Arlington had been running from the person and tripped on the stairs. Or maybe the person had intentionally pushed her.

I lifted my hips to reach into my back pocket for the car keys, because I didn't see them on the dash where I thought I had tossed them. My pockets were empty except for the skeleton key. I felt around on the floor. Not there either. I must have left them in the house, and yet I couldn't remember having them inside. I checked in my satchel, which now sat on the passenger side floor, where it held my computer and wallet. No keys.

I drummed my fingers on the wheel. I'd just have to wait here until the police arrived. Even if the intruder was long gone, that house had a creepy vibe.

The car was growing hot and stuffy, and Diva's panting sounded like she was practicing Lamaze. As I reached over to give her a reassuring pet, she gave a low growl and looked past me out the driver's side window. I turned slowly. Someone had just come out of the shadows of the shrubs and was heading straight toward us.

Keys, where were those keys? I cursed the antique car that didn't have a keyless start. Diva sat upright and was panting so hard that her entire chest was damp with drool. I was doing a bit of panting myself as I tried to send Tom another text. I was so nervous that the phone slipped out of my hands and fell right into the tight little crack between the seat and the console, and I could do no more than graze the phone with my fingers in the tight space.

A man who fell in age somewhere between Richard and Horace rapped his fist on the window. He was fit in black jeans and a black T-shirt, and he had the kind of suntan that suggests a lot of outdoor time. His face was creased deeply around chocolate-brown eyes, and his tanned head of close-cropped snow-white hair reminded me of those nonpareils my sister and I used to eat. He was holding work gloves in one hand and made the *roll down the window* motion with the other.

Despite Diva's wagging tale, it seemed too much of a coincidence that someone who looked like a landscaper had shown up just minutes after an intruder exited the front door.

The man motioned again.

Even if I wanted to unroll the window a bit just to hear what he had to say, the automatic windows wouldn't work without the car turned on. This car was half in and half out of the twenty-first century. Time for an upgrade.

He looked like he would win any tug-of-war over a partially opened door—I kept it locked. Diva climbed across my lap and put her paws to the window, her tail slapping my face. As I pushed her furry form back to the passenger seat, I finally caught sight of the keys in the spot where she had been sitting. I retrieved them, started the car, and felt the welcome relief of the AC before cracking the window.

"Who are you?" the man demanded. "Where is Mrs. A, and why do you have Diva?"

"Who are you?" I asked, just as forcefully. Better to go on the offensive when under attack, my uncle always says. "Why are you sneaking around the house?"

"I'm not sneaking around," he said defensively. "I'm here to check the house for storm damage. And for God's sake, let Diva out. She's claustrophobic. Look at her—she's hyperventilating."

I turned to look at the pup, who was now panting so hard I thought she might pass out. Drool matted the fur on her chest, and the seat where she sat had a dark splotch.

Before I could react, the man strode around to the passenger's side, yanked at the locked door, and peered in angrily. I opened the lock, and when he wrenched the door open, Diva's small body fell to the ground in an explosion of damp fir. The man bent to pet her and whispered soothing words. I'd had no idea dogs could be claustrophobic.

"You haven't answered me," he said as I climbed out of the car. "Where are you taking Diva? Where is Mrs. A?"

I was about to explain, because I realized that the guy probably did work for Mrs. Arlington, when a whoop sounded and a cop car screeched to a stop. Both officers emerged cautiously. Kip's hand hovered over his weapon, and Tom had pulled his.

"Everything's okay," I hollered. The last thing we needed was for someone to get shot. "This is . . ." Well, that stopped me, because I didn't have a name.

"Mark Goodwin," said the man, who carefully lifted his hands in full view and placed them atop the Subaru, a gesture that seemed familiar to him. "I help Mrs. Arlington out. I was checking for storm damage. This woman has Mrs. A's dog, and I haven't been able to reach her all morning."

Kip and Tom cautiously moved closer. Diva barked. The tension was palpable.

"Easy, girl," said Goodwin.

Tom stared at him. "Don't I know you?" he asked.

"Rec Center gym," Goodwin replied.

Thank goodness it took only a moment more for the situation to diffuse.

Mark Goodwin asked again about Mrs. Arlington, and this time Kip explained.

"She hired me to write her obituary," I added. "I had some questions, and I couldn't reach her, so I came over in person."

"You're the obituary writer?" he asked, peering more closely at me.

"Yes, Winter Snow."

"She mentioned you. Said you came highly recommended, but I had no idea you'd be so young."

"Did she say why she needed her obit by Friday?" I asked, ignoring his reference to my age. I get that a lot, along with *What's a nice girl like you doing in such a morbid business?* and *Can't you find something more cheerful to write about?*

"We were talking about our dogs," said Goodwin. "She wondered who would care for Max—that's my shepherd—if something happened to me."

It seemed clear how a discussion of postmortem pet care could segue into his employer talking about hiring an obituary writer. I was about to ask what details Mrs. Arlington had shared when Officer Kip Michaels began grilling him.

"Were you in the house at all today?" he asked.

"No, I was about to go inside because I saw a strange car in the driveway . . . this car. I thought someone was stealing Diva."

"Speaking of Diva," I interrupted. "Can you care for her until Mrs. Arlington is out of the hospital?"

I didn't miss the look that passed between Tom and Kip. Even if she did awaken, we had no idea what extent of brain injury she might have incurred. She might never be able to return home. Goodwin must have come to the same conclusion, because his coloring suddenly took on the shade of bleached flour as he slid through the open door of my car, oblivious to the dark-stained seat.

"Diva would be dog food if she came home with me," he said, rubbing his hands over his face. "Max—he's very protective, especially around me."

I offered to get him some water and hurried to the house with Diva at my heels, entering by unlocking the side door. I gave Diva a refill and retrieved a bottle of water from the fridge for Goodwin. The empty house still gave me the jitters, and I left the outer doors open for Diva as I hurried out.

A minute later the puppy dropped her shoe toy at my feet and wagged her tail. What was I supposed to do, play toss and fetch? I wasn't much of a dog person, so I looked to Goodwin for advice. Kip and Tom had stepped away to confer out of earshot.

"No, Diva," Goodwin said sternly. "You know you're not allowed to chew on things that don't belong to you."

I picked up a dark-blue sneaker, about size seven, still muddy, though clumps had started to dry and fall off. Mrs. Arlington would be like Cinderella's stepsister trying to squeeze into a glass slipper, but maybe it was Brittany's. I recalled her boots—the out-of-sync-with-the-weather boots she had been wearing yesterday. Maybe she kept a change of shoes at the main house.

"I'll put it in the mudroom when I go back inside," I said, wondering about its lost mate.

Kip and Tom returned to the car, and Mark Goodwin, now feeling well enough to stand, hovered near the car hood and answered a few more questions, including whether he had a key to the house. No, he didn't need one, because Mrs. A kept a spare on the doorframe in the mudroom. He also said he hadn't seen anyone besides me on the property today.

"Going to answer that?" asked Kip with a nod toward the car, where my cell blasted its eerie ringtone.

"I can't," I said, indicating my problem.

Kip chuckled, and for the first time his eyes traded brewing storm for smiley face. It was a nice look, though I couldn't enjoy it. I had a hard time resisting a ringing phone, and while I could just graze it by sliding my hand between the seat and console, I could only inch it forward a tiny bit more.

Promising to be available for more questions, Goodwin recited his contact info to Kip and Tom before trudging off in the direction of the pool house, where he'd left his truck on the service lane. With his shoulders slumped, he shuffled away, looking very much like he had just lost his best friend—which maybe he had.

Chapter Nine

"Did you clean up here?" Kip asked with a frown.

The three of us were again standing in the entry hall where I had found Mrs. Arlington, and I had just gone into great detail about the intruder's exit through the squeaky front door.

"I didn't want Diva traipsing through. Why?"

"If this turns out to be a crime, you just tampered with the scene."

"Look at you, Mr. CSI," Tom said. "If we thought it was a crime scene, we would have secured it before we left."

Kip's scowl deepened as we climbed the staircase, leaving Mrs. Arlington's slipper on the step as we passed.

The second-floor landing mirrored the front-to-back bottom-floor entry. Unlike the downstairs, however, this landing had two narrow hallways funneling off it, one to the left, the other to the right. Neither had any paintings on the plaster walls or carpets on the hardwood floors. While over time the downstairs had experienced a facelift or two, the antique upstairs hadn't aged well.

Both long narrow hallways were lined with closed doors, reminding me of a dormitory. I could think of several houses in town that had once served as boarding schools, including the Victorian that houses the Ridgefield Police Department on East Ridge and a colonial on High Ridge with original brass dorm room numbers, all restored and polished by the new owners, who wanted to preserve the history. Maybe this house had once been a school.

We chose the hallway to the left first, because Kip said that was where we'd find the master suite. Kip and Tom cleared a string of smaller rooms before reaching wide-open double doors, a welcome relief from the tunnel-like atmosphere of the rest of the second floor.

Through the doorway was a small vestibule with a table and two side chairs. An ornate gold mirror hung above. A large bowl on the table held several keys, one of which I recognized as a twin to the antique skeleton still in my back pocket.

"Do you think all the doors use the same key?" I asked.

"Probably, why?" asked Tom. He then took the key from the bowl and placed it in the bedroom lock. It turned with a click.

"The doors were all locked when I got here, so the intruder would either have had a key or would have been let in by Mrs. Arlington, who would have then locked the door behind them."

"Or they could have known that Mrs. Arlington keeps a key above her doorframe," said Kip.

"That too, although why take the time to put it back and then relock the door from the inside?" I asked.

I stepped into the master suite.

"Wow," I said.

The room was large, with an expanse of casement windows overlooking the back lawn and the swimming pool beyond. One window was cranked open, and I swear I could smell the fragrance of the sweet peas growing in the garden below. A horizon of trees was broken by a sliver of silver, a distant lake, and beyond that the unmistakable shadowy outline of tall buildings.

"Is that what I think it is?" I asked.

"Manhattan," confirmed Kip.

I didn't doubt it. Ridgefield is only sixty miles northeast of New York City, with an elevation high enough in some places to view the city skyline. On 9/11 you could see the smoke pouring from the Twin Towers.

The decor in Mrs. Arlington's bedroom was much simpler than the ornate palette of the downstairs. A muted blue carpet with matching walls made me feel like I was floating at cloud level. A king bed rested against a wall, perpendicular to the windows, so its occupant could look out while snuggled in. It was covered in a silver duvet that was rumpled and had been pulled down, as if Mrs. Arlington had been in bed before she was disturbed. An unlit lantern sat on her nightstand. On the opposite side of the room was a comfortable sitting area with two chairs and ottomans facing a fieldstone fireplace.

This is the kind of money that must make it hard to die, I thought. Kip stood in the center of the room and studied each segment, doing a slow turn as he did.

"Nothing seems out of place," he said.

I followed him through another doorway, this one leading to the master bath, where more opulence made that little green monster rear its ugly head. *It's only money*, I reminded myself. Although it was hard not to be impressed when I had so little of it myself.

Another doorway led to a dressing area. Kip continued his appraisal, looking for something out of place, while Tom wandered to the windows to stare outside.

"What about that?" I asked, pointing to a dressing table with several drawers on either side and a mirror above it. One drawer had a tiny red speck peeking out, a nip of cloth caught by a careless close. Kip took out a bandanna from his pocket, wrapped it around his hand, and gently eased the drawer open. We peered inside.

"Just scarves," I said, disappointed. "Was this scarf sticking out like this when you checked the house earlier?"

"I can't remember," said Kip, shaking his head. "Tom?"

Tom turned away from the window and joined us. "We were mostly looking for someone else in the house or something to indicate why she lost her balance. I wasn't focused on drawers unless it looked like things were messed up. Which it didn't."

"Someone searching through Mrs. Arlington's belongings could have cut it short when they heard me," I said.

"*If* someone was even in here searching," said Tom.

"Do you think I'm making up the opening and closing of the front door? I know what I heard. Diva heard it too."

"Some of these casements up here are cranked open. You probably just heard them blowing in the wind," said Tom, dismissing me.

"No," I insisted. "Windows creaking don't sound like a squeaky door slamming shut."

Kip said nothing.

We covered the rest of the house, checking the places someone could have hidden—more bedroom suites, a door to an attic filled with a lifetime of stuff, and a small room on the opposite end of the house with the same grand view as the master that looked like Mrs. Arlington's office. It housed a desk, file cabinets, and built-in shelves holding an array of books crammed so tightly together that I wondered how one could even be pried out.

Papers were stacked on the desk, pens overflowed a caddy, and the wastebasket held several crumbled castaways. A sleek-looking rose-colored MacBook Air sat closed on her desk. It looked like a place someone worked in rather than something choreographed for a magazine. The only thing off-putting was the tightly shelved books that looked almost painted in place. The well-ordered tomes misaligned with the well-used space and the old working bones of the house.

"This office door was locked earlier," said Kip. "We didn't bother to open it, because by the time we got down here to this end of the house, we were pretty sure it was empty."

"Looks like you were wrong," I said.

Kip's cheeks flushed, and he rubbed his hand across his brow.

"We had no reason to believe anyone was in the house," said Tom. "Still don't."

"What about the now-unlocked study door?" I said. "Someone had to open it."

Tom gave me a look.

"What, you think I opened it?" I asked.

"You were the one who pointed out that the same key opens every door," he said.

"Leave it alone, Tom," said Kip. "If Winter heard an intruder, then this was probably where he was hiding."

The room didn't look disheveled, just well used. I wrapped my shirt bottom around my hand and opened one of the drawers.

"Hey, guys, look at this."

Kip physically grabbed both my shoulders and firmly guided me away from the cabinet.

"Stop touching things," he said, before peering into tousled files.

Papers jutting out of bent manila folders were crumpled, as if mashed down quickly to allow the drawer to close. The files were in no order. Whoever had invaded Mrs. Arlington's office had been in a hurry.

"Looks like my mother has been here," said Tom, chuckling. "You could eat off the floors, but don't dare open a closet."

I knew people like that. One wrinkle in the bedspread and they freaked out, but open the pantry and the chaos would keep you from cooking. While not an anal neatnik who organized for appearances, Mrs. Arlington didn't seem like the type to tag files with a label maker and then stuff them haphazardly into a drawer.

Kip echoed my thoughts. "Half these files aren't even right side up, let alone alphabetical."

I leaned closer, careful not to touch. As if reading my mind, Kip pulled his pen out and gently lifted so we could read labels. There were the obvious ones like *Frontier, Eversource, Comcast*—utilities folders where she probably saved paid bills. Then there were things like *Contributions* and *Home Repair*. Just normal household files.

The next drawer down was more personal, and I noted one that said *Medical*. If I could just peek inside, maybe I'd have the answer to the question that had been eating at me since she first called.

"Winter," said Kip. "We aren't opening any of these files because of the privacy issues."

I looked up, startled, and nodded.

We continued to skim the file labels—*Travel, Botanical Gardens, Book Club*. This was her personal life drawer, and if ever there was a treasure trove of information for an obituary, it could be found here.

The book club file interested me. I am always curious about what types of books people read and how friendships born out of a mutual interest in books can be so enduring. My mom was a fan of medical mysteries—no surprise there, since she was a nurse. She hated historical novels, anything with a love story, and nonfiction. She didn't last long in her book club because her tastes weren't varied enough.

I was less interested in what the book club was reading and more curious about the gaps fellow members might fill. This club had been important enough for Mrs. Arlington to list with her other interests and hobbies.

"I'll be right back," I said. "I'm going to check on Diva."

Instead, I headed toward the master bedroom.

"Don't touch anything," Kip yelled after me. That guy seemed to know my intentions almost before I did.

Sure enough, *Premonition* sat on the bedside table. Sticking out amid the pages was the familiar Books on the Common bookmark. If Mrs. Arlington frequented our local independent bookstore where area book clubs registered their selections, maybe they could provide contact info for other members.

Downstairs, I wandered back to the living room window, where I watched Diva hot on the tail of a rabbit. She put the brakes on when she came to the pool. Taking advantage of the lead, the rabbit skittered across the pool patio and buried itself in shrubbery. Diva sniffed, assessed the water, and made a quick exit in the opposite direction.

Great, a claustrophobic dog afraid of water.

From the living room I quietly stepped into the front-to-back hallway and tiptoed across to the large sunroom where Mrs. Arlington and I had spent yesterday afternoon. Next to the useless portable phone, her iPad was like that sweet you can't resist.

I flipped it open and then closed it again. Even if Mrs. Arlington's electronic devices held the answers to my questions, hacking was way beyond my skill set. And if I could open the iPad, it would be like reading her diary. I was about to put the small black device back where I found it when another thought struck. Maybe I should hide this so no one else tried to unlock the secrets it might hold. I lifted the cushion on her chair and shoved it underneath just as I heard Kip and Tom heading toward the stairs.

Chapter Ten

I had just made it back to the hallway, where I pretended to be watching Diva from the French doors, when I felt Tom breathing down my neck.

"Where did you disappear to?" he asked, standing way too close for comfort.

"Just checking on Diva," I said, inching closer to the door.

I jiggled the handle. Locked, of course.

Suddenly a large hawk swooped down toward the dog. I was instinctively reaching to my back pocket for the key to open the doors when Tom pushed past me. He produced the key he had taken from the bedroom, turned the lock, and flung open the door.

Diva, who looked a little uncertain over what the outcome of her battle would be, dashed through the doors and hovered closely behind my legs. I reached down, picked up the shaking puppy, and buried my face in her fur.

"Let's get this place locked up," said Kip. "Winter, where did you put the key you used to get into the house?"

My cheeks felt on fire as I continued to nuzzle Diva. What would Kip think if he saw the outline of the skeleton key branded into my jean pocket? And why had I kept that key? I told myself it was in case I needed something for Diva. In truth, this house held secrets that my insatiable curiosity was having trouble ignoring. Relinquishing that key would close the door on the opportunity to find answers.

Besides, I rationalized, Mrs. Arlington had invited me into the most intimate details of her life. The fact that she had left so much unsaid didn't mean she didn't want me to do my normal due diligence to get her obit done well.

Sure, Winter, keep telling yourself that.

"I think I left it in the kitchen," I lied.

Tom relocked the French door, and before he could pocket the skeleton, Kip suggested they check with Fire and Dispatch to see who the key holder was for the Arlington estate.

Some people left keys with the police and fire departments in case their homes had to be entered while they were away. Others asked neighbors to be key holders and hold alarm codes. From the small white electronic panels evident on the first floor, I deduced that Mrs. Arlington had an alarm, so it wasn't a reach to think she would have provided a way for responders to enter her home.

Tom stepped out the front door, eyes glued to his cell in search of a signal. A minute later he returned and let us know that emergency responders had access through a neighbor named Burton Hemlocker. Something flitted across his face when he said the name before he mumbled that he would put the key back where he found it and hurried up the staircase.

Hemlocker was a well-known name around town, and not only because he'd joined the ranks of some of the wealthiest Ridgefielders. The Nosy Parkers had had a lot to say when the financier married his trophy wife, a woman over twenty years his junior. As I recalled, their opulent estate, often the highlight of house tours, was also somewhere near West Mountain Road, not far from Mrs. Arlington's house.

The officers waited as I gathered the dog bed, a couple of toys I found in the pantry, a bag of dog food, and a half-eaten bone I found on Diva's bed. I stuck the bone into my back pocket, hoping it would disguise the outline of the key I still had. My intention, I told Kip and Tom, was to drop Diva and her stuff with Brittany and her boyfriend at their cottage.

We left through the mudroom door. I now either had to fess up that the key normally kept on the doorframe was in my pocket or come up with another way to lock the door behind us.

"Wait a minute," I said, and hurried into the kitchen. This would have been a good time to remove the key from my pocket and bring it back out to Kip and Tom as if I'd just remembered where I had left it. Instead, I removed the key on the hook near the phone and, back in the mudroom, waved it toward Kip.

"This should probably be left above the doorframe," I said as I placed it in his outstretched hand.

Kip locked both doors and then surprised me by pocketing the key. "If we know about it and Mark Goodwin knows, others might also. I'll leave it at the station."

Was he taking the key so I wouldn't sneak back?

Diva appeared at my feet with that stupid blue sneaker in her mouth again.

"Fine," I said, because I was through trying to control this willful animal. The sooner she was out of my hands, the better.

And then a thought hit me. An uncomfortable one. Where was Brittany? Surely she would have heard the sirens coming and going.

Diva and I climbed into the Subaru and followed Kip and Tom out of the circular drive and down to the small guest cottage that

Brittany shared with her boyfriend. The skeleton key and the dog bone were now tucked into the car's door pocket.

"There's no one home," I said, after ringing the doorbell. Diva looked dejected and headed back to the car, where I had left the door open.

"That's for sure," said Kip, who had been looking in windows. "They've cleared out."

Tom, looking bored, stayed leaning against the cruiser, swiping at his phone.

"What do you mean, cleared out?" I asked, trying to peer past Kip to see through a large picture window to the right of the front door.

"Take a look," said Kip, moving aside so I could get a better look.

The house had bare-bones furnishings—a carpet, couch, and chairs—but no personal touches like photographs or throw pillows. I could see an open-floor-plan kitchen and island with stools. The countertops were empty save for a toaster and a coffee maker. There wasn't a stray dish or even a piece of mail in sight. The house felt abandoned. I returned to the front door and turned the knob. The door swung open.

Kip pushed past me. "Let me check," he said, calling out as he entered the house.

A minute later, when he returned shaking his head, I did my own appraisal. Closets were devoid of clothing. The bathroom had no toiletries. There was nothing more than a few dishes in the kitchen cupboards and an open box of baking soda in the fridge. Brittany and her boyfriend must have planned for this exit, because the house was clean, with no signs of a hasty retreat.

"Great," I said, as reality began to sink in and we headed back to the cars. "What am I going to do with Diva?"

"ROAR will probably take her," said Tom, who was now within earshot.

"I can't take her there. What if Mrs. Arlington recovers and we've sent her off somewhere else to live?"

"Looks like you'll have to dog sit for now," said Kip.

"Why me?" I didn't know the first thing about taking care of a willful puppy. Surely this must fall under the category of *protect and serve*.

I reached my car and slid into the driver's seat. Before I could pull the door shut, Kip leaned on it and surprised me with a smile— a very nice smile that lit up his serious gray eyes.

"Why do you think?" he asked, and nodded toward the passenger seat, where Diva was curled contentedly with no evidence of her earlier claustrophobia. With her was her favorite new chew toy, the ratty blue sneaker. Next to it was my cell phone.

"How did you get that out?"

Diva wagged her tail.

"She's a pretty clever little thing," said Kip. He indicated a line of claw marks that raked over the cloth mat, now shifted out of place in front of the seat. She must have pawed at it until she moved it enough to pull my cell phone free.

"Great, she just destroyed the carpet," I said.

Kip took in the old clunker, with its stained cloth seats and pockmarked exterior from a hailstorm encounter. "No one will even notice." And then his smile faded as he relinquished the car door.

"Stay out of here, Winter," he warned. "We could be looking at a crime scene."

Chapter Eleven

"She'll get used to it," said the saleswoman from Ridgefield Pet, who I had called to explain my need for a leash, a collar, and a curbside delivery. She laughed when I told her about Diva's claustrophobia and said, "Let's hope that doesn't extend to neckwear."

The poor dog writhed on the passenger seat, squirming in an effort to escape the new collar.

"Does she have a license?" asked the saleswoman, who true to her word had brought all the items to the car. "You'll need proof that she's up to date on her shots."

More problems—and more money. I'd reluctantly consented to the collar, a leash, and the latest biodegradable plastic poop bags.

"Is that expensive?" I asked, suddenly seeing my New York City fund start to dwindle.

"It doesn't matter; they're required."

Then I had a thought. Looking for Diva's license gave me a legitimate reason for returning to the Arlington house.

"I think I have that all in a file," I said.

"Even better. You'll also want to keep an eye on how tight the collar gets. Great Pyrenees grow fast."

No worries there. I didn't plan to have her long.

Back at the cottage, I took Diva for a short walk and then placed all her things, ratty blue sneaker included, near her bed, which faced the window so she could look out. Just as the saleswoman had predicted, the collar took second place to all the new corners to sniff at the cottage. She finally settled onto her bed, turning her big eyes toward me and then letting them droop to a close.

Before I could open my laptop to delve into my work, my cell phone rang with a number I didn't recognize. I got ready to have a little fun if it was a spammer. Robocalls always got a hang-up, because you can't talk to a recording. Spammers who tried to separate me from my money were a different story. They got retorts like "Your mother would be ashamed of you if she knew what you did for a living." I would probably have to alter that now that a recent documentary had reported that scamming was often a family affair.

Although I didn't really need that kind of distraction now, the ringing phone, as always, reeled me in.

"Winter, hi, this is Kip Michaels. How's it going with Diva?"

Suddenly, I was tongue-tied.

"Winter, are you there? Can you hear me?"

"Um, Diva—yes, she's fine. A lot of work, but fine."

"Good. Glad to hear it. I'm calling because I wondered if Mrs. Arlington gave you any information on next of kin?"

My heart sank. She must have died.

Kip immediately realized the flaw in his approach, because he quickly added, "She's still in a coma, which is where the doctors want her to stay—something about resting her brain. I think I should at least notify her family of her condition. And then there's the house. I don't know who is supposed to be watching it, and I can't seem to reach that Goodwin guy."

My relief turned to curiosity.

"Didn't he say he was going to the hospital to check on Mrs. Arlington?"

"That's what he said, though according to the nurse who has been on duty today, no one by that name has been in to check, and he's not answering his cell."

"Hold on." I gathered Mrs. Arlington's papers.

I hadn't really spent much time on the basics yet, because I had been more interested in the woman's story. Next of kin and contributions didn't require much creative writing and were usually just listed toward the end of an obituary. I now skimmed the forms she had filled out and found what Kip was looking for.

"She has a brother named David Wysocki, who lives in Stamford, Connecticut. She mentions a younger sister who predeceased her and gives no additional specifics. She also mentions several nieces and nephews, and again, there is no detail."

I spelled *Wysocki* for him.

"I was going to try to track down her brother," I added. "If you get his phone number, can you share it with me?"

"Why?"

When I explained the need to verify some facts for my obituary and perhaps gather anything additional her brother might want to add, Kip agreed.

"Speaking of sharing," he added. "Do you want to grab a bite for dinner?"

Had the very attractive, sexy Kip Michaels just asked me out? My inner alarm was ringing. He wasn't just an ordinary guy, and I knew danger when I saw it. According to the therapist who'd talked me off a ledge more times than I could count, this was just your usual psych 101. My fear of commitment stemmed from losing too many people I loved.

"Full disclosure," added Kip, before I could answer. "Tom and I thought we could pick your brain some more about Mrs. Arlington's accident. I told him you were probably too busy, but you know Tom . . ."

I suddenly felt foolish for assuming Kip might be interested in me. It was Tom who had leered when he pressed his phone number into my hand. I felt a punch to the stomach realizing that Kip was helping him by disguising a fix-up as an information-sharing dinner.

"Sure," I said. What harm could dinner with the two of them do? Maybe I'd find out what the drive-by schedule was for the Arlington house—just in case I decided to go looking for Diva's dog license.

The power at Gallo Restaurant had now been restored, so we made a plan to meet there.

When we disconnected, I added Kip's number to my contact list and then felt Diva's muzzle at my ankles. She had dropped the sneaker at my feet and was now staring at me, tail thumping.

"What is with you and that shoe?"

And then my cell rang again.

"Winter, what's going on?" It was Scoop, his voice impatient. "You haven't been answering my calls."

I explained what had happened to Mrs. Arlington and how I'd found her. I then told him about Diva.

"I just got home and got her settled," I said. "Now I'm trying to get some work done."

"I knew it." He sounded excited. "I heard it on the police scanner."

Scoop's police scanner runs 24/7, and while he keeps it on low so as not to disturb the people in the funeral home below his apartment—at least the live ones—he is still constantly barraged with chatter. I don't know how he can get any work done. He says he barely notices it anymore, although certain key words jump out.

"The second I heard West Mountain Road, I knew you'd be in the thick of things."

"Why would you say that?" I asked. Scoop hadn't even known I was returning there today.

"Because trouble follows you."

Time for a topic change.

"So, what's up?"

"Pop's—I thought there might be a story there."

"Pop's Place? You mean that new guy hangout?"

"That's the one," said Scoop. "I decided to check it out. I dressed cool, you know, like I might belong in a swanky place like that."

"Tell me you didn't wear the suit."

Scoop's vintage Nehru, a royal-blue affair lined in brilliant gold, had been a standout in the window of the town's popular thrift shop, a well-stocked space that could rival a small department store. At five ten with boyish good looks and a slight physique, Scoop could pull off the look—if he was going to a costume party.

"I might have been a bit overdressed," he admitted.

"Not exactly undercover, were you?"

"No," said Scoop with a giant sigh.

"What did you find out?"

"Nothing sinister. It's just a nice little bar with a pool table and a dart board with guys hanging out, shooting the breeze and using the f-bomb like it was the only word in the dictionary. It would make a really great human interest feature . . ." He let that trail.

"But?"

"But if I wrote about it, it would defeat the purpose of all these guys going there to just let their hair down in private," he said.

Whoever said journalists could be unbiased had it wrong. Every day writers make choices about which stories to tell, which facts to include, and which to leave out. Scoop's dilemma wasn't unique, and whatever decision he made would have consequences. Pass up the story, and someone else might do it anyway. Tell the story and risk losing newfound friends, not to mention potentially destroying the vibe the place had.

"Any new news about Croak?" I asked, changing the subject.

"To tell you the truth, I feel a little guilty. I haven't thought about him today. I'm too busy with the kittens."

"Kittens?"

"Didn't I tell you? Four of them, all climbing on top of each other and mewing like crazy, were left in a box at my back door. Cute little fellas. I'm writing about them now to see if I can find homes." He paused. "But it's odd. There was a note in the box."

"What did it say?"

"It was written in bright-red marker—all caps, as if it was shouting. It said *MIND YOUR OWN BUSINESS*."

Ah. The real reason for the call.

"Have you been snooping around anywhere? I mean, besides Pop's Place?"

"Not really," he said.

My suspicious nature kicked in. He had a reputation for not letting go of a story. Whatever he was working on might have put him in the line of fire.

"You need to report that threat," I said.

"You think it's serious?"

"I don't know, Scoop," I said. "Just make sure you keep all your doors and windows locked. And watch your back."

Chapter Twelve

Reclusive Ridgefield philanthropist Leocadia Arlington, who shied away from recognition for her many contributions and whose generosity supported such organizations as the Ridgefield Library, the Boys and Girls Club, ACT of Connecticut, The Ridgefield Playhouse, and many more, died TBD of complications from an accidental fall at her home. She was 81 years old.

I scrolled through the obituary I had written about this formidable lady who might not live to see tomorrow, and I knew that somehow I needed to breathe some life into her story.

I plugged away, trying to remember any interesting details from yesterday's conversation. Lottie was a night owl, often staying up into the wee hours watching a favorite old movie like *Die Hard* or reading a Louise Penny mystery. She rarely awoke before midmorning. Even Diva had learned to sneak out of the room and wait for Brittany to take her out. No obit fodder there.

Earlier, when Mark Goodwin had rattled off his phone number for Kip and Tom, it had rolled around in my head like a jingle you couldn't stop singing until I entered it into my contacts. Maybe he could fill in some of the gaps I was missing.

There was no answer, so I left a message and, for good measure, sent a text.

Now what?

There was that one loose end—her book club. Why mention it unless it was important?

The folder in Mrs. Arlington's file cabinet would probably have a list of members. Maybe even the iPad I had hidden under her seat cushion or the MacBook I'd seen on her desk could give me a few names. I sighed. An obituary contract didn't necessarily entitle me to invade her privacy. I'd just have to hope her club members were registered with Books on the Common, which I would visit tomorrow.

* * *

A short time later, I left Diva engaged with Richard in a tug-of-war with an old sock at his Village Square bungalow. I opted for the short walk to Gallo.

Power in this area had been restored, and the Hideaway, billed as a casual gastropub with craft beer and comfort foods, had its usual crowd overflowing under tented dining. One of the silver linings to the COVID cloud was the abundance of outdoor dining spots that had popped up all over Ridgefield, many with tables and added shrubbery, reminding me of a Paris streetscape.

Gallo's tent life had been short-lived—they really did need their parking spots. Instead, a vine-draped trellis now separates intimate tables from the sidewalk adding much desired open-air dining. Tonight, the popular restaurant just down the road from the Hideaway looked like it might have standing room only.

"Guest bartender night," said the hostess. In response to my questioning look.

These popular fundraisers were hosted by celebrity residents from various organizations, who filled drink orders in exchange for hefty tips. Part of the proceeds were then donated to local charities ranging from playgrounds to cancer support. No honest cause was off the table.

I waved to a couple of people I knew, including the Nosy Parkers, as I followed one of the regular waiters through the chic bar and headed to an enclosed porch with large windows thrown open to the outdoors.

"Sorry, it's a busy night," said Tom, who stood as I took my seat. "I guess we could have chosen someplace a little quieter."

"It's fine," I replied, though I knew that when Gabby and Abby realized I was dining with two cops, their busybody chatter would begin.

"Kip is running late," said Tom as we both slid into seats.

"So, what riddle couldn't you solve yourselves?" I asked, thinking that the sooner this apparent fix-up was over, the better.

He grinned in that way that gave me the shivers. "For starters, are you dating anyone?"

"Not interested," I said. "I'm moving to New York in a few months."

"We could have a lot of fun until then." He reached out and stroked my hand, which I quickly yanked away.

Was this how guys hit on girls these days, or was this just Tom's unwelcoming style? Either way, I wasn't having any of it, and I rose to go.

Tom practically took the tablecloth with him when he jumped up and grabbed my arm. Feeling eyes on me, I glanced toward the adjacent bar, where I now had the full attention of the Nosy Parkers.

"Hey. You can't blame a guy for trying," said Tom, still muscling my arm.

Envisioning the red marks that would erupt on my fair skin, I pulled from his grasp. I was contemplating a glass of water in his face when a voice behind me said, "Is there a problem here?"

Kip was dressed in a light-blue shirt and dark pants. His hair looked slightly disheveled, as if he had paid careful attention to dressing but had forgotten to run the comb through. He carried a helmet and wore sturdy boots.

"Just a slight misunderstanding," said Tom. "Sit. I'm buying."

I slid back into my chair, resigned to stay now that Kip was here. And then it hit me. I hadn't even combed my hair or put on lipstick, because I'd been frazzled by the dog delivery to Richard. The same jeans I had on earlier had smudges of mud from my trek around Mrs. Arlington's sopping yard. At least my royal-blue top, which I'd been told brought out the color in my eyes, was a change. As were my high-heeled sandals, though the polish from my last pedicure could use a refresh, and I curled my feet under my chair out of view.

"Glad you could make it," said Tom to Kip, though he looked anything but.

One of my favorite waiters slid a glass of Benziger Chardonnay in front of me, a perk of being a local regular.

"Ginger ale," said Kip. "I'm on my bike."

Tom announced that he was off duty and ordered a martini. Judging by the dregs of the glass in front of him, it was his second.

A few minutes later Fred was back to take our orders—the eggplant appetizer for me, Sciuè Sciuè for Tom and Kip. Richard's hobby of sharing new recipes was beginning to challenge my wardrobe, so I ignored the temptation to change to the scrumptious signature Gallo dish.

After some small talk, Kip got to it. "I just had an update from the hospital. Mrs. Arlington has a brain bleed. They're keeping her in a medically induced coma to reduce swelling."

"Did you reach her brother?" I asked.

"Not yet. He hasn't returned my calls."

"You didn't tell me you found her brother," said Tom, slurping his martini like it was all an oasis had to offer.

Kip shrugged. "I just followed up on some info Winter had."

Tom glared. "Hope you're getting this, Winter."

Whatever I was supposed to be getting was overridden by the waiter, who parked an oversized Parmesan wheel near our table. My mouth watered as he began tossing spaghetti with cherry tomatoes into the Parmesan bowl, scraping the cheese into the concoction as he went. The aroma of the garlic infused Capri-style dish was intoxicating. *Skinny jeans be damned*, I thought. *Next time.*

Over dinner the conversation drifted from Mrs. Arlington's accident to Ridgefield happenings and eventually to my fledgling business.

"That's what pays your bills? Obituaries?" Tom asked with a shake of the head. "It sounds, well, kind of depressing."

"The last words written about a person carry weight," I said defensively, and repeated my mantra about how the internet had upped their importance because they were used as historical documents.

"I have a friend who is a history buff and is always digging up old obits to share," I added. "They give me a taste of what Ridgefield was like when that person lived here. I love knowing that our town has longevity and that it is sustained and enhanced as each person adds their stamp."

"Still weird," said Tom as he knocked down a glass of Brunello he had ordered to accompany his meal.

Kip did a quick room scan, obviously uncomfortable that Tom was so into his cups. It was rare to see a police officer having a drink in the town where they worked. Many of Ridgefield's officers lived in other communities where their lives weren't under such scrutiny. I could only imagine the field day Abby and Gabby would have with this tidbit.

While I sipped tea and Kip nursed his ginger ale, Tom ordered an after-dinner grappa. His halting conversation was beginning to sound like one of Uncle Richard's records playing on a burnt-out turntable stuck on slow speed.

"Have you reached Mark Goodwin yet?" I asked as the waiter produced the bill.

"Still no answer," said Kip. "He might have pulled a fast one."

Keeping my own efforts to reach Goodwin to myself, I asked, "What about the house?"

"What about it?" asked Kip.

"Someone broke in, hid inside, rifled through Mrs. Arlington's papers—what if they go back?" I asked. "It's not just the files—she has an iPad, a phone, and a computer that could hold important information."

Tom perked up. "I'll sign on for the house checks. With all those valuable electronics . . ."

"It's taken care of," interrupted Kip.

"Sounds like you're running your own back-end investigation," Tom said.

"Tom, you left in a hurry after we got back to the station, remember? I did the wrapping up. We'll catch up tomorrow. Right now, I'm getting you an Uber."

Kip stood and, phone in hand, exited through a side door.

"That's the thing about trying to work with Kip," Tom said, startling nearby diners with a table pound. "He's a loner. You should keep that in mind."

"Why would I need to keep that in mind?"

"You two must think I'm blind."

I picked up the check.

"This is mine," Tom said, tearing it from my hand and fumbling for his wallet.

The bar crowd had thinned, though the Nosy Parkers were still at it and Gabby waved energetically.

"Who's that?" asked Tom as he swayed past.

"Abby and Gabby," I said. "Sisters. They live at Village Square near my uncle and they thrive on local gossip, which is why we have to get you out of here."

I sent a wave in their direction, then arm-hooked Tom and led him outside.

"I saw that you came in on foot," he said as he fumbled, then dropped his keys. "I'll drive you home."

I got to the keys first.

Kip held up his cell for me to see that there were no Ubers in the area.

"I'll take him home if you can follow and pick me up," I said to Kip, ignoring Tom, who was now fussing about being sober enough to drive.

When I climbed behind the wheel of his Ford Bronco, he gave up. After muttering his address, he laid his head back against the seat and fell asleep, snorting and snoring all the way. He awoke with a start as we pulled into the short gravel driveway of a small ranch tucked off Chestnut Hill Road in Ridgebury—the same road where Maurice Sendak, writer and illustrator of *Where the Wild Things Are*, lived and worked.

Tom slurred something that sounded like "Do you want to come in?" He seemed to already know the answer, because he staggered to the front door without looking back.

I caught up, dangled the keys in front of his face, and asked, "Which one?"

He squinted and pointed.

Inside, I did a quick appraisal. The decor of the small house was orderly and looked like inherited hand-me-downs, nice but dated. I dropped the keys in a large silver tray sitting on a table by the front door. Tom pushed past me into a family room, flopped onto a brown leather sectional, leaned his head back against the pillows, and was out cold.

There were any number of reasons why Kip might not show, and I nervously considered my options as I waited for him. I hoped he wasn't trying to thrust Tom and me together by abandoning me. It was a three-mile hike back to my cottage on narrow winding roads and not one to make in the pitch-black.

Just as I was about to call Richard or Scoop, a flicker of light bumped up the road, and Kip eased his shiny machine into the driveway.

"I thought you forgot me," I said, studying the black-and-gray Indian motorcycle with some trepidation.

"I stopped home to pick up this," he said, and handed me a helmet.

The second I climbed onto the bike and wrapped my arms around Kip's waist, I felt safe, although holding on to him felt a little too comfortable.

We coasted smoothly along Ridgebury Road. Residents living in this part of town, with its wide-open spaces, farms, and equestrian centers, think it is worth the extra mileage to the village center. We roared past McKeon Farm, protected as the last working farm in town through generous donations, and I made out the silhouette of the Henny Penny llama resting among the grazing sheep.

When Kip eased his bike to a stop at the intersection of Ridgebury and North Salem, he turned his head for me to hear.

"I think Tom thought we were—you know—hanging out behind his back. Maybe you could cut him a little slack."

"I'm not looking for a relationship," I said, annoyed. "Especially not with a drunk guy fifteen years my senior who leers at every woman he sees. Besides, I'm planning on a part-time move to Manhattan in a few months."

"I see," said Kip, and we didn't pause to talk again until we reached Richard's bungalow where I would retrieve Diva and my car.

"Thanks for the ride," I said, handing back the helmet.

Kip buckled it over the bar and revved.

"Listen, Kip, the electronics at Mrs. Arlington's house might be an important clue as to what happened there."

"Leave it alone." Kip revved again.

"Wait, before you go, you were going to give me David Wysocki's contact information."

"I'll call with it tomorrow. And Winter, stay out of trouble."

Now why would he say that?

Chapter Thirteen

It was six AM—an hour earlier than I usually awoke—when a cool breeze wafted through the window, announcing that fall was knocking at the door. A gently snoring Diva was burrowing into my side. I wondered how her little body had reached the great height of the bed, and then I zeroed in on a bench, lower to the floor, and newly positioned sometime in the night. I jostled the pup awake.

"See this?" I said, placing her in the corner, where I had fashioned a blanket into a makeshift bed on the floor. "This is yours."

She wagged her tail.

Once downstairs, the leash in my hand, we exited the front door. Of course, I had to return moments later to retrieve the environmentally correct waste removal kit. This dog business was consuming.

Generator groan reverberated across the lake—a nonstop reminder of Mother Nature's vicious attack. However, most wires and debris were now cleared, suggesting we were just a few days from full power restoration. Maybe I should check to see if Mrs. Arlington's house was still dark.

After a breakfast of leftover avocado toast for me and kibble for Diva, I carried my tea to the train room. The segments with sculpted mountains dusted in snow were in direct contrast to the hot muggy New England August we had been having, yet they were a reminder of what was in store. Newer residents were always startled at how much snow dumped on Ridgefield compared to our neighbors. The high elevation probably hadn't been a consideration when droves of city folk fled to escape COVID confinement.

Just as property in Ridgefield was scarce, places to build in the train room were becoming harder to come by. However, there was a small spot next to the newly added cemetery and overlooking the lake where I would add the cottage I had decided would be my next project.

I was about to go online to see what kinds of kits I could find to build when my phone rang its haunted tune. The clock read seven forty-five AM.

"I'm terribly sorry to call so early," came a woman's breathless pitch. "I need an obituary written and was told that you were the one to call."

"Sorry, who is this?" I asked. "And who might the obituary be for?"

"Oh dear, I'm so out of sorts. My husband died yesterday." Her words came in the frenetic staccato of someone who might still be in shock.

"And you are?" I prompted again.

"Marietta," she said in a breaking sigh. "I cannot believe it. They took Burton's body away yesterday afternoon. One of the officers—Bellini—told me to call you."

"Marietta Hemlocker?" I asked, connecting the dots.

Marietta was married to Burton Hemlocker, key holder to the Arlington house. Was that the call that had sent Tom and Kip on the run yesterday? If so, why hadn't they mentioned that Mrs. Arlington's key holder was now dead?

79

"Yes, that's me," she said with a sniffle. "Can you get it done?"

Bereaved families rarely prioritized an obituary before more immediate concerns. There was the emotional tsunami to absorb, even in an expected death. Then there was the litany of calls to family and friends and the personal shuffling of the survivor's schedule. Aside from the obvious impact on the departed, death was also highly inconvenient for the living.

Burton still had a bit of a journey ahead of him before any funeral plans could take place. After the state medical examiner's office was notified, an autopsy might be required, which would be performed at the thirty-thousand-square-foot facility located at UConn Health in Farmington, about an hour away. Dying wasn't a simple matter of picking out viewing clothes and setting up a funeral date. It was a complicated process beginning with the loss of life and ending with a death certificate.

Being called so soon to do the obit was a surprise, though I gathered it was due to Tom's recommendation. I cringed at the thought of having to thank him.

I slid behind the desk in the study and pulled out a pad of paper and pen to start jotting notes as Marietta talked. We agreed to meet later in the afternoon, because she didn't want to wait until funeral arrangements were completed before sending out the obituary. "So many people will want to know. I'll need it out by Friday," she said.

First Leocadia Arlington and now Marietta Hemlocker—both insisting on a lightning-fast turnaround.

*   *   *

I spent the remaining part of the morning answering calls and setting up appointments in the city for the next few weeks. The agent who was helping me look for an apartment, had space to show me. A

CFO from a well-known corporation wanted to meet to discuss how to preplan his funeral arrangements. A nurse from Danbury Hospital had read some of my COVID tributes and asked me to write one for her mother, who'd passed away from "plain old A-G-E," as she put it.

After another walk with Diva, a shower, and a quick bite for both of us, I was ready to face the afternoon. Before meeting with Marietta, I would visit Books on the Common, keeping my fingers crossed that they could give me a name from Lottie's book club. I loaded my satchel with the tools of my trade—a notebook, multiple pens, my phone with its voice recorder, an obituary kit I put together for my clients, and of course, my laptop.

I then packed Diva's things—her leash, her waste removal supplies, everything she needed for an afternoon with Uncle Richard. I left her shoe toy home.

A short time later, I was standing outside Books on the Common, totally perplexed about what to do next. Was it safe to tie Diva to the bench while I went inside, or was that akin to pet abuse?

Tom's booming voice broke into my thoughts, and I looked two doors down to Tazza, where he sat at one of the outdoor tables. Kip sat opposite, pointing a finger in his face.

"Hey, you two," I called as I waved and headed to their table. "It looks like you're plotting a take-over."

"Winter, hi," Tom said, looking uncomfortably surprised. "We're just reviewing some work stuff."

I couldn't read Kip's expression, and he was politely distant as he said, "Hello, Winter," before leaning down to give Diva a pet.

Tom's eyes were bloodshot from last night's binge. What should have been a crisp uniform looked like it had spent the night crumpled on the floor. Kip, on the other hand, looked razor sharp as he stood and offered me his seat.

"I can't stay. I have an appointment with Mrs. Hemlocker to write her husband's obituary. Thank you for the referral, Tom."

"Maybe that will make up for my behavior last night," he replied.

"Apology accepted. I do need a favor, though." I explained my Diva dilemma.

"Hemlocker? Wasn't he Mrs. Arlington's key holder?" interrupted Kip. "When did you find out about him?"

Tom shrugged. "I heard about it yesterday after work."

"I'm surprised you didn't mention it last night. It seems like an important piece of information as it relates to Mrs. Arlington," pressed Kip.

"Look, I had a bit too much to drink," said Tom. "It didn't really cross my mind."

"Well, I for one appreciate that you gave my number to your friend," I said, trying to diffuse the undeniable tension between the two.

"Not a friend, just an acquaintance," said Tom. "I've only met her a couple times."

People don't always know how to proceed when they find that a loved one has died, and the police department is a go-to place for all sorts of questions. Maybe Marietta had called a cop she knew for help.

Just then a nearby parked car erupted in honks and whistles. Diva yelped in surprise. Tom jumped from his seat, splashing coffee on his rumpled pants.

"We could take her for a few minutes," said Tom, as he wiped at the dark stain with a napkin. "But hurry, because we're on duty."

The storm clouds I had come to associate with Kip in only a day were on the horizon. I couldn't decide if he was mad at me for asking the favor or frustrated with his partner's behavior the night before and his lack of information sharing. When I held out my hand with the leash, he was the one who took it.

The building Books on the Common occupied had once housed the multiple levels of Bedient's Hardware—a place where every imaginable tool or household gadget could be found. It had been the sort of place that might have invented the phrase *If we don't sell it, you don't need it.* I walked across creaky floors, passing wall-to-wall book displays, to the front desk in hopes of finding one of the store owners.

Instead, a very helpful salesperson told me that while she sympathized with my plight in trying to find friends of Mrs. Arlington, she did not feel she could share private information about individual book club members. She did agree to contact all the registered book clubs and ask them to volunteer anything they could about my client. Although I gave her my contact information, this felt like a dead end.

Back outside, Kip and Tom had resumed whatever heated conversation they had been engaged in when I showed up. Diva sat at their feet, looking from one to the other and cowering as their voices grew louder. When she saw me, she stood and wagged her tail, and the conversation screeched to a halt. Before I could ask Kip again for David Wysocki's info, he handed me back the leash and said a hasty goodbye. Tom echoed his partner as they hurried to their parked cruiser.

"You don't happen to know what they were arguing about, do you?" I asked my furry friend, who seemed to be growing by leaps and bounds.

She wagged her tail in response.

We walked up Main Street and crossed toward Catoonah, where Scoop's apartment was located. When we got to his place, his scooter was gone and there was no answer to my knock.

Downstairs, the funeral home, with its dark-stained shingles and crisp white trim, was always meticulously maintained and gave off a peaceful vibe. I had been to countless wakes and memorials there and would no doubt attend many more. It was where many residents in our small town assumed they would be taken care of after the fact.

When I stopped to say hello, I found a funeral assistant, Carla, at the desk.

"Where'd the dog come from?" she asked, looking Diva over with a frown.

"I guess I shouldn't be bringing her in here." I could envision Carla hurrying to vacuum up the flurry of Diva's fur that had already reached the carpet.

Carla led me out a back door, where she diplomatically said the dog might like a little fresh air.

"I thought I'd check to see if there are any details on Burton Hemlocker yet," I said. "I'm doing the obit."

"Wow, that was fast," said Carla, liberating a piece of gum from its wrapper. "Want one?"

I shook my head no, and she continued.

"No details yet. You know the drill. He might have to have to go up to the state, although he was old and everyone's talking heart attack." Carla snapped her gum vigorously and said apologetically, "I gave up smoking."

"Never too soon," I said. "How old was Burton?"

"I believe he was close to eighty."

Carla herself was somewhere in her thirties. She had dark-brown corkscrew curls that framed a round, cherublike face with full cheeks and pale-blue eyes. Plump arms, which she usually covered with long sleeves during work hours, were shrouded in tattoos. I'd once asked her what they were about, because they seemed to spill into each other.

"Survival," she answered. "Each one signifies a major challenge I've overcome. They remind me not to quit."

I recalled the guilty thought I couldn't suppress—hers was probably a story I'd enjoy writing.

"Not even eighty? That's not terribly old these days. We've had presidents that age." Some people say seventy is the new fifty, the mark Uncle Richard wasn't far from crossing.

She shrugged. "The state looks at age as a factor when they decide whether or not to do an autopsy. I'm guessing with Burton's age and whatever medical problems he had, they might skip it. They like to release a body as quickly as possible, especially at that age. Bereaved families don't want to wait forever for their loved ones."

"Will Burton's remains be buried or cremated?"

Carla snapped her gum again, twirled on one of her curls thoughtfully, then shook her head. "I don't know yet."

"Keep me in the loop if you can. I've got to get this done right away."

"Sure," she said. As she turned to go, I thought of one more thing.

"Carla, when were you notified about Burton?"

"We got the call yesterday—midafternoon."

"Do you recall which officer was on the scene?"

Maybe Tom had been informed by a fellow cop and then taken it upon himself to call Marietta to recommend me as a way of gaining favor. But then why not mention it at dinner last night?

"Sorry, I don't have any idea. I could ask for you. I'm seeing one of the cops—you know, like dating him."

She looked at me shyly and smiled.

I smiled back, hoping it wasn't anyone I knew. The last thing sweet Carla, survivor of many challenges, needed was someone like Tom in her life. And then there was Kip. *Don't go there*, I told myself.

"Great," I said. "Let me know."

Chapter Fourteen

Diva and I still had enough time to hoof it around the village for some exercise before I had to meet Marietta. Dog ownership was a whole new world for me and a deviation from my earbuds-in, fast-walk routine. Diva stopped to sniff almost every tree and bush. When dog walkers and their owners paused to chat and pet, she sat poised as if on a throne. Thank goodness for a town initiative that placed tasteful biodegradable dog poop bag dispensers around the village, because I had forgotten mine.

During our slow stroll, I had ample time to scan the Museum in the Street, a series of plaques placed throughout the town identifying historical sites. We finally reached the fountain, a large white structure at the intersection of Main and West Lane that had been donated in the early 1900s by notable American architect Cass Gilbert.

Like other wealthy New Yorkers, Gilbert fled the oppressive heat and smells of city summers for the fresh country air of our quaint little town, just sixty miles to the northeast and accessible by train. His home, now the Keeler Tavern Museum, which has a long history of its own, sits diagonally across from the fountain. As local lore goes, Gilbert donated the fountain to replace the ugly watering trough visible from his home. The elegant structure still watered the horses and yet was a majestic addition to the triangle where the main road from New York meets historic Main Street.

The poor architect would turn over in his grave if he knew how many times his marble masterpiece had been hit by a distracted or inebriated driver. When a Hummer plowed into it a while back, a protective planter was erected around it. While the barrier is still an occasional victim to vehicular abuse and the fountain now sits a foot or two higher than the original, it has become the quintessential symbol of Ridgefield. Decorated seasonally with flowers, it's the gateway to my beautiful hometown's Main Street of historical homes, churches, and museums. Ask any number of Ridgefielders what first attracted them to our town, and they will say, "Hands down, the ride from the fountain to the village."

By the time Diva and I got to the top of Main, my appointment with Marietta Hemlocker was approaching.

"Let's pick up our pace," I said, and surprisingly, Diva seemed to understand.

We trotted past two once identical houses, built by brothers, that were always a source of amusement to me. As the story goes, when the siblings had a falling-out, one of the brothers ripped off his charming porch and cupola, leaving his house looking unfinished next to its beckoning neighbor. Talk about cutting off your nose to spite your face.

Ridgefield is robust with such stories, and many of the colonials lining Main Street have their own secrets to tell. By the time we reached Lounsbury House, Diva and I were both winded. We crossed over and took a minute to sit at one of the benches near the Veterans Memorial and soak in the day. Lounsbury House, called the Community Center back when my parents held their wedding there, looked particularly beautiful today, with flower baskets hanging on the wraparound porch. With Diva curled at my feet, I had an overwhelming sense of well-being. Ah, if only it could last. But Marietta Hemlocker couldn't wait.

* * *

Diva ran straight into Richard's welcoming arms when we got to his bungalow. He would bring her back later, because Horace and a few others were joining Richard's blackout party.

"By the way, the garage refrigerator is stuffed," said Richard. "I knew you wouldn't mind if some of the neighbors used it to keep their perishables alive."

"*Alive* is a word we avoid in my profession," I said, and Richard chuckled at my lame joke, the gallows humor we both had adopted since I'd started my business.

* * *

Hill Manor was on Oscaleta Road, a winding horseshoe accessible on either end by West Mountain Road and just to the east of the Arlington estate. With the substantial resources that the Hemlockers enjoyed, I doubted the switchback driveway I was now navigating would be much of a problem during winter. Heated asphalt or well-paid snow-plowers could take care of that. And if the couple were snowbirds like many well-heeled Ridgefielders, they would escape to warmer climates during the harsh winters. For pocketbooks like mine, though, a driveway like that would be a challenge.

The house I finally reached was a stiff oversized white-brick affair that could have been softened by lush landscape—had someone bothered. Instead, with only a few shrubs anchoring the corners of the house, it rose barren and unattractive, as if it had been planted there and failed to thrive.

The woman who answered my knock, on the other hand, was jaw-droppingly beautiful. This was the first time I'd seen the woman whose photos graced *068 Magazine* and the *Ridgefield Press* on a regular basis. Dressed in an all-white fitted jumpsuit that hugged her slim body in all the right places, she shot past my five-foot-five frame by a few inches. She reached a slender hand toward mine and looked at me with wide green eyes glistening with tears. If I hadn't already known she was in her midfifties, I wouldn't have guessed her age from her unlined face and well-toned body.

"Thank you for coming," she said, tossing a strand of shoulder-length auburn hair away from her face.

Still hanging on to my hand, she led me inside to a large living room that had so much shimmer I felt like reaching for my sunglasses. She indicated I should sit on a U-shaped silver sectional flanked on either side by black high-gloss tables. A round glass coffee table that filled the space between the sectional and a black granite fireplace showcased ornamental crystal. Two chairs on the opposite side of the room faced a wall of window. Beyond was the breathtaking view—an ever-changing kaleidoscope of color that forgave the stark exterior.

"I'm sorry for your loss," I began as she finally released my hand. "Please accept my sincere condolences."

Marietta wiped a tear that threatened to escape from the jail of long thick lashes.

"It was dreadful, finding Burton like that. He was just—well, just lying there."

She described how her husband had been out in the yard gardening while she had been inside preparing dinner, a pasta dish made from fresh garden vegetables picked that very morning. One of their favorites that she simmered for hours to enhance the flavor.

I let her talk as I observed her clasped hands, recalling their softness when she led me inside. Those were not gardening hands. It must have been Burton's hobby.

Marietta continued with her story, detailing her exact movements throughout the house, first upstairs in the master to change her clothing, then downstairs to check her sauce. It sounded like she was rehearsing for a play.

"Would you like to tell me a little bit about Burton?" I asked, hoping to steer her toward the reason I was there. "What were his hobbies?"

That opened the floodgates. I learned that her late husband had an antique car collection. His passion for Broadway spilled over to Ridgefield's equity theater, ACT, and he'd even made a cameo performance in last spring's show. It was the kind of color that made for a good obituary.

"And did he grow his own vegetables?"

Marietta's perfect lips pursed. "Oh God no. He could kill a plant by looking at it. I'm not much better. We have someone to help with that."

There were no plants in the interior landscape. Actually, there wasn't much of anything besides stark edgy furniture, large contemporary canvases adorning the walls, and lots of glitter in the form of crystal lining the glass shelves and the chandelier hanging from the ceiling. There were no photographs or other kinds of personal things that people filled their homes with. Inside, at least, this house was magazine cover perfect.

"Sorry," I prodded lightly. "You mentioned he was gardening when you found him."

Marietta looked momentarily surprised, then clarified, "Walking in the garden."

We moved on to the basics of the obituary, covering arrangements, and I outlined what would happen next.

"Do you think we could fudge a bit on his birth date?" she asked. I'd been asked a lot of things, but never that.

"We don't print birth dates anymore. Too many bad guys are out there trying to find identities to steal. We keep details like that to a bare minimum. We'll just print his age."

Marietta looked alarmed. She should be. Nearly a million and a half thefts a year in the United States was not nothing.

"It's just that he was sensitive about it, with me being so much younger and all," she said. "If we could shave off just a few years, I think he would like it better."

I didn't think Burton was in any position to like or dislike anything. Printing a lie, however, was out of the question, no matter what the compensation. I would not be the one to distort a historical record. Writers and reporters rely on obituaries as a source for information about a person, particularly those penning historical accounts, and I was guessing that someone of Burton's stature would have many people writing about his death.

Marietta must have sensed my discomfort over such a request, because she added, "Oh, never mind. People who Google him will find out his age anyway. Besides, his age is probably what killed him. His doctor told him that if he didn't alter his lifestyle, he was on track for a heart attack. But Burton always said life was intended to be lived to its fullest."

Marietta was babbling, jumping from one thought to another. I find that a lot when I interview people who have just lost a loved one. My job was to help her through this by keeping her focused.

I explained that we could make the *News-Times* but it was too late for this week's print version of the *Ridgefield Press*. It would be posted on both online sites as soon as it was completed and approved. We would have to add the service details later, and I would check with the papers to see if there would be an additional fee for those edits. In addition, Burton's obit would run in the *New York Times* as well as a college publication and a few smaller papers servicing areas where his relatives lived.

"I don't care about the money. I'm going to have the memorial at Le Chateau. I'm sure we'll need that large space, because he knew so many people."

I jotted down the info about the former restaurant turned private event mansion, which was only a few minutes away, just over the New York border in the hamlet of South Salem.

Having everything I needed, I told Marietta I would be in touch.

"Winter, would you stay for a glass of wine or a drink?"

I avoid the pain my clients wash over me by keeping my distance. When I first began writing obituaries, I would get so involved that I had trouble sleeping at night, especially if the deceased was young or had died tragically. Now I put up a wall. I was about to respond with a tried-and-true escape when Marietta added that she just couldn't be alone yet.

"Please?"

It was approaching five o'clock, and I'd need to get home to help with Diva while Uncle Richard fed the neighbors. Curiosity, though, made me reconsider. And now that Marietta's tears had stopped dripping over her pretty face, I wondered if I might learn a little more about her esteemed neighbor. In the end, I think it was the *please*—pitiful and defenseless—that won me over.

After she poured a double martini for herself and a white wine spritzer for me, I followed her through a kitchen that would make *Architectural Digest* salivate. Every appliance, cabinet, countertop, and accessory was as high-end as you could get. Sadly, though, none looked used. My uncle, who always insisted that true decorative beauty was where function reshaped form, would not approve.

Passing by a sprawling family room I could barely take in, we ended up outside on a large stone patio with furnishings that actually looked comfortable. I squinted at the horizon, which was even more stunning than what I had seen from Mrs. Arlington's bedroom window. With a tiny remote, Marietta released an awning that blocked the sun from our faces while still allowing for the expansive view.

I was sipping my drink and trying to find a way to segue into a conversation about her reclusive neighbor when Marietta solved the problem.

"Officer Bellini told me that you were the one who found Lottie," she said. "How dreadful. Burton and Lottie were close—do you know what happened?"

"She fell down the stairs."

"Yes, I heard that. Maybe she tripped over that little dog she has?"

"It's possible. For now, the doctors are keeping her in a medically induced coma."

"I heard that too," she said.

I was surprised that Marietta, busy with finding Burton and making arrangements, was also following the play-by-play of her neighbor's plight. Which was curious. If she'd found Burton yesterday while Kip, Tom, and I were at the Arlington estate, then when would she have contacted Tom? And how was she getting all these updates in the throes of her mourning?

"So, what's going on with the dog?" Marietta asked, interrupting my thoughts.

Maybe now that she was widowed and lonely, Marietta would welcome a pet, even if only temporarily.

"She's with me for the moment, but I live on a lake, and I don't think she likes the water. I'm not sure if she can even swim. Any chance you would like to watch her until Mrs. Arlington is better?"

"No, I don't really like dogs. Best thing to do with it is to send it off to ROAR," said Marietta, wrinkling her nose in distaste.

Great as ROAR is at caring for and placing neglected or orphaned pets in forever homes, it wasn't a pet hotel where you could just check in for a night or two. I would just have to care for Diva until Mrs. Arlington returned home and was able to reclaim her pup.

"Do you think she'll get better?" Marietta asked, now taking more of a neighborly interest. "I mean, she is quite old, and she fell down a very large staircase. People that age are nearing the end anyway, so maybe it's for the better."

I peered at Marietta through squinted eyes. Suddenly I thought she didn't look so pretty anymore.

Chapter Fifteen

Reeling back in, I focused on Marietta's account of Burton's friendship with Leocadia Arlington.

"They were buds," she said as she sipped her martini. "Totally buds."

"So how did they meet?" I asked.

"Doctor's orders—he had to walk to keep his heart healthy. Apparently they ran into each other on one of his walks."

Marietta took more sips, closed her eyes to the waning sunshine, and kept talking. "There's a path between our houses."

More into the conversation, I learned that Burton and Lottie shared a love of books and that it hadn't taken long before they were traveling back and forth almost daily.

With flushed cheeks and a petulant look, Marietta confessed that their friendship annoyed her.

Good grief, a woman who looked like Marietta could not be jealous of an eighty-one-year-old recluse with big feet, could she? Although, her husband did share two key things with Lottie: one was their love for the written word, and the other was age. Maybe there came a point in the life of a man with a trophy wife when he craved conversation with someone who might at least have been alive when JFK was assassinated.

I mused over all these things as I drove home. As I came close to the Mamanasco cottage, I could already hear the music as it echoed off the lake. Uncle Richard must have expanded his feed-the-neighbor event, because it sounded like a party in full swing.

I entered through the kitchen and almost tripped over a heavily panting Diva, her version of a panic attack. I scooped her into my arms and held her close while she calmed. Of course, because my arms were full of fur, my cell rang.

Trying to balance the puppy in one arm, I let my satchel slide off my shoulder to the table and fumbled inside for my phone. The caller ID read *Kip Michaels*.

"Hi," I said loudly, because the music reverberating from the out-door speakers was at rock concert volume.

"Sounds like you're having a party. Sorry to bother you," said Kip.

"Not me, my uncle. He feeds the neighbors who don't have gen-erators when we have power outages. If you're hungry, you should come over."

Now where had that come from?

"I was calling to see if you wanted to come with me to see David Wysocki tomorrow," he said. "And I'm actually starving. I can be over in about fifteen minutes, and we can talk then."

Fifteen minutes. I hadn't combed my hair all day. I wore no makeup and had on the same jeans I'd been in yesterday when I'd found Mrs. Arlington. I looked down at multiple strands of white fur and bits of dried mud clinging to my ankles. The jeans clearly needed washing, and Diva needed a brush.

After giving Kip directions, I tore upstairs, Diva at my heels. The cool air in my bedroom settled the pup, who now curled on her bed, suddenly oblivious to the muffled sounds from the deck. I changed from black jeans to white jeans and donned my royal-blue top. I added eyeliner and lipstick and stared in the mirror.

I felt the familiar stomach clench. Even after nine years, catching a glimpse of my sister in myself could spiral me downward. My uncle often reminds me that the reason I'm so good at my job is because I know what pain feels like. *Embrace it*, he always tells me. *Turn a negative into a positive.* Most of the time I push past the loss of her. At moments like this, even though I was suddenly excited about seeing Kip again, I almost couldn't resist the desire to wipe the makeup off and climb under the covers.

Diva nuzzled my ankles. She had the shoe again. I bent to pick it up and studied it. As I had originally thought, a size-seven dark-blue sneaker, almost mudless now, with a few tiny rhinestones I hadn't noticed before sparkling across the top.

"We have to find Brittany."

Diva looked at me with her soulful eyes and thumped her tail.

I left the shoe on the vanity in the bathroom, and the dog returned to her bed as I headed downstairs to the party. Diva probably wouldn't gravitate toward the loud music, though it wouldn't hurt to leave the door ajar, just in case.

Tonight's feast included Uncle Richard's homemade fried chicken along with lots of sides brought by the guests. It was a good old-fashioned picnic with people from the lake, most of whom I recognized, though there were a few new faces. I was surprised to see the Nosy Parkers.

"We heard about poor Mrs. Arlington," said Gabby, who had beelined for me. "And we heard that you found her. Is that true?"

Gabby, short and stout, had a penchant for loose, flowing dresses. She lived up to her name, because she spoke almost nonstop, with seemingly no plan on where she was taking her conversation. Abby, even shorter and so reed thin she'd have trouble finding anything to wear if it wasn't in the children's department, was the one who always introduced the intrigue.

"Mrs. Roth Arlington's an odd one, Winter," she said in a conspiratorial whisper. "She was hiding something up there on that hill, make no mistake."

"Like what?" I asked.

"Like something she didn't want people to know about. Mark my words, she was up to something, and I'll bet someone pushed her down those stairs. It must have been terrible finding her like that."

The girls were scavenging for bits of information. Their seemingly innocent questions were bait, and I was wary of falling into their trap.

"What do you base that on?" My old reporter skills kicked in protectively. *Ask the questions, don't answer them.*

"We hear things," said Abby.

"Tell her about Henry," said Gabby. "He lived up there with Roth and Lottie. They had some sort of threesome going on."

"That's not how it was," said Abby. "I told you, Roth and Henry were the couple."

Gabby pouted. "Doesn't explain the *Mrs.* in her name. What does your cop friend say?"

She nodded toward Kip, who I was surprised was already here and engrossed in conversation with my neighbor.

"He says I should mind my own business," I said, and left the two women with their mouths agape as I worked my way to Kip.

"I see you've met Horace," I said as I joined him.

Bent, frail, and balding, Horace still had that twinkle in his eyes as he appraised me. As usual, his eyebrow wiggle was akin to a smile.

"You clean up well," he said, and toasted me with his Heady Topper.

"Oh no," I said.

"Problem?" asked Kip.

"I should have invited Scoop," I said, and hurried inside to make the call.

"You were right. I went back to Bennett's Pond again, and I swear I saw Croak hanging out with the other frogs," Scoop said when he answered. "Hey, is that music I hear? Are you having a party without me?"

I explained and invited him to join, but he was working against deadlines.

"I found some interesting background about Roth Arlington. I'll email it. I also started researching Burton Hemlocker, because we're doing a story on him. He was a big shot in town. Gave a lot of money to good causes. He was an early hedge fund guy, self-made, and his family tree goes back about as far as the *Mayflower*. It's funny, though; I can't find much on his wife. Her family tree seems to start and end with her."

We said goodbye, and I rejoined Kip, who had moved from Horace to Uncle Richard.

"Winter, I'm sorry about invading your privacy. I had no idea this would get so big," said my uncle.

"Yes you did," I said, with a grin that mirrored his. "But it's nice to see all the neighbors having such a good time. How is it that the Nosy Parkers are here?"

"The who?" asked Kip.

I explained.

"Aren't they offended by being called that?" asked Kip.

"Are you kidding me? They love it," said my uncle, then he turned to me. "They said they had coffee with you and then saw you again at Gallo, so I figured if they were friends . . ."

"They aren't friends," I said, rolling my eyes. "We just bumped into each other, twice."

"Sorry about that," said my uncle.

"Richard, they mentioned that Roth Arlington and Henry Harmless were a couple—have you heard anything like that?" I asked.

Richard shrugged. "You'd have to ask Gabby and Abby. Their information comes in steady drips, like an annoying faucet you can't quite turn off."

The night wore down, and when I joined the cleanup, it felt comfortable to have Kip help.

Uncle Richard had indulged in several glasses of his very fine wine, and he wandered off with Horace to have coffee next door. He would stay here tonight. Kip and I carried cups of chamomile outside, and a few minutes later I turned to see Diva pawing at the slider.

"Good grief, I forgot all about her," I said, horrified that the helpless little thing needed a walk, food, and water. When I widened the doors, however, I noticed the sneaker.

Not so helpless after all.

She had somehow managed to get the shoe off the vanity where I'd left it. I didn't even want to think about the mess she might have caused in her attempts.

While Diva took care of business on the small patch of grass, I could hear Richard and Horace deep in conversation. Back inside, Kip had already filled her food and water bowls.

We returned to the deck, where I turned on portable fans to ward off the onslaught of mosquitoes that viewed my fair skin as dessert. As we sipped our tea, Diva appeared, carrying a doggy chew bone, and plopped herself contentedly next to the cracked door. The shoe had again disappeared.

"I believe you when you say someone was in the house. And I saw those messy files for myself," said Kip. "Tom, he's skeptical."

"The Nosy Parkers think that Mrs. Arlington has a secret that someone doesn't want spilled." I told him about my conversation with the women.

After we made a plan to visit David Wysocki, the conversation drifted away from mystery and murder.

I learned that before coming to Ridgefield, Kip had been a Danbury police officer. He was still in training, which meant he was assigned to shadow Tom, adding that he couldn't wait to get the all clear to work alone.

"Why?" I asked.

"I don't know; something about that guy bothers me," he said, and left it there.

We talked more about our backgrounds. Kip was the only child of a former police officer who had been killed in the line of duty when they lived in Brooklyn. He had been twelve years old at the time, and his mom had relocated them to Danbury, where she was a professor at WestConn, the same place my uncle taught mathematics. I wondered if they knew each other. Kip went on to say he'd stayed in the Danbury schools until high school, when he'd gone to Wooster, a private day school just over the Ridgefield border.

I recapped my own résumé—Ridgefield High School, UConn in Storrs, and my own tragic loss of my father.

"So, your uncle raised you?" he asked.

"My mom was stuck—she couldn't move forward, so Richard booted her back to work and stepped in."

I didn't mention losing my sister, Summer. Those kinds of stories with their heavy baggage didn't need to surface so early in a friendship.

"By the way, I'm sorry we rushed away and left you there. I can't believe we didn't check the house more thoroughly," said Kip. "I had to put that in my report, so I'm sure there will be repercussions. Our only saving grace was that we were responding to an urgent call."

"Hey, don't kick yourself too hard. We were in the middle of a crisis trying to get help for Mrs. Arlington. All the doors were locked from the inside. And there was no apparent disruption to the house—unless you count me breaking and entering. Why would you think that someone was lurking?"

Kip furrowed his brow. "I missed that whole key thing. I probably still wouldn't know that one key opens all the doors if you hadn't said something."

He looked pointedly at me. Did he know that I still had a skeleton key in the pocket of the Subaru door? I felt my cheeks grow hot. *Here come the freckles*, I thought.

"Do you think Mark Goodwin could have been the guy inside?" I asked. "He made no bones about the fact that he planned to check the house before he saw Diva and me in the car."

Hearing her name, Diva sat up expectantly. She remained at the edge of the sliders, still fearful of stepping out onto the deck, and in her mouth was that shoe.

"Diva is a smart dog," Kip said. "But just because she knew Goodwin doesn't mean he wasn't the guy sneaking around inside. He's not responding to any of our calls, and I'm beginning to wonder if I screwed up when I let him go."

Diva had put one paw out on the deck, as if testing it for safety. She repeated her efforts until both front paws were outside and her hind legs inside. The damn sneaker was still in her mouth.

"She's fixated on that shoe, and I wonder if it has some significance," I said as I watched her.

Kip leaned forward and reached out his hands in a welcoming gesture.

Diva inched her way from the door. Her eyes looked downright frantic as she took another step.

"She is terrified of water, and yet here she is, trying to get up the courage to come out on the deck to deliver the shoe," I observed.

Finally reaching us, she dropped the sneaker and scurried back to the safety of the door.

"It looks about your size," said Kip as he studied it more closely. "Maybe she wants you to have it as a gift."

"Well, it wouldn't do me much good without its mate. It's interesting. She never chews on it. She just deposits it at my feet and stares at me with those big eyes. What is she trying to say?"

We both looked at Diva, who was sitting back safely inside the sliders, tail thumping and staring back.

"I have no idea, but . . . ," Kip started.

"What if it has something to do with Mrs. Arlington's fall down the stairs?" I finished.

Kip was nodding.

"The shoe is small. Maybe Brittany's size," I said. "Brittany could be responsible for Mrs. Arlington's fall, and that's why the hasty retreat."

As soon as the words left my mouth, I knew I was wrong, and so did Kip.

"There was no hasty retreat," said Kip. "The day you met Brittany, she was already packed up and ready to pull out."

So, did Diva miss Brittany and want to return her shoe? Or had Brittany, with bags all packed, taken one last trip to Mrs. Arlington's house? And if so, why?

Chapter Sixteen

Daylight was still struggling to emerge through a misty morning when Diva nudged me awake, and we made our way groggily downstairs. Grabbing our walk essentials, now conveniently kept by the front door, I loaded up and stepped outside. Diva halted at the doorstep.

Surely she wasn't afraid of a little rain. But despite my efforts, she stayed stubbornly in place. And that's when I felt the hairs on the back of my neck prickle.

While I saw no one watching me, there were many places someone could hide and not be detected. I decided to trust my instincts and those of the little dog. We retreated inside and locked the door, feeling silly. A deer watching us exit the house, a raccoon caught in the act of scavenging, a dog who'd barked so long his owner scooted him out—I could think of countless reasons I might feel eyes on me.

Through the bank of windows highlighting the lake, the morning light was still wrestling with the remnants of the night. Though I might not be able to see much outside through the foggy mist, with the lights still on, someone could see inside. I switched them off and waited. Every instinct in my body told me that outdoors, the cool gray morning offered nothing but trouble.

A half hour later, when the poor dog burst outside to do her business, there was no hint of anything sinister, and I chastised myself for overreacting. And yet there had been so many times in my life that instinct had overruled sensibility. Often, my instincts had proved right.

After dog duties, I stepped into a warm shower and then readied myself for the visit to David Wysocki. With the casual wardrobe I had adopted since the pandemic and my tight budget, my clothing options were limited. To avoid looking like Diva's lint brush, I chose my white jeans, this time adding an aqua top, a step up from my normal T-shirt. A quick coat of blue polish on my toes improved the look of my wedged sandals.

I was surprised to see Kip in jeans and a button-down dark-blue shirt.

"No clean uniforms?" I asked.

"Off duty," he said, rubbing a hand across his brow, something I noticed he did when he was uncomfortable. "Is she coming?"

He was pointing to Diva, whom I had totally forgotten about.

"Hold on," I said. I settled Diva on her bed with her toys and left Richard a note saying he was in charge. I would just have to hope she didn't feel suffocated into doing any damage before he awoke.

"So . . . why does David Wysocki think we're visiting him if it's not official?"

Kip put his Jeep Wrangler in gear and sighed.

"I told him that the person who found his sister wanted to meet him."

"You didn't tell him I was the obituary writer? Did you tell him you're a cop?"

"Look, something is off, and I don't know what," he said, giving his brow another rub. "The department is ready to call Mrs. Arlington's fall an accident. I'm not so sure. So, yes, I'm acting solo, although I did tell him I was a police officer."

"Are you going rogue?"

"Not rogue exactly. I'm just following a hunch."

Well, I certainly understood that itch.

* * *

David Wysocki answered the door of a modest home in Shippan Point, one of Stamford's wealthiest neighborhoods, which overlooked Long Island Sound. The resemblance to his sister was startling—big bones, large hands, the same shock of white hair. And that's where their similarities ended. Where she was stern, her brother was not. His merry eyes twinkled, and he met us with a welcoming smile, as if we were old friends.

"Come in, please." He ushered us through a small hallway into a tastefully decorated living room with views of the sound.

"Lousy weather today," he said, following my gaze. "Normally the view is stunning."

"Do you have to worry about hurricanes?" asked Kip.

"Definitely. My wife and I put up with the steep flood insurance because we love it here. When we evacuate, our son lives up off High Ridge Road, so we stay there with his family."

"Even with the mist and rain, it is beautiful, Mr. Wysocki," I began, and he held up his hand.

"Please call me David."

"And please call me Winter, and this is Kip."

"I thought you said you were a police officer when you called," said David, turning his eyes toward Kip.

"I'm off duty, sir," said Kip.

"We came because we thought we'd like to learn more about your sister," I added hurriedly. "As Kip said, I found her."

"I don't know what I can tell you. Lottie and I haven't ever been close. She left for college when I was twelve and my younger sister was ten. Is there some reason why you want to know about her?"

"Have you stayed in touch over the years?" I asked.

"After Alice died five years ago, Lottie and I reconnected. Before that . . ." David shrugged.

"Alice was your younger sister?" I asked, and David nodded. Mrs. Arlington's notes hadn't mentioned her sister by name.

"How much did you know about Lottie?" I asked. "Do you know any of her friends, by chance?"

David looked at me curiously, and his smile was beginning to fade. "What's with the twenty questions?"

I wasn't sure what to say. Should I tell him about my job, or my suspicions that someone had been after his sister? That sounded too much like my overactive imagination kicking in.

"Your sister asked Winter to write her obituary," Kip interrupted. "She was probably putting her affairs in order, as many people in their eighties consider doing, and Winter is a professional obituary writer."

"You're kidding," said David, staring at me. "That's what you do for a living? Write obituaries?"

"Yes, and your sister contacted me to say she wanted one done by today."

"Why? What's so special about today?"

"We were hoping you might be able to give us some insight into her motivations," I said. "I also hoped you might know the names of some of her friends or book club members."

David looked at me in surprise. "Book club members? I wouldn't know. And I've never had insight into my sister's motivations or her friends. Lottie is—how should I say it?—self-absorbed. She always took care of Lottie and barely paid any attention to me or Alice."

"Sounds like she isn't your favorite sister," I said.

"Look, we had a bad history. She managed to suck my parents dry financially. College, help with her apartment in New York, clothes—you name it, Lottie needed it. When it came time for Alice and me to go to college, there wasn't anything left. By the time my parents were gone, Lottie was working at a big job in the city, and she barely visited. I was the lucky one. I went to school on a full scholarship, and between my wife and me, we did okay."

The resentment in David's voice dribbled out. Revenge could be a strong motivation for harming someone, although the man in front of me looked more sad than angry. And as I looked around the room, I'd say David and his wife had done more than okay. We sat on a pale-blue sectional surrounded by the kind of edgy furnishings that came with large price tags. Getting rid of Lottie for any money he might inherit seemed a stretch.

"Bitsy's out at the club this morning—her tennis group meets rain or shine. If she was here, she would attest that Lottie and I weren't close," David said defensively. "I'm not sure why you're asking all these questions. You said my sister fell down the stairs, but you make it sound more like someone pushed her. Well, I promise you, it wasn't me or my wife."

"Look, David, we're just trying to figure out what happened to Lottie," said Kip. "No one is accusing you or anyone else of anything."

"Are the police investigating this?" His voice rose in alarm.

"No," I said hastily. "It was my idea to meet with you. I wanted to learn more about your sister for her obituary. And because I'm curious as to why she needed it by today. I thought the whole thing was odd."

"You don't seriously think she jumped off the staircase, do you?" asked David with a laugh. "If she was suicidal, that wouldn't be a very reliable way to go. Besides, Lottie was too self-absorbed for that."

"We don't think she tried to kill herself," said Kip. "It appears that she tripped."

"She might have tripped over Diva," I added.

"Who is Diva?"

"Oh, that's her puppy," I said.

"Wow, that's a bit out of character. Lottie taking care of a pet. Lottie was always just about Lottie," said David. "But that definitely rules out suicide. People who are considering killing themselves give things away. They don't acquire new things, especially a puppy that would be left homeless."

My thoughts exactly.

"Can you tell us a little about Alice?" I asked.

David sighed and looked out the window at the sheets of rain now pummeling the yard. His mood had plummeted since his first cheery greetings, and I felt terrible for ruining his day.

"Alice wasn't so lucky," he finally said. "She worked as a nanny and ended up getting fired when she got pregnant. No one ever said who the father was, though it was hard not to point the finger at the man whose children she was nanny for. I suspected it was the guilty father who put her up in a nice apartment and sent the income Alice lived off. Bitsy and I filled in where we could, but Alice kept to Alice. After the baby was born, she moved to the Midwest. We'd get a yearly Christmas card. Still do from her daughter. Now, that gal did okay. Married a nice fella, and they have a few kids. After Alice's granddaughter, Brit, got older, she started sending us cards too." He smiled momentarily at the thought of it.

"Brit?" I asked.

"Alice's granddaughter," he said, looking a bit startled.

I looked at Kip with a question on my face. Could Brit be the Brittany we were looking for? The same Brittany who worked for Lottie Arlington?

"Do you have contact information for Alice's daughter and for her granddaughter?" asked Kip.

David looked at us warily.

"Why would you want that? They don't even know Lottie," he said, though he glanced quickly at a desk sitting against the wall.

"Do you happen to have a photo of the granddaughter?" Kip asked.

"Look, I'm not sure what this is about, but I don't have anything that would help you," said David, who was growing increasingly agitated. "We're not in touch with any of them in any meaningful way."

"Your sister had a young woman working for her named Brittany," Kip said. "She disappeared right around the time of Lottie's fall, and we'd like to ask her some questions."

David rose abruptly from his seat. "I hope you aren't suggesting that Brit had anything to do with Lottie's fall. How do you know if it's even the same young woman?"

David wrestled his hands and looked to the front door, as if he could usher us out by desire alone.

"Brittany is somewhere around late teens to early twenties," I pushed. "Is that about the age of Alice's granddaughter?"

David stayed on his feet. His face looked like he had been sitting too close to the fire. Our meeting here was just about over.

"Winter met Brittany, so if you had a photo . . ." Kip still pressed, but David was digging in his heels.

"I seriously doubt that Lottie, who never stepped up for anyone in the family, would start now by hiring her great-niece."

"Maybe she felt guilty about deserting you guys when you were little," I offered. "Maybe Brit needed help and asked for it. If she was in touch with you, maybe she was also in touch with your sister."

"I would think that Brit would ask Bitsy and me for help if she needed it," he said angrily. "We've always made it clear that we're here for her and the rest of the family."

So not such a distant relationship after all. David Wysocki was beginning to trip over his lies.

"Maybe she preferred to ask someone who didn't have a son and grandchildren. Do you know who your sister's estate goes to when she passes?"

If humans could produce steam, it would be wafting out of David's ears right now. He clenched his jaw and was beginning to turn beet red.

David Wysocki, 75, died of heart failure after being falsely accused of pushing his sister down the stairs.

"How dare you? Are you suggesting any of us had a motive to harm Lottie? If you did a little homework, you'd figure out very fast that my sister has enemies, and they aren't family members."

"Help me out: Who are these enemies?" Kip asked.

"I don't know who her enemies are. I just know that Lottie stayed far away from my family, even though we live fairly close to each other. When I asked if we could put the past behind us and be a family again, she said it was safer for us if she kept to herself so her enemies wouldn't have anyone to take things out on. Now, I have a busy day, so if there is nothing else, I'd like you to leave."

Chapter Seventeen

"You were pretty brutal with David," said Kip, once we had belted in and started back toward Ridgefield. "Are you always so accusatory? The poor guy looked like he might blow a gasket."

"I think Brittany is Alice's granddaughter. Even if David doesn't need the money, maybe Brittany does. Or maybe the enemies David mentioned reemerged, making Brittany hightail it out of there. Either way, she might have some answers."

"No picture, no last name—how will we ever figure out if Brit and Brittany are one and the same?" asked Kip. "We don't even know how to reach Alice's family, and I doubt David will help."

"I have an idea," I said, and pulled out my phone.

I plugged *Wysocki* into my Facebook and Instagram. It was a reach, because Alice's daughter had married and probably taken her husband's name. Still, some people wanted to be found by old friends and listed their maiden names.

I sighed. That was not the case here.

I then tried *Lottie Arlington*, *David Wysocki*, and finally *Bitsy Wysocki*. I got a hit with Bitsy on Facebook, although none of the photos on display included the Brittany I knew. Frustrated, I stopped searching.

And then it hit me.

"What was I thinking? Alice never married. I'll search for her obituary and see if there's a next of kin listed. At the very least, we could contact the funeral home, which would have a death certificate."

"Good thinking," said Kip.

I hoped that Alice's obituary was as thorough as those I wrote. While *Wysocki* turned out to be the Polish version of *Smith*, I was able to eliminate many names because they didn't fit Alice's profile. It finally came down to one midwestern woman who'd died five years ago at the age of sixty-eight.

I clicked on the obituary and scanned.

Alice is survived by her daughter, Alicia (John) Bennett, and grandchildren, John Bennett II, James Bennett, and Brittany Bennett . . .

I went back to social media and began scrolling through the hundreds of Brittany Bennetts. I plugged in Alice's midwestern hometown to narrow the search. More scrolling, and then suddenly there she was. The pretty young face with lots of ear piercings and an edgy haircut. Mrs. Arlington's assistant and grandniece.

"Bingo," I said triumphantly.

"Don't keep me in suspense."

"Mrs. Arlington's assistant Brittany is Alice Wysocki's granddaughter," I said. "Brittany Bennett is family."

Kip reached over and squeezed my hand.

"Great work."

"Kip, when we get back to Ridgefield, why don't we stop at the Arlington house and see if Brittany or Mark Goodwin has returned."

"Bad idea. Entering her home unofficially would be trespassing. Besides, Tom already thinks I've gone rogue on him."

"Is that because Tom doesn't really believe I heard anyone in the house, and you do?"

Kip sighed. "It's also something else. He's acting a bit weird over the whole thing."

"What do you mean?"

Kip explained how Tom had pushed hard to get the house-checking beat. "He's acting proprietary—not wanting anyone else to take over. He also insists that there was no evidence that anyone would want to hurt Mrs. Arlington and that she tripped on the stairs while she was alone in the house."

"I know what I heard, and I know what I saw. You saw it too. Mrs. Arlington would never have tossed her files in the drawer that way. Plus, didn't you say her office had been locked earlier? When we returned, it was unlocked. Does he think I did that?"

"Probably. I think Tom was originally willing to overlook his suspicions because he had a thing for you, but now he's shifting blame in your direction. Tom has some anger issues, and you seemed to have triggered them."

"How mad could he be? He gave my name to Marietta Hemlocker so I could write Burton's obit."

Kip did the hand-to-brow thing.

"What's the matter?"

"I can't figure out when Tom would have told Mrs. Hemlocker to call you. Tom did cut out of work early, but there wasn't much time between then and when we met at Gallo. When I called to say I was running late, he was already at the restaurant."

"She could have texted him," I said. "Plus, there was that short window between work and restaurant."

"Maybe, but then why wouldn't he just say so when we had dinner? It seems like he would have wanted to impress you with the recommendation."

"He didn't talk to anyone the night it happened, that's for sure," I said. "She could have called him before we went to Gallo or maybe the next morning before she called me, though it was really early. Something else is bothering me. She sure knew a lot about Mrs. Arlington's fall."

"Like what?" asked Kip.

"Like that I found her and that she was still in a coma," I said. "Where did she get all the information so quickly?"

* * *

Pelting rain saturated the ground, and trees continued to uproot around town, dragging the restoration timeline further into the future. Still, little by little, Eversource was chipping away at the damage, and at day four, many households had power. As we pulled into my driveway, the generator buzz told me mine wasn't one of them.

"Kip, do you have power?"

"My landlord has a generator," he said.

"Where do you live?"

"In a garage apartment on New Street," he replied, referring to the appealing road close to the town center dotted with a number of vintage homes, many of whose owners had turned extra space into income-producing apartments.

I lured Kip inside with the promise of leftover fried chicken, and I also heaped his plate with potato salad, adding two chocolate chip cookies for dessert. We carried trays of food into the living room, where we had a full view of the smoky sky melding into the stone-colored water. When lunch was over, I had an overwhelming urge to ask him to stay longer. Instead, we said goodbye with the promise of sharing any new information we found.

While cleaning up lunch remnants, I rolled around the idea of sending Brittany a friend request, then nixed it. It might scare her into hiding.

Mrs. Arlington had painted an unflattering picture of the girl. Maybe she had become wary of her. Brittany could easily have snuck back into the house and either pushed her great-aunt down the stairs or scared her into the fall and then left her there to die.

What in the house, particularly the study, would Brittany be searching for? Something about her family? A copy of the will? And why would Brittany need to sneak back into the house if she had access all the time? Nothing was making sense.

Maybe Diva had been trying to point her furry little paws at Brittany by depositing the sneaker at my feet. I raced upstairs to the dog's bed. No sneaker. I looked in all the spots she liked to curl up, but all I found were strands of fur, reminding me that I needed to buy her a brush.

I called Uncle Richard. "Does Diva have that blue sneaker with her?"

"She wouldn't leave home without it. Personally, I think it's gross and I'd like to toss it, but she's very protective."

"I think it might have something to do with Mrs. Arlington's accident," I said, and explained my thoughts.

"So, you think someone snuck into the house while the lady was asleep to rifle through her files?" asked Richard.

"Maybe," I replied thoughtfully. "More likely the intruder came to search the files, took off her shoes for quiet, and then Diva hijacked one of them. The intruder, who we have to assume was a woman, if the shoe has anything to do with it, was searching for it when I showed up."

"People don't usually look for lost shoes in file cabinets," he said.

"Her shoe could have gone missing after she rifled the files," I said.

"And then you interrupted, so she hid," said Richard.

My head was spinning, and I needed a break. After disconnecting, I wandered into the train room, where I studied the scenes. A few trees had been added to the cemetery, giving it a strangely calming effect. As soon as I had time, I would contribute that cottage I wanted to build.

I dusted engine wheels and placed the cars back on the track. I then rearranged some of the tiny vehicles poised on the town streets. The small antique Ford Sedan was now traveling over the mountain pass that paralleled the train track, and I imagined excited children in the back seat waving at the passing caboose.

A short time later, I was back in the living room rereading Mrs. Arlington's papers. Now that I knew a little more about her, it was hard not to read *selfish* into her motives. How had she convinced Roth Arlington to marry her, and where did Henry Harmless fit in?

According to David, Lottie was all about Lottie. Did the altruistic actions she described in her life story hide her true motives of greed and deception? That was probably what David would say. And yet, his depiction of Leocadia Arlington didn't jive with my instincts about the person I'd met just days ago.

At the very end of the obit Lottie had drafted, there was a handwritten scribble, one I hadn't noticed before. I squinted yet couldn't read the faint writing. I retrieved a magnifying glass from the kitchen junk drawer and studied the writing. In the margin near next of kin, it read: *Henry Harmless (?)*

I fingered the thumb drive and was about to plug it into my computer when my cell rang with a number I didn't recognize.

"Is this Ms. Snow?" asked a heavily New York accented voice.

"Who's calling?" I geared up to respond to the potential spam with one of my usual quips.

"Sondra Milton," the woman said in a nasal reply. "I'm Mrs. Roth Arlington's attorney. I've been instructed to call you about her obituary."

I was momentarily disappointed that I wouldn't be able to have a little scammer fun, and then it sank in. Mrs. Arlington had been serious enough to contact her attorney to make sure I met my deadline.

"Yes, she wanted her obituary done by today," I said. "Although I was hoping to have a few more days to breathe some life into it, especially because I recently found some of her relatives and I'd like to include them. And of course, I'll have to add details of arrangements at a later date."

"Skip any additional next-of-kin detail. Lottie was specific about that. Can you deliver by today? Oh, and I'll need your billing info."

Maybe I could pick Sondra Milton's brain about her client. Before I could change my mind, I blurted out, "What do you know about Henry Harmless?"

"Henry was a dear friend of hers," replied Sondra coldly. "Is there a problem?"

"There's a reference to him in Lottie's notes," I said.

When Sondra remained silent, I continued, "Look, there's some chatter about his relationship with Roth Arlington, and I don't want to fuel the local gossip. The last thing I'd want to do is turn the obit into a soap opera—I'm wondering if I should leave his name out."

"Lottie was very confident in your abilities. I'm sure whatever you include will be worthy," End of subject. "In the meantime, she authorized payment before her fall, and it is stipulated that I have the obituary in hand before I make the disbursement." Attorney Sondra Milton then gave me a figure that startled me.

Temptation tingled my fingers. That was enough to accelerate my New York City plans.

"As much as I appreciate it, I'm afraid that is much more than I usually charge," I said. "If I had a little more time to fill in the gaps, perhaps I'd feel I was giving more value, but right now I can't accept that much money from her."

"Admirable, but isn't beauty in the eye of the beholder? I'm sure that Lottie would find the obituary worth every penny. Trust me, Ms. Snow. Lottie always did her homework. When she called me Tuesday evening, she instructed that I send this amount if you delivered the obituary by Friday at midnight."

"Did she say why Friday?"

"No, and I too questioned the sum, and she was insistent," said the attorney. "Lottie was legendary when it came to her sixth sense about people, and after she met with you on Tuesday, she said she knew her instincts had been spot on."

"She was so alone in that big house, so I asked her to come stay with me until her power was restored. I have a generator. When I couldn't reach her the next day, I decided to bring her warm tea as an excuse to check on her. That's when I found her."

"Well, there you go. She knew a good person when she met one. By the way, where is Diva?"

"My uncle and I are caring for her, though I keep looking for someone to take her—if you have any ideas, let me know." And then I had another thought. "Do you know who the beneficiary of Mrs. Arlington's estate might be?"

"Why do you ask that?"

"Maybe that person could take Diva."

I thought back about how defensive Lottie's brother had been when I asked the same question.

"And maybe a bit curious about who would benefit," I admitted.

"Curious, or suspicious that someone might have a motive for getting rid of her?"

"So, you have your suspicions too," I suggested.

"She's been acting odd lately. Not that she didn't always act a little different than most people, but she was in such a hurry to put things in order. It was almost as if she was in a race against time."

"And yet she has a puppy only a few months old," I said. "That doesn't sound like someone who knew just a short time ago that she might need an obituary so soon."

"I don't understand it myself," said Sondra. "Now about that deadline."

A wave of panic set my heart fluttering. It was already one o'clock.

Despite Sondra Milton's insistence that I leave out additional next-of-kin references, I thought I should include Brittany and her family.

"I'll have it to you by midnight," I said. "I'll leave the service specifics blank to be filled in later."

"That won't be necessary. I have those details for you," she said. "Lottie died an hour ago."

Chapter Eighteen

With a heavy heart, I disconnected. I contemplated calling David Wysocki and then decided that the very efficient Sondra Milton would probably do that. I scrolled through recents on my phone to find Kip's number, and just as I was about to punch it in, my eerie ringtone blasted.

"Winter Snow?" came a male whisper.

"Who is this?"

"Mark Goodwin. I got the messages you left on my cell." He sounded like he was calling from a library.

"Mark, everyone has been trying to reach you. Where are you?"

"Lying low. Mrs. A is dead." I heard the pain behind his words. "Can you meet me at her house? I think I might know who killed her, and the proof has to be there."

"Then you should call the police."

"I can't. Just meet me there in half an hour. Don't get there before one forty-five, because they've got a cruiser checking the house every hour on the half hour. And Winter, I won't show if you bring anyone."

Click. He was gone.

He didn't pick up when I tried to call him back.

Was he the bad boy who'd rifled through Lottie's files, and if so, what did he want with me? Thank goodness Uncle Richard still had Diva, because I couldn't pass up the chance to learn more about what was going on.

* * *

The short connector from Mamanasco to Old Sib could rival any of San Francisco's hilly streets. The Subaru groaned as I gunned the engine, and I checked my rearview to make sure I wouldn't hit another vehicle if I rolled back after the stop sign.

Catching sight of a black pickup closing in on my space, I got the same prickly feeling I had gotten this morning. Whoever had been watching me then might be following me now.

The truck stayed with me through the winding back roads until I turned right on Old West Mountain. I was relieved when it turned opposite toward town. I slowed to see if it would cut across Eleven Levels, which would also land it on West Mountain Road, another way to get to the Arlington estate. It did not.

I admonished myself for being so paranoid. Mrs. Arlington's secrets were getting under my skin. Still, just in case, I put my phone on speaker and called Scoop. Someone should know that I was about to meet Mark Goodwin.

"Mrs. Arlington died. Call me in half an hour. If I don't answer, send the cavalry," I said.

"I'll come with you," he offered.

"Goodwin said he wouldn't show if I didn't come alone."

"I'm going to park somewhere and hike up close—no one will see me, I promise. If you don't answer, I'll call the police, and I'll at least have eyes on the house until they get there."

The thought of Scoop close by helped to quell my queasy stomach. With Mrs. Arlington now dead, I was becoming more and more convinced that her fall had something to do with her urgent need for her obituary. Call it premonition, intuition, or maybe a downright threat, but she'd known she was going to die.

Someone had been inside her house either before or after she fell, and my guess was it had been both. Maybe Diva had alerted her to a trespasser and Mrs. Arlington had fallen while trying to escape. Or maybe she had been pushed, though as Kip pointed out, that would hardly be a reliable way of getting rid of her. Unless she had been pushed in anger by someone who wanted something from her. Someone with a size-seven shoe. Someone like petite Brittany.

Aside from looking for Diva's dog license, which I could probably get at town hall, I had no good excuse for trespassing. Regardless, I had to hear Mark Goodwin out.

I debated choosing the service road and hiking back up to the house the way Goodwin had done the other day and then thought better of it. I didn't have time to mess around in search of back entries. Besides, if I did get caught, I wanted to appear justified in looking for Diva's license.

The key to the Arlington house was still in my car door pocket. I plucked it out and slid it into my jeans. I put the keys to the car on the dashboard, left my car out front, and followed the driveway to the side door I had entered through just days ago. It hugged the treescape and presumably connected to the service road. In the grand days of service entries, this was where deliveries would be made.

I was standing there, debating whether to go inside or wait outside, when Goodwin stepped out of the shadows, startling me so much that I jumped. He cranked his head to look over my shoulder and around the corner.

"I came alone. Now what is it you want to tell me that you can't tell the police?"

"Mrs. A trusted you. She told me how she checked you out before calling you to do her obituary."

"Well, that must have taken about five minutes," I said. I couldn't even imagine what she was checking.

"She was a thorough person. That's why I'm trusting you."

I held up my hand to stop him from talking and said, "Mark, whatever you want to tell me, you can tell . . ."

"No, I can't."

He ran his hand over his snowy buzz cut.

"There's some things in my past—Mrs. A knew about them. By God, nothing could be kept secret from that woman," he said, and I could hear the admiration in his voice before he grew solemn. "I'm sure that's what got her killed."

Mark again looked over my shoulder toward my car. I looked too, relieved. If Scoop had arrived on foot, he wasn't visible.

"Maybe we should move your car," said Mark. "The police will be checking again soon, and we won't want them to see it."

I pulled out my cell phone. It was exactly 1:45.

"Look," I said. "I plan to be out of here by two fifteen. If whatever you want to show me takes longer than that, you can tell them when they drive by."

Mark turned the outer door handle.

"Damn, it's locked. It's never locked," he said. "Mrs. A keeps the key to the inside door over the doorframe in the mudroom."

"The police locked it when they left," I said.

"We have to get in there." He banged his hand against the door. "The answer has to be in her files."

I reached into my pocket, inserted the key, and opened the door. Mark looked at me as if reassessing.

"I had it in case Diva needed something. Turns out she needs her license."

"That's probably also in the files. Let's hurry," he said.

Once inside, I handed the key to Mark.

"Put this back on the doorframe when we leave."

We climbed the back staircase, both of us being as quiet as we could, though I couldn't think why. The house was tomb silent. A musty closed-up smell was beginning to permeate the place, especially with no AC.

On the opposite side, Mrs. Arlington's bedroom was ajar.

"Wait," I said, and hurried down the long expanse to peek inside, Mark trailing after. The small vestibule looked just as it had a couple of days ago.

Two steps in, and I stopped so short that Mark bumped into me. Clothes were strewn around the room; shoes were tossed randomly from the closet, and Mrs. Arlington's bedside table had been ransacked.

"This changes things," I said, pulling my phone from my pocket.

"Not yet," said Mark, and like a parent leading a resistant child, he pulled me down the long hallway.

I wasn't sure which was greater—his determination or my curiosity.

"Let's see what you think killed her," I said, vowing that the second he showed me, I would call Kip.

Mark gave the study door a hard shove before it opened. When it finally gave, I could see files piled like fuel for a bonfire.

"We're too late," said Mark, stooping in dismay and thumbing through them.

"What are we looking for?"

"She was writing her memoirs," he said. "They told everything."

"About what?"

He looked around in frustration.

"Her book club," he said, brandishing an empty file with the label *Great Dames Book Club*. "She and her so-called book club members collected secrets about people. Then they used them as leverage to get something they wanted."

"She told you that?"

"I put two and two together." Mark abandoned his efforts and stood.

"Explain," I said as I pulled my cell from my pocket. "You have one minute."

Mark was quick. One swift slap, and the phone went flying to the floor. Surprisingly agile for his age, he got to it before I did. He then placed it out of my reach on the file cabinet.

"I'll explain," he said in what sounded like an agonized growl. "And then you have to give me time to disappear."

My heart was trying to climb out of my chest. I must have read this man wrong. I prayed that Scoop had followed through and was outside watching the house, though that wouldn't help me inside. I crossed my arms over my chest to disguise my shaking hands and tried to look in charge.

"Back then, I worked for Mrs. A," Mark muttered.

"Back when?"

"In New York, before she got together with Mr. A. I helped the girls dig up information, the kind of information that people normally left off their résumés. She and these friends of hers . . ."

"What friends?" I interrupted again. Although I had a million questions, at the moment I didn't trust my voice beyond two words strung together.

"Some women she used to hang with from the city," he said. "That was what I was hoping to give you—the file with their names and the secrets they collected. Maybe even a copy of the memoirs. These women used the secrets to get things they wanted. It was how she got together with Mr. A."

"They blackmailed people?" I asked.

"They never called it that," he said. "It was more like trying to right a wrong. Then she tried to squeeze Mr. A—"

"Because he was gay and didn't want anyone to know," I finished. "Did she blackmail him into marrying her?"

"It wasn't like that," he said. "He did her a favor, and she did one in return."

"Henry Harmless," I said.

"Henry was Roth's partner. Times were different back then. Not everyone was accepting. Hell, look at things today. There are still those who deny someone's right to love who they choose."

"Start from the beginning," I said, eyeing my phone and wondering if I could go for it.

"Mrs. A was Roth's protégé, and she figured out that he and Henry had a secret relationship."

"What was it she wanted?" I asked.

"Mr. A had a lot of influential friends—she wanted him to use his contacts to right a wrong," said Mark as he watched me through cautious eyes.

I waited as he leaned down and plucked a file titled *Diva* from the pile and handed it to me. I opened it and glanced through her pedigree. Four months old in a couple of weeks. Great Pyrenees, originally from Montana. Poor Diva. Had she come by her claustrophobia innately, or was it because she had been transported cross-country in a cage? A copy of her up-to-date dog license and a shiny blue tag were also inside the folder. I closed it, placed it on the desk, and stayed quiet.

"Mrs. A knew my secret," he said, and then began his story.

As a bright young man with few opportunities, Mark had joined the army, hoping to take advantage of the GI bill. By the time boot camp was almost over, he was on a fast track to Vietnam.

"My buddy and I talked about deserting all the time. Every time we had a plan, my buddy backed out. His dad was former military, and my friend knew deserting would destroy him. We were both opposed to the war, and the closer to deployment we got, the more desperate we were, until he finally agreed. And then one day I found him, his face blown off in a training accident."

"Accident?" I asked.

"Not sure." Mark shrugged. "It took me only a second before I saw it as an opportunity. I switched dog tags and IDs, smeared blood on his uniform name tag, and took off for the East Coast."

"How in the world did Mrs. Arlington find out?"

"When I took a job as a janitor in the building where she worked, she would always stop to say hello. I was flattered. A classy lady like that paying attention to me, a twenty-four-year-old janitor. We got to be good friends. I had a huge crush on the lady, and she knew it. Anyway, I kept my backstory as close to the truth as I could, because I didn't want to trip over a lie. But I asked too many questions and she suspected I wasn't who I said I was. By then I was worn down from carrying the burden alone, and it didn't take much for her to pry my story out of me. I didn't tell her my buddy's name, but she figured it out. She was a relentless investigator. She should have worked for the CIA." Mark paused a moment and smiled. "She was something."

Mark explained that by the time he'd changed his identity and crossed to the other side of the country, it had begun to sink in how devasted his friend's family would be over the desertion.

The Last Word

"It was in every newspaper. I died and he deserted. He was even a suspect in my so-called accident."

"What was your buddy's name?" I asked.

Mark smiled. "Mrs. A was right about you. You're smart. You know how to put pieces together."

Chapter Nineteen

"I think the whole book club thing started as a lark—a little fun for Mrs. A and her friends. Then they found some serious stuff, and I think they started to think of themselves as angels of sorts."

Now that Mark had started, the floodgates were open, and there was no stopping his story.

"How so?" I asked, back to two-word sentences.

"Like the guy she had me follow, who was dating one of her coworkers. The poor girl was picking out wedding china, and it turns out he had an entire family, including a pregnant wife, in New Jersey."

"How did Lottie know?" I asked.

"That's the thing. It was almost like she had a sixth sense about people. When she met the guy, something felt off to her." He shook his head in wonder. "She threatened to tell all if he didn't break up with her coworker. The problem was, with a few successes like that, the club got a little overconfident. And they took some payoffs to keep some potentially damaging secrets quiet."

"Why did you stay?"

"Are you kidding me? When my buddy's family finally knew the truth, I could live again. Once she and Roth got together, she focused her energy on doing good. And I had a great job driving her places, escorting her when Mr. A was in the country with Henry. I even helped research the philanthropies she supported. We were friends."

Friends with benefits? I couldn't be sure.

"What about Roth?" I asked.

Mark shrugged. "He was upset at first. Who wouldn't be? His protégé, the person he took under his wing, blackmailing him? He was hurt, but he wanted the carrot she dangled badly. Besides, I don't think she would have ever disclosed his secret. She cared for him too much."

I wasn't sure I agreed.

"So, they married to squash any rumors about him and Henry?" I asked.

Mark smiled. "Something like that."

While Mark's secrets were fascinating, how far might he go to keep them quiet? Were Mrs. A's memoirs motive for murder? And why tell me?

"What about Brittany?" I asked.

Mark narrowed his eyes and stiffened. "What about her?"

"Did you know she was Mrs. Arlington's great-niece?"

"Who told you that?" he demanded.

"Her brother mentioned a grandniece named Brit," I said. "Kip and I—that's the cop from the other day—visited him, and David let it slip. We think she might know something about Mrs. Arlington's fall."

"She doesn't know anything. Leave her out of this," he said with finality.

Suddenly my cell rang its eerie tone, startling us both. From where it sat on top of the file cabinet, Mark could read the caller ID.

"Scoop," he said.

"If I don't answer, he'll send the cops."

Mark frowned. "So you told someone you were meeting me here."

"Yes, my reporter friend."

Mark grabbed the phone and held it out to me. "Give me a little time to disappear," he pleaded.

Then get going, I thought, though he waited as I swiped.

I could have remained mute and signaled for help, but something about the plea in Mark's voice rang true.

"I'm not quite finished," I said into the phone. "I'm on the second floor looking through files. Where are you?"

"Outside. Since Goodwin didn't turn out to be an ax murderer, catch me up later," he said. "The kittens are being checked out at the vet, so I'm heading back downtown to pick them up."

"Any more threatening notes?" I asked, trying to keep him on the phone. Mark stood so close he didn't need speaker for him to hear Scoop's loud voice.

"Nope, but I have a lead on the kittens' origin."

"Oh?"

"I'll tell you later; the vet is calling me back."

I clutched the phone as if I could hold on to the connection. But no, he was gone.

I was about to tell Mark to disappear when he startled me by taking the phone back.

"What are you doing?"

He held up the skeleton key, and before I could move, he was out the door with both key and phone in hand.

"What is the code to your phone?" he asked through the now-locked door.

"Why should I tell you?"

"I need to unlock your phone and call your buddy Scoop to come get you out. Otherwise, it's going to be a long time before he figures out that you're still here."

Talk about blackmail. I gave him my code and then heard his footsteps racing away.

Great. Scoop wouldn't miss me until after he picked up his kittens from the vet. Would Mark be good to his word and call him? At least the police would be doing their drive-by soon and see my car, but how would I explain what I was doing there amid an obvious break-in?

Mrs. Arlington and her secrets. Ugh, I could kick myself for getting involved.

I slumped down on the desk chair. The only secret I cared about was the one that had caused all this mess, and it wasn't likely I would find any more answers here. I picked up my Diva folder and thumbed through, distracted.

I still didn't know what the intruder had been looking for, though I now suspected it could be the memoirs. There could be a secret that the book club had used for leverage, and someone who knew about it might have been afraid it would be revealed.

Who knew?

Brittany, of course. On the day I'd first met her, she'd mentioned that her boss was working on her memoirs. Was there something in there that might damage her family—tarnish Grandma Alice's name?

Mark had good reason to want to get rid of Lottie. His secret might land him in jail if she shared it. Maybe he and Brittany were in it together. He'd been protective when I asked about her.

And where were those memoirs? Mrs. Arlington's computer and iPhone were missing. Like an *aha* moment, it came to me. If someone

133

was still searching, they must be looking for either a hard copy or another device—maybe even the iPad I had hidden under the seat cushion in the sunroom.

What secret had resurfaced after all these years? Or was it something new?

I got up and began pacing, ignoring the private files that seemed to beg me to snoop. I stopped in front of the bookcase—something about it was off. I studied the books more closely and noticed that none of the books on the lower half had covers. The glossy attractions most people enjoyed keeping on their books even after they were read were all missing. I ran my hand over some of the spines. I tried to pull an Agatha Christie off the shelf. It didn't budge. It was as if it was glued in place.

I looked at the top shelf and saw the Michael Lewis collection. Oddly, those did have covers. I dragged the desk chair to the shelf, climbed up, and carefully balancing so the wheels didn't propel me off, began pulling out those with covers. One by one, each slid out easily. I dropped them to the floor. Once they were all heaped along with the files, I was staring at a folder that had been hidden beneath the collection. Just like the one from her drawer, it read *Great Dames Book Club*, only this one had something inside.

File in hand, I climbed gingerly off the chair, sat down, and rolled to the desk. This file I could not ignore.

The first page held a piece of paper that read *GAME ON* printed across the top. Below was only one line: *Your secret is safe with me, but you have to pay to play.* The next page bore the title *Great Dames*, below which were listed several names in alphabetical order, *Leocadia Wysocki* at the bottom. I didn't recognize the other names, and there were no addresses.

First on the list was a Barbara Balkan—likely a maiden name. I grabbed for my phone to start searching through obituaries. Maybe

I could find Barbara the way I'd found Brittany Bennett. Of course, my phone was gone. I couldn't even take a photo. Privacy or not, this file was just going to have to come home with me.

Two additional pages titled *The Players* listed names of people I presumed had been blackmailed, and a paragraph on each described how they had been "leveraged."

I scanned down and found Roth Arlington's name. This file was going to make the time stuck in Mrs. Arlington's study go by very quickly.

It was then that I heard noise. There was no clock in the room, so I could only guess at the time. I had arrived with Mark Goodwin around one forty-five. He had probably been gone by a little after two, so my guess was that it was now close to two thirty—time for the police check. Thank goodness I had left my car out front, because whoever was doing the police drive-by would surely see it and come check out the house.

I said a silent prayer that it wasn't Kip, because it would be hard to explain to him what I was doing here. On the other hand, I didn't want to be confronted by Tom either.

My thoughts were interrupted by a distant steady high-pitched beep. I strained to place it. Mrs. Arlington's cell phone, maybe? She might feel the same way I did about ringtones—pick something odd so it doesn't sound like everyone else's.

No, it didn't sound like a ringtone. Before I could completely register the sound, I caught a whiff of something burning.

Denial was my first reaction. And then I sniffed again. Something was on fire, and from the sound of the beeping I now surmised was the smoke detector, it was close by. With no alarm panel in the room, it was hard to know for sure.

Unreasonable as it was, I rattled and then kicked the door. The solid old wood barely shuddered.

A sick feeling overwhelmed me. I was trapped in a burning house.

Chapter Twenty

Dear God, Mark had locked me in here and then started the house on fire. What an idiot I'd been to agree to meet him alone. I couldn't believe that I'd read him so wrong. And yet, he didn't seem crazy—he seemed afraid. And he certainly hadn't seemed like he was ready to lock me in a room so I would die from smoke inhalation.

The bare-bones study had no curtains, though there was a swag over the window. I rolled the desk chair over, balanced myself on it, yanked at the rod, and pulled the swag free. I stuffed as much as I could beneath the door. I ran back to the window and looked straight down at the two-story drop to the flagstone patio below. I was going to have to chance it if the firefighters didn't get here in time.

Then I had a terrible thought. Would they even know to come here? The house had a fire and alarm system. That much I'd seen on my first visit. What if Mrs. Arlington had skimped on the second-floor detection the way she had with the decor? Mark might have set the fire up here to destroy evidence and to delay the fire's discovery.

Smoke travels up. How long would it take for the smoke to be thick enough to reach down the stairs, where I had seen alarm code panels? And what if they were just for show? Lots of people never bothered activating existing systems. Maybe the beeping was from one of those battery-powered alarms not even connected to a central monitoring location.

I thought back to the Mamanasco cottage. It was no longer hard-wired like in the old days, when lines literally ran to the firehouse and police headquarters. We were now connected via the internet with a backup battery for power loss. Would Mrs. Arlington, who didn't even have a generator, have an updated system?

No sense in thinking about something I couldn't change. I would just have to hope that the fire department had received the alert.

The Arlington estate was less than four miles away from the antique firehouse on Catoonah Street that still serviced the town. For once I was grateful that the new emergency operations headquarters being built away from the village center wasn't yet completed. I hoped that the smoke now seeping into the room wouldn't outrun the help I prayed was only minutes away. While I waited, I would do whatever I could to survive.

After I'd announced to my uncle that I would be moving to New York City, he'd given me a book for Christmas called *Dr. Disaster's Guide to Surviving Everything*. I think he thought it was funny, but the more I read through how to survive bear encounters and chemical attacks, the more prepared I vowed to become.

Grizzly bears did not inhabit this part of the country, and the black bears frequently spotted around town weren't interested in people. All you had to do was retreat slowly without turning your back, and you could both go your separate ways.

Chemical attacks required covering your face as much as possible, exiting as fast as you could, and stripping down naked to douse yourself in water even before help arrived. Not something I would relish.

Most useful in my current predicament was fire survival. What had I read? In a high-rise fire, avoid elevators unless you want to end up akin to a roasted turkey. That one was etched uncomfortably in my brain.

What else? Fires needed fuel to burn, and homes built a hundred years ago didn't always provide the same fuel opportunities as new houses with synthetics and plastics. Hopefully Mrs. Arlington's old house with its plaster walls would slow the flames.

Fires also needed oxygen. Well, so did I.

I hoped the window I now tried to lift wouldn't attract the flames. As much as I put all my strength into it, the old frame wouldn't budge. Too many coats of paint over the years had secured it so tight it might as well have been nailed shut.

By now the smoke had seeped into the room enough to make my eyes water. I was also beginning to cough.

What secret was still in here that was worth killing for? Had Mark lured me here knowing that I had been the last to speak with Mrs. Arlington? He might have been trying to determine what I knew and who I might have told before getting rid of me. I had the sick feeling that I had just placed Scoop in mortal danger.

A racing heart, clammy hands, and the desire to climb out of my body told me I was also in the throes of a panic attack. The smoke was still coming from the gaps surrounding the door and had risen, hanging like a cloud overhead. The swag wasn't enough. I crawled to the door, sticking low to the floor. I pulled the swag out to reposition it and then jumped back in terror as a thick haze of black wafted into my face. Coughing, my eyes stinging, I hurriedly stuffed the swag back. I then kicked off my shoes and tore off my jeans, which I stuffed tightly into the remaining gaps.

The smoke confirmed that the fire was heading my way, if not already nearby, and I was going to be out of options soon. To have any chance of survival, I would have to break that window and lower myself as close to the stone patio as my five foot five inches could reach.

I searched for something, anything to break the window. Aside from the few books I had previously removed from the shelf and had already thrown at it, there was nothing strong. I wished I had the bucket I had used on the downstairs door when I first broke in. Even the wastebasket was useless, because it was wicker. As a last resort, I took the chair and, with all my strength, flung it. One of the plastic wheels fell off as the window cracked. I tried again. The window still held.

Before I could throw the chair again, I heard sirens. Relief was only momentary, because the cloud of smoke now felt like fog surrounding me. I tried to breathe into my arm and then pulled my shirt up over my face, gasping for air.

Between the smoke and panic, it was hard to get a breath of any kind. The overwhelming sorrow I felt as the realization sank in that I might die today stalled me for a moment.

No way, I thought. I'd throw the chair again and lower myself out the window. I'd risk the drop to the cement patio. Irrationally, I decided I would not leave the room without revenge. I grabbed a scrap of paper from the desk, scribbled a note, and stuck it in my bra—*Mark Goodwin locked me in and started the fire*. If I died of smoke inhalation, someone might at least find it. Unless, of course, my body was roasted.

STOP, I told myself. *Think.*

I knew from my survival reading that there was something called back draft, and I tried to remember if this was the type of environment that would create an explosion. The door still felt cool, so the flames had not yet reached this part of the house. The smoke, however, was a rude reminder that the fire was heading this way fast. I decided to risk it and threw the chair again.

More cracks riddled what I could now see was a double-paned window. I thought I heard the driveway alarm over the incessant smoke detector, and noise outside told me that the firefighters were here. Somehow I would have to let them know where I was trapped.

Stuffing the cracks with my jeans and the swag had bought me some time. I quickly dropped to the floor, where the smoke was less dense. I would wait here until I was sure the firefighters would be able to hear me when I threw the chair at the window again. I would then keep doing it until I made enough noise for them to notice.

Burying my face in my arms, I pressed my back against the bookshelf and listened. A loud click caused something to shift behind me, and I fell backward into a cool black abyss.

What the heck?

The bookshelf, with its glued-together tomes that I hadn't been able to tug off the shelves, had been a decorative way of treating a closet door—a well-sealed closet door—which had now opened. I knew I needed to shut it again, and yet it was so dark—what if I got stuck in there and no one ever found me? Didn't they tell you not to hide in closets when a building was on fire? I might be locked in the walls of the burned-down Arlington estate in perpetuity. My poor family would never know what had happened to me.

Cloudy thinking aside, when smoke chased me inside the closet, I knew I had no choice but to slam the door against the murderous gasses. A few minutes later I was feeling less oxygen deprived, though my breathing and heart rate could still rival that of an Olympic sprinter. It was pitch-black, and as my hands moved over the wall, I felt enormous relief at finding a light switch. That is, until I flicked it on and off. *Idiot*, I thought. *Power has not yet been restored to West Mountain.*

As if blind, I moved my hands around. It appeared that this was Mrs. Arlington's office supply closet. Trying to call out with a raspy voice wasn't working, so I continued investigating the space.

Eyes straining in the darkness, I cursed Goodwin for taking my phone. I could have called for help. I could have used my flashlight app. Of course, that was his plan, wasn't it? Take my phone, start the fire, and goodbye, Winter Snow, the woman who had been nosing around and now knew his secrets. Hadn't he said he had a truck? Maybe the black truck that had been following me was his.

The roar of water from heavy hoses slapping against the house somewhere still sounded so far away. I called out, and my voice sounded like Croak's. I tried again, louder. Still no response. Feeling like a caged animal, I suddenly understood Diva's claustrophobia.

"Calm down. Breathe," I told myself aloud.

I did a few inhale/exhale exercises.

I could probably wait out the fire here in this well-sealed closet, where very little smoke had followed in after me. When the fire was out, I could exit the way I came in, I told myself logically. Of course, that was assuming it was a fire that could be put out before it destroyed the rest of the house. Flashbacks of a flaming mansion on High Ridge a number of years back, rumored to be arson, trailed in my brain. That fire had flattened the entire structure like a pancake of ash and debris.

I felt back for the door I had come through, and sure enough, there was a normal knob. Thank goodness the door still felt cool. The fire hadn't spread inside the room where I had been trapped. *Okay*, I thought. *Stay in control, and all will be fine.*

As tempted as I was to crawl back and retrieve my jeans, I left the door closed. Fine or not, I was not reentering that smoke-filled coffin. Instead, I continued feeling my way around the closet. My fingers moved over what felt like a three-hole punch, extra file folders, and so on. Mrs. Arlington could compete with Squashes, our former office supply store on Main Street.

And then, suddenly, I heard the unmistakable sci-fi ring of my cell. How could that be? I followed the sound. No light flickered anywhere to indicate where it might be. If I could find it, I could turn on my flashlight app. I could text 911 with the address. Maybe this high up on the second floor, I'd even have enough of a signal to call the fire department to let them know the house was occupied.

I worked my way around the closet, passing over more shelves of supplies and something that felt soft, like a blanket. Where had that been when I needed it? Finally, I reached the opposite side of the cramped space where the ringtone was loudest.

And then it stopped.

In this blackness, there was no way I would find it. Still, I continued feeling toward the direction the sound had come from.

A moment later it started again. Still no light indicating that it was here in the closet, although it could be hidden under something. I picked up my pace as I continued to feel my way toward the ringing phone. Just as it stopped again, I reached what felt like another door. Moving my hands over it, I easily found a knob. I touched the door to feel for heat. Nothing. Slowly I pulled the door open, ready to slam it against any deluge of smoke. However, the large room diluted what smoke there was. This was the room farthest from the master bedroom and closest to the back staircase. As I took one step inside, I tripped over something and went flying into a face-plant.

My hands smarted where they had slapped the floor to break my fall, and my shoulders hurt. My jaw didn't feel broken, though it would be bruised. I ran my tongue over teeth that I was relieved to find still intact.

Pulling myself to my hands and knees, I looked to see what had caused me to trip. The smoke mixed with the light from the window made the room look like a misty morning, and I blinked several times to refocus eyes that stung. And then I blinked again.

Mark Goodwin lay in front of the door I had just exited. The loosening of his muscles made his cheek bones protrude, as if he had had too many fillers injected by an incompetent physician. His deeply tanned face was now the color of unbleached flour, and his head was contorted at an odd angle, with blood pooling beneath it.

My cell phone rang again.

Mark's back pocket lit up like Broadway. Just as I pulled my cell from his pocket, the door cautiously opened and a firefighter in full gear entered. He squawked something into his radio, took in the scene, and came straight for me. It was then that I remembered the two files I had left on the desk in Mrs. Arlington's study. Too late to go back now. And also too late to retrieve the iPad hidden under the seat cushion in the sunroom.

Chapter Twenty-One

"**I** know how this looks," I said to Kip, who had been waiting outside with half the cops and firefighters in town. "Mark Goodwin called me to meet him here. He thought we'd find a clue about why Mrs. Arlington died."

Kip probably wasn't shocked to see me emerge from the house—he would have seen my car. He might, however, have been surprised to see me standing there, cheeks burning with humiliation, in skimpy hot-pink bikini underwear.

When the firefighter led me down the back staircase and out the mudroom door, I was surprised to see that someone had moved my car out of sight to the service side of the house. Either it had been in the way of the fire trucks or Mark had moved it to give himself more time to run. Either way, it explained why no police had come to look for me.

With Kip on my heels, I was escorted to the waiting ambulance, where an EMT promptly wrapped my arm in a blood pressure cuff. From the surrounding chatter, I gathered the fire was out and damage was now limited to water and smoke.

I had no idea if the room where I had been held hostage was destroyed and along with it the folders I'd left on the desk. I didn't even want to think about my jeans, though they were replaceable, as were Diva's dog tags. Not so much the book club file.

Poor Mark Goodwin. He'd probably been telling the truth when he'd said he just wanted a head start. He must have seen the flames or smelled the smoke and come back to let me out. He would have ducked into the end room to get out of the smoke-filled hallway with the intent of reaching me through the Jack and Jill closet. Had he seen the arsonist? Was that why he had been killed?

"I don't think you know how this looks," said Kip, as an EMT handed him a blanket to wrap around me. "A firefighter found you taking something from a dead man's pocket. The fire looks like it was started intentionally, and one of the firemen who cleared the house said some of the rooms had been ransacked. You were the only one inside."

"Actually, not true. Mark Goodwin was inside, though admittedly dead. I was only taking my cell from his pocket."

"I rest my case," said Kip, and he did his brow sweep.

"Look, I went to meet Mark because he said that Mrs. Arlington blackmailed people, though he called it leveraging. Anyway, he thought he could find proof that her death wasn't accidental. You can check my cell. Then he told me his story, took my phone, and locked me in the study. I wanted to call you, but he wanted a head start. I thought he started the fire, but he couldn't, because he's dead—so who did? We have to get back in there to get the files."

"You're rambling," said Kip, and pulled the blanket more securely around me. "It looks to everyone who responded like you started the fire to get rid of Mark's body."

"You can't seriously think I would do that," I said. "What would be my motive?"

I didn't add that if I were starting a fire to hide evidence, I'd start it in the room where the dead body was instead of on the other side of the house. And I wouldn't trap myself in a room and then give up a good pair of jeans to keep the smoke from killing me.

I thought that the poor EMT who was taking my vitals must be having a hard time following our conversation. Professional that he was, he said nothing and continued with the job of checking me out.

"I'm just telling you what it looks like," said Kip.

"I was locked in a room and fighting for my life. I can show you if we can get back inside. And I can show you the file I found if the room is still intact—the one that links Mrs. Arlington's past with what has happened to her. In fact, I think someone returned to look for a file with secrets and wore a size-seven sneaker. That's why Diva carries it around. She might not be able to talk, but she's trying to communicate."

Kip stared at me with troubled gray eyes.

"I think you're in shock," he said. Then, taking advantage of the EMT releasing me from the blood pressure cuff, he wrapped his arms around my trembling shoulders and gently rubbed my back.

I pushed away angrily. "You think I'm making this up."

"You are really something else," he said as he released his hold on me. "First you break and enter, now you're close to being accused of murder and bordering on shock, and all you can do is be angry. Add to that you want me to go back into the house to retrieve files. Winter—that is not going to happen."

"Fine. If you should ever decide to do your job, you will see that the door to Mrs. Arlington's study is locked. You will also see that the room adjacent to her study has a closet that acts as a Jack and Jill between both rooms. It was in that room that I tripped over Mark's body while I was trying to escape the smoke. If you want any more information, call me."

"What is a Jack and Jill?" asked Kip, and I could see he was truly puzzled.

"You know, like when there is a connecting bath between two rooms—well, this is a connecting closet," I said. "Now, I'm going home."

"You're not going home," said a gruff voice behind me. "You're coming downtown with me for questioning."

I turned to see Tom. He was staring at me as if we had never met. Boy, he really must be mad at me for turning his dating offer down.

Kip rolled his eyes and shook his head, though Tom looked deadly serious.

"You were seen emptying the pockets of a dead man. Come with me without resistance, or otherwise I'll arrest you."

"Ms. Snow is going to the hospital," said the deep, booming voice of the EMT. While his bold elocution didn't go with his small, fit body, it stopped everyone in their tracks. "Smoke inhalation is nothing to be casual about."

"I feel fine now; just a little raspy throat." My voice sounded like I had spent the evening with Croak and his friends.

"How long were you trapped in there?" asked the EMT.

"I don't know, though I was starting to feel light-headed," I admitted.

"You need to get checked. Your blood pressure is understandably a little high, and we are not taking any chances," said the EMT.

"Could I go in my own car?" Maybe I could swing home for some pants.

"Not advisable, miss," he said. "We'll take you in the ambulance."

"Don't leave town," said Tom. "There will be questions." He stormed away.

"I'll get your car home for you," said Kip, who then followed Tom.

* * *

The ride with Ridgefield's professionals proved to have a tranquil effect, as they calmly provided me with information about smoke inhalation. Because Ridgefield's EMTs are also firefighters, I quizzed them about how the blaze started. They wouldn't provide any details except to tell me what I expected to hear. I was lucky they'd been able to knock down the fire so quickly and that it hadn't gotten inside the walls. If that had happened, the entire place could have been gone in minutes and I would have been a goner.

Danbury Hospital checked me out quickly and provided recommendations to take it easy over the next few days. A kindly nurse had provided me with scrubs, so I didn't have to go home half-naked. When I finally exited the ER, Uncle Richard was waiting, and his face registered relief when he saw that I was okay. By his side was Scoop.

As we rode home, I relayed the entire story that Mark Goodwin had told me.

"I think he thought there'd be something in Mrs. Arlington's files that would show who was behind her death. Someone got there first," I said.

"Well, it's a darn good thing I had to stop home to trade my scooter for an Uber before going to the vet," said Scoop. "I heard over the scanner that there was a fire on West Mountain. The sirens were already screaming on Catoonah Street. I put two and two together and called your cell, and there was no answer. I texted you about the fire. And then I kept calling. Finally, someone answered."

"Mark. What did he say?"

"All I heard was some heavy breathing, like he was running, and a loud noise blasting—probably the fire alarm. Then he told me, 'I'll get her,'" said Scoop.

"Anything else?" I asked.

"I don't know," said Scoop. "I was already jumping on my Vespa to try to get to you myself. I got to West Mountain on the tail of the first fire truck."

"Mark could have seen you calling on my caller ID and might have checked the messages to make sure you weren't already sending the police," I said.

"He could have heard the alarm, or maybe he saw the smoke," said Scoop.

"Either way, wherever he was had to be close to the house," I said. "He obviously had time to get back and get himself killed before the first responders arrived."

"When I got to the Arlingtons' driveway, it was already blocked and I could see smoke curling up over the treetops," said Scoop. "I wove in as close as I could get on my Vespa, and when the fire police stopped me, I told them I thought you were still in the house on the second floor. After that I just kept calling your cell. I didn't know what else to do."

"You saved my life, Scoop," I said.

I repeated what the EMTs had told me about how the materials used in homes could influence how quickly a fire spreads. That and the fact that the Arlington house had a closed floor plan with multiple shut bedroom doors lining those long narrow hallways—all had been helpful in stopping the spread, although there was a heck of a lot of smoke. And smoke, they told me, is what usually kills you.

While my uncle maneuvered around traffic built up on I – 84 and Scoop checked his cell for messages, I pulled the paper from my bra accusing Mark Goodwin of starting the fire and crumbled it. Mark had said he wanted a head start, and yet he hadn't traveled too far from the house.

"Mark would have been able to listen or read my voice mail transcription, because he had my pass code," I said, and imagined him packing his bags and then dropping everything because he'd either smelled smoke, heard the alarm, or received Scoop's message to me. He would have raced to get back to let me out. Someone was either still in the house trying to spread the fire or had followed him back inside the burning building.

"Do you think someone started the fire to cover up Mark's death?" asked my uncle.

"No, the timing was wrong for that—Mark wouldn't have returned to the house to get me unless he knew about the fire," I said. "Someone might have been trying to cover up the fact that Mrs. Arlington's bedroom and study had been ransacked."

"Maybe they didn't even know you were trapped in the house," said Uncle Richard, no doubt reassuring himself that no one wanted me dead.

"Maybe," I said, though I wasn't sure. "Scoop, you need to tell the police what you told me about the phone call to Mark before they start thinking I'm the killer."

Scoop laughed. "Right. Like you, who has a soft spot for everyone in the world, would murder another breathing soul."

"Tell that to Kip and Tom."

Chapter Twenty-Two

Diva was panting like an out-of-breath swimmer as she greeted us with a tail wagging hard enough to fan my legs. Her need to escape confinement rivaled even my worse panic attacks.

"This is Diva?" asked Scoop, and immediately he was on the floor petting and cuddling her. Diva looked at me with those big eyes that seemed to be saying, *See, this is how you're supposed to take care of your pet.* I leaned down, gave her a rub, and left her to Scoop.

Uncle Richard and I surveyed the damage Diva's escape efforts had left in her wake. There were deep scratches in the moldings around both the kitchen and front doors, though there was no evident damage on the doors leading to the deck and water beyond. In the study, where the windows were low to the floor, she had taken a bite off part of the sill.

Suddenly I felt overwhelmed. What was I going to do with this determined dog now that Mrs. Arlington was gone? And then I had another terrible thought. Where was Max, Mark Goodwin's shepherd? I envisioned him trapped in Mark's hideaway or maybe loaded into the truck with no food or water.

Gerri Lewis

That at least was worth a text to Kip. *Goodwin's dog Max is alone somewhere.*

He texted back almost immediately. *I've been looking. No luck yet.*

I sank into the living room chair, feeling drained, as I watched Scoop and Diva wrestle over a knotted toy. The humiliation of being escorted from the burning building in my underwear still smarted.

"Stop thinking about it," said Scoop, eyeing me.

"What?"

"Whatever is making your freckles look like leopard print. They're always a dead giveaway, especially when you're mad or embarrassed. Or lying."

"When have I ever lied to you?" I asked.

"Plenty of times—by omission, that is. Like holding out on details you don't want me to write about."

Thankfully, that was the moment that Richard barged into the living room, nearly tripping over Diva and Scoop's floor exercise as he entered.

"I'm rustling up some dinner. It'll be ready in ten," he said.

Scoop begged off. His vet planned to drop the kittens at his apartment, because he only had a scooter and it was too late to rely on an Uber in small-town Ridgefield.

"I could drive you," I said, by way of apology.

Scoop rose and gave me a goodbye cheek peck.

"You rest," he said. "And don't worry about not telling me everything. I don't tell you everything either."

"Don't erase your recents," I hollered after him, knowing that the record of Mark's voice answering my phone might be all that stood in the way of me and arrest.

* * *

152

When the evening shadows shrouded the lake and the twinkle of lights in houses across Mamanasco announced more power restoration, I suddenly realized with relief that I no longer heard the steady drone of our generator.

I idled over the past twelve hours. Mark had died probably because he had come back to do the right thing by saving me. If the smoke had been too thick or the fire had been closing in on the study door, he would have entered the last room at the far end of the hallway, oblivious to the murderous stalker who followed him inside.

Whoever started the fire had probably done so to cover their tracks after they ransacked the bedroom. That, and maybe whatever secrets they didn't want revealed were still filed away somewhere in the house. Thanks to Diva, we still had the blue sneaker.

Dinner was a vegetarian panini, oozing with cheese and just slightly overcooked because Uncle Richard hadn't mastered his new panini maker yet. Even in my state of depression, I had to admit the flavors were delicious, despite the burnt bread.

While my uncle walked Diva, I sent the lawyer Sondra Milton an update about the fire along with Mrs. Arlington's obituary. I wanted to wash my hands of anything related to her, her house, and the mysteries surrounding her life.

After Uncle Richard returned with Diva, he took an appraising look. "Are you sure you don't need anything else?"

"I'm fine now," I said with a reassuring smile. The last thing I wanted was to worry my uncle.

Once he was gone, Diva and I padded upstairs to my room, where I did a quick version of my bedtime routine and crawled under the covers. Sensing my displeasure over the damaged millwork or maybe concerned over the next steps in her search for a forever family, Diva dutifully went to her makeshift bed, rested her head on her paws, and gave me a woeful look.

It felt like only minutes later that my phone jarred me awake, and I groggily fumbled for it. I was shocked to find that I had been sleeping for twelve hours. Diva, who had transitioned from floor to bed, was pressing against my side.

"Did I wake you?" asked Kip.

"Yes," I said grumpily.

"Sorry, but we have to talk right away. Tom seems to be building a very convincing case against you."

"Did you talk to Scoop?" I asked, shaking the fog from my brain.

"Yes, and Tom is trying to say that Scoop is just covering for you," said Kip. "Where is your phone?"

"Right here in my hand . . . you are calling me on it, remember?"

"Right, sorry; this whole thing with Tom has got me rattled. Don't let it out of your sight, and for God's sake, do not delete a thing. I'll be there in half an hour."

* * *

Half an hour later I was showered and dressed in my comfort clothes—yoga pants and UConn sweatshirt. My hair was still damp and stringy, though remembering yesterday's embarrassment when I'd emerged in hot-pink Hanky Pankys, I took time to choose nice underwear. I didn't bother with makeup.

After the humiliating events of yesterday, I had barely made the midnight deadline for Lottie Arlington's obituary. Now, Saturday morning, I realized with a pang of regret that I had missed the deadline for Burton's last words. Time to face the music.

When I called to explain that I had run into personal problems and asked if Marietta would like a recommendation for someone else, I was surprised when she asked if I could still write the obituary.

"I've changed my mind," she said. "I now realize that it is better to have the obituary accompany the service notice. Please say you can still do it. I promise to make it worth your time."

It didn't take more than a second for me to agree. I wanted—no, needed—Burton's obit in my portfolio, and I promised to get right on it. *That is*, I thought, *until I'm arrested for murder.* I'd have to ask Kip if I would be allowed to bring my computer to jail.

Kip arrived in blue jeans and a casual shirt. His tousled dark hair said he was riding his motorcycle.

"I guess you're not on duty." I said.

"No, it's not my shift."

At least he wasn't there to arrest me.

The head-to-toe he then gave me made me feel like a specimen under a microscope.

"Are you okay? What did the doctor say at the hospital?"

"I'm fine," I said. "No asthma or COPD, so no danger that the smoke I inhaled would trigger either of those things."

I didn't tell him that my throat felt like someone had run a rake over it.

"You could have died in that fire, Winter." Kip put his hands on my shoulders and to my surprise pulled me close, nearly smothering me in his arms.

"What was that for?" I asked, when he loosened his grip.

Kip did his brow rub and completely ignored my question. "Can we talk?"

By now Diva was downstairs and pacing near the door.

"She has to go out," I said, nodding toward the pup.

"I'll go with you."

As we walked down Mamanasco and across North Salem Road to the high school campus, Kip told me that despite finding Goodwin's South Salem rental, he had not located Max.

We were almost back at the cottage when a black pickup truck, the same type that had been behind me yesterday, cruised slowly by. The license plate started with *AV*.

"What kind of truck did Mark Goodwin drive?" I asked.

Kip studied me. "Why do you care?"

I explained about the pickup. "I think someone is following me."

"It's not Goodwin's truck—that's at the pool house. Besides, Goodwin is dead."

"Good point," I said.

Back at my own cottage, I put a K-Cup in the Keurig for Kip and the pot on to boil for my tea. Kip filled Diva's bowls with water and food. We then sat at the kitchen table with our morning brew.

"This must be very pretty in the fall with all the leaves turning," he said, studying the lake outside the window.

"It is. In fact, it's pretty in every season."

"Then why leave for New York City when you live in one of the prettiest places in one of the best towns in Connecticut?"

And there it was, the question that kept me up at night, wrestling between my love for my hometown and my desire for a clean slate.

"I'm trying to build my business," I said in practiced explanation. "A lot of my clients are in the city, and it will be easier to network. I would have a much larger audience in New York just by virtue of the population."

"In other words, more people die in big cities and you'd have more work."

"When you put it that way, it sounds pretty morbid," I conceded.

Even before working with Mrs. Arlington, I'd prewritten a few obituaries. It was better than waiting around for people to die to grow my business. I explained my thoughts to Kip.

"Lots of Ridgefielders commute to Manhattan," he said.

"I guess, though it's not the same as being based right there in the city, where you can respond to a client at the drop of a hat. And face-to-face is how I do my best work."

I didn't tell him that getting away from a place filled with so much history, where even in the train room a new cemetery had popped up, might be a refreshing change.

"I haven't preplanned my funeral," said Kip. "And I wouldn't want to have anything written about me yet—I hope to accomplish a few more things in life before I think about obituaries."

"You aren't my target audience. People are more interested in obituaries when they're on the back end of their lives. That's when they want to leave their mark."

Diva had disappeared, and I was pretty sure I knew where she'd gone. Sure enough, she interrupted our conversation by dropping the blue sneaker at Kip's feet.

"Cinderella's shoe," I said. "If we could find out whose foot fits in this, we might at least find the person who ransacked Mrs. Arlington's bedroom."

"Tom thinks it was you who did the ransacking," Kip blurted out. "You might want to call a lawyer."

I looked at his solemn face. "You're serious, aren't you?"

He nodded.

"Maybe if we solve the mystery, I won't need a lawyer."

"That's what I wanted to talk to you about. You have to promise to stay away from the Arlington estate. If you do that, I'll try to help you."

"Why?" I tucked a wayward strand of hair behind my ear. Maybe I should have put on some makeup after all.

Kip reached in his pocket and pulled out a small blue piece of metal that I recognized immediately.

"You went back to the house," I said, fingering Diva's license. "Why?"

"A few things aren't adding up." Kip splayed his fingers and began ticking. "First, the obvious—Mrs. Arlington's need for an obituary right away. Second, confirmation from FD that you were truthful about being trapped in a locked room. Your jeans, by the way, weren't salvageable."

I flushed. Lots of people now had firsthand knowledge of my underwear preference, including Kip.

He grinned. "At least it was warm out."

Serious again, he continued. "There was only smoke damage to the study. Diva's file was still there unharmed on the desk, so where was the book club file you left? I sifted through the mess on the floor in case it had been knocked off, and it wasn't there either. My guess—someone went back for the file after the emergency responders left and before I got there this morning."

"You must have gotten there early," I said, remembering the call that woke me.

"Very. I knew that the state investigators were going to be on the scene all day today. I had to sneak up the back way so I wouldn't be seen by the guys watching the place."

"That was risky," I said.

Kip shrugged. "I didn't go near the room where Mark was found, and I steered clear of the area where the arsonist obviously used an accelerant, but yes, I could get in a lot of trouble."

"The book club folder—I should have taken it with me," I said.

"Can you remember anything in it?"

Some folks can remember names like they're their own. I wasn't one of them, and new facts slipped out of my head as fast as they registered. That's why Google and I were BFFs. I shook my head no.

"The fact that Brittany and her boyfriend have disappeared points some fingers in their direction," said Kip. "Mrs. Arlington could have held one of her infamous secrets over their heads."

"So you believe me about the secrets she kept."

"Of course I believe you. And I believe David Wysocki who said his sister had enemies—enemies she probably made because of her blackmail schemes."

It felt as if he had just lifted a ten-pound weight from my shoulders. If I had him on my side, it might at least dampen Tom's efforts in trying to have me arrested.

Kip bent to pick up the shoe that sat at his feet, and Diva wagged her tail in approval.

"Size-seven women's shoe with no mate. The break-in was confined to Mrs. Arlington's bedroom and to her study. It was as if someone was looking for two things—the sneaker, so they couldn't be implicated, and a file, so they could destroy whatever secret it held. Do you have a bag we can put this in?"

"If the secrets are from days gone by, why come back for the file now?" I asked as I retrieved a paper grocery bag from a hook in the pantry and slid it toward Kip. "There has to be something that triggered everything. Like maybe the fact that she was writing her memoirs."

I told Kip about her taking those memoirs upstairs to work on them the night of the storm.

"We didn't find any electronics anywhere, and you'd think that her memoirs would be on her computer."

This was not the time to tell him about the iPad I hoped was still hidden under the seat cushions.

"You sure you can't remember anything from that file?" Kip prodded.

Dashing the hope in his voice, I said, "I glanced at the list, didn't recognize anyone, so moved on to the *Players* list. I thought it would make good lockdown reading. And then the fire alarm went off."

"I think whoever ransacked her home, started the fire, and killed Goodwin has to be from her past. Maybe a book club member who doesn't want her name revealed in the memoirs," said Kip.

With the lost file a dead end, Kip turned his attention to Scoop's messages.

"Can you play back his voice mail?"

Kip's brows rose in surprise as I lifted my shirt, the edge of which reached well past my waistband where my phone was tucked, and said, "No pockets."

"Aha." Embarrassed to be caught ogling, he looked away, and I suppressed my smile.

Facial recognition acknowledged me even with the purple bruise covering the bottom part of my chin. I navigated to voice mail, where Scoop's pitch rose with each message, all of them delivered in rapid succession. From calm to frantic, the messages and subsequent text told the story.

One of Scoop's calls had presumably been answered as Mark was running back into the house, probably just moments before he was murdered.

"Mark could have listened to my messages—he had my pass code. He would want to know if Scoop had already called the police so he could assess how much time he still had to run. If he didn't know it already, he would have heard Scoop alerting me to the fire."

"You notice the details, don't you?" asked Kip, the smile lines around his eyes creasing.

"I have to pay attention to detail. When you're writing an obituary, it's often the smallest thing that brings it to life. Like the fact that someone loved potato chips or dabbled in painting or swam every day well into their nineties. Those little tidbits tell you something about a person."

"Let's hear it again," said Kip, nodding toward my phone.

I was acutely aware of our heads almost touching as we listened. "Get out! The house is on fire!" came Scoop's desperate voice. We could hear sirens blaring in the background.

"Doesn't this prove that I was telling the truth?"

"It does to me, but I already believed you. Let's put that thing in a plastic bag and bring it down to the station."

And then, looking at the horror on my face, he said, "What's the matter?"

"My phone is my lifeline to my business. It's my lifeline to everything. I can't give you that."

"Well, if we have any hope of proving that Goodwin took it from you, we have to protect any fingerprints that might still be on it."

"Wouldn't mine wipe out any others?"

"Not necessarily, though it is a long shot."

"I can't live without my phone," I insisted stubbornly.

"Let's secure it and then go get you a burner. You can have your number forwarded until we get yours back."

"Wait," I said as I started swiping. "My Google maps tracking locator is activated."

Kip's brows shot close to his hairline.

"If I leave my phone somewhere, I can hunt it down to my last location. I'm also a *be prepared* kind of person—if I'm lost or kidnapped, someone can track my location."

"Do you usually get lost or kidnapped?"

"I'm practicing for when I move to New York City. Besides, I personalize my phone so all my apps can't track me."

"And you aren't worried about all the reasons not to have tracking on? Trust me, with that app activated, you can be tracked anywhere. It's pretty uncanny how much someone can learn about you from your GPS."

"I wasn't worried until now." I sighed as I swiped. "Anyway, maybe this will confirm that Mark was close by." I thought a moment. "Tom seems a bit too cocky to let one little turndown bother him," I added.

"I don't think it's about that," said Kip thoughtfully. "But I can't think why he's in such a big hurry to pin everything on you."

I could feel Kip's breath on my neck as I went to significant locations on my phone, verified Face ID, and studied the places that popped up.

"It's not always precise, because you might drive along a road yet not stop somewhere with a known address, although it's a pretty good indicator of where my phone has been."

"That's a little unnerving," said Kip as he reached for his own phone and began swiping.

"As I mentioned, unless you have location services on all the time, it won't work. Here we go. Check this out."

My phone showed David Wysocki's address in Stamford earlier yesterday. It followed my tracks to my Mamanasco Lake address and then my travels to the Arlington Estate, again with an address. Sure enough, it showed that a short time later my phone had been at another location on West Mountain Road, this one with no address. However, the radius on the map indicated that it was just a stone's throw from the Arlington manor and in the direction of the pool house.

"Close enough to walk," said Kip, observing the little dot.

"Or run," I added. "He definitely could have beat out the emergency responders from there."

"We found his truck on the service road right behind the pool house."

"He didn't seem like the kind of guy who would leave without his dog," I said.

Kip shook his head from side to side. "There was some evidence that Goodwin stayed in the pool house. There were a couple of blow-ups in the dressing rooms and a dog bed and dishes in the main room. Unfortunately, no Max."

"Do you think Mark was targeted or just collateral damage?" I asked.

"Not sure," said Kip. "Whoever started the fire probably saw him running back to rescue you."

"Why kill him, though?"

"To keep the flames burning," said Kip. "Or maybe they assumed he knew what his boss knew."

"So it would be someone familiar with Lottie Arlington's life," I said.

"Brittany," we both said at the same time.

"Aside from the brother who says his sister had enemies, the locked door to the study, which proves you were telling the truth, the missing file, the dead body, and the cell phone messages, what else do we have?" asked Kip.

"Diva's fixation with this size-seven shoe. By the way, for the record, I'm a seven and a half and my left foot is closer to an eight. I could never squeeze into that shoe."

"Okay, we'll rule you out due to foot size. You do know that makes you the ugly stepsister, right?"

"I deserve ugly," I said with a laugh, though I could feel the heat rise to my cheeks. "I'm not looking my best today."

Kip's eyes penetrated as he gently touched my bruised chin. "I don't think you could ever be ugly."

Please, please, please don't let my freckles flare, I thought.

"Trust me, I look pretty bad in the morning."

"I'd like to see that for myself."

We sat, both grinning awkwardly for a moment, before Kip fingered the shoe.

"Brittany might stand to inherit," he said thoughtfully. "That would give her motive to get rid of her great-aunt."

"According to Mrs. Arlington, Brittany was dumber than a brick. Maybe it was the boyfriend encouraging her to accelerate her inheritance claim." I tried to put myself back in the moment when I'd met Brittany. While she had been annoyed as I dripped all over the foyer and guarded the house like a Rottweiler, she hadn't seemed inept when I told her she could turn off the driveway alarm from the inside. She had seemed reluctant.

"Kip, what if Mrs. Arlington warned Brittany to beware of strangers?" I said as I walked him through that stormy afternoon.

"Okay," he said, drawing the word out in thought. "If you're right, then why?" He was still holding the sneaker. "If this is evidence, it's been pretty well compromised."

"True," I said. "Diva has carried it everywhere. I wish I had figured out that it might be important sooner. Maybe there's some DNA to be gained from the inside of the shoe."

Kip wrinkled his nose. "Not my area of expertise, though I'm pretty sure the chain of evidence has long since been destroyed. Didn't you say you and Diva play toss and fetch with it?"

"Maybe if we find the mate . . ."

"It would be a pretty stupid intruder to leave the mate hanging around," interrupted Kip. "It's bad enough to have some clever little dog steal and hide one of your shoes. Who knows when she'll drop that evidence in front of someone who will get suspicious? The more I think about it, the more sure I am that this is one of the things the intruder was looking for."

"So what I'm hearing is that you think the intruder is a woman—probably Brittany—and that she returned to find her shoe, and also to find something important in the file cabinet. And then she tried to cover her tracks with the fire."

"Something like that," said Kip. "When she couldn't find what she was after, she might have left to get an accelerant, which is when you arrived. Didn't you say you thought Mark had moved your car?"

"Yes. After he locked me in, he moved it out of view of the front of the house so the police wouldn't see it during a routine drive-by."

Kip stood and began pacing. "She might have seen him climb into the car and head around the house toward the service entrance and the back exit to the estate."

I tried to picture it. *She trashes the house and now realizes that not only is her DNA everywhere, but she still hasn't found the shoe or whatever it was she needed from Lottie's house. So she goes off to look for an accelerant so she can burn the place down—maybe to the detached toolshed where the landscaper's equipment is kept. That would be when she hears my car in the driveway, so she stays hidden until she sees the car exit around the corner of the house fifteen minutes later. She goes back inside through the front door, douses some of the furniture in the living room with gasoline she's found in the shed, uses the fireplace lighter to start the fire, and hurries out.*

"She might have escaped from the side door—away from the area where the fire was now underway. That's when she would have seen that my car was still there," I said.

"So instead of escaping, she hides to see what's going on, and she sees Mark running back into the house to try to rescue you," said Kip.

"Mark wouldn't have been quiet," I agreed. "She could have followed him into the room without him hearing her and . . . and what? How did he die?"

"A hefty blow to the back of the head followed by another to the temple."

I grimaced.

"The smoke was already pretty thick in the upstairs hallway," I mused. "How would that work?"

"When she saw Goodwin run into the mudroom door where the fire had not yet reached, she must have decided to take the risk. She had to keep him from stopping the fire's spread. Killing him was probably impulsive." Kip was warming to his theory.

"It seems pretty dumb to think that one person could possibly stop a fire like that from spreading," I said.

"Maybe she thought Mark knew where the incriminating evidence was and that he went back to save it so he could pick up where Mrs. A left off." Kip sighed in frustration and slid back into the chair. He didn't like that I was poking holes.

"How did she get away? Except for my car, there were no other vehicles in the driveway."

"Her car might have been hidden in the detached garage when you arrived. She wouldn't have wanted it left in view of anyone who was checking the house. How long were you stuck in there once the fire was underway?"

I tried to remember. In my panic, I'd felt like I was in there forever, but in reality, it probably wasn't more than ten or fifteen minutes before I became aware of the fire.

"She had plenty of time to start a fire while I was locked in that room," I said.

"She wouldn't need more than five minutes to knock Goodwin over the head and then get out of Dodge before the fire department got there."

I wasn't as excited about our scenario as Kip. Why would Brittany feel the need to sneak into a house that she presumably spent a lot of time in? Unless she didn't want to retrieve whatever she was after until she was ready to leave permanently.

Diva thumped her tail, an indication that it was time for her pet. I sighed, reached down, and gave her a cuddle. When I looked up again, Kip was staring from me to Diva.

"What can I say?" I said. "She's a needy, claustrophobic, aqua-phobic, willful dog."

"But not stupid," said Kip excitedly. "What if we're on the wrong track? What if the intruder didn't know about Diva way back on that first day when you found Mrs. Arlington? She's just a puppy. Mrs. Arlington couldn't have owned her for long. If the intruder didn't know about the dog, she wouldn't have realized that she might be detected and that the dog might steal her shoe. The house is so big, you could sneak up that back staircase, head to the study, and spend hours in there without anyone realizing it."

"That would mean the intruder wasn't Brittany, because she was in the house every day with Mrs. Arlington and Diva."

"Exactly," said Kip. "So who else wears a size-seven sneaker?"

Chapter
Twenty-Three

O ur scenario had plenty of holes, which we weren't going to fill without more information. First, though, I needed a phone, if Kip was going to share mine with his chief. We left his motorcycle at my house and climbed into the Subaru. I wasn't in the mood for more chewed windowsills, so Diva clamored in behind us.

At the Verizon store, the manager assured me that I could have my number temporarily rolled over to a burner. He did add that unless I designated a name to my burner, the number would not be recognizable to those I called.

Because my biggest worry was clients calling me, I didn't bother with any of that. Kip stayed in the car, keeping Diva busy.

Burner now in hand, we left Verizon and a few minutes later pulled into the driveway of the Victorian house on East Ridge, home of the Ridgefield PD. At various times the house had been a private residence, a boarding school, a multi-family, and the state police barracks. I wondered what would become of the beautiful building once the new fire/police facility was built on Old Quarry Road. It anchored a row of majestic homes overlooking the Veterans Park School Field, but returning it to a single-family didn't seem logical, because it had an unappealing cell tower on the property. Condos, maybe?

I was contemplating these things as I sat with Diva in the driveway, waiting for Kip's return. Diva listened, ears alert, as I chatted away while familiarizing myself with the new burner. I began to have second thoughts. There was always a learning curve with new electronics, and I wanted to race inside and retrieve my phone, fingerprints be damned.

"How long?" I asked when Kip climbed into the Subaru.

"Not sure," he said.

"Did you play my messages for your police chief?"

"I did. And I showed him the GPS locations where your phone had been. He said it didn't prove anything. You could have left and then come back to kill Goodwin."

"Did he say why I would want to kill Mark?" I asked. "And doesn't the locked room prove that I was telling the truth?"

"He found ways to refute everything I put forward. I'm guessing Tom got to him first, but he didn't seem like he was about to send someone to arrest you. I suspect he believes you and wants to dot the *i*'s and cross the *t*'s. I think you should leave it in a lawyer's hands."

"I was hoping it wouldn't come to that," I said.

Kip gave me a sideways glance. "Maybe you should err on the side of caution."

I didn't want to spend my precious New York City fund on a lawyer if I didn't have to, but I wasn't about to tell that to Kip.

"Where to next?" asked Kip, looking hopeful that there was more for us to accomplish.

I explained that I had an obituary to write and had to get back to work. Kip exited onto East Ridge and took Governor to Main.

Downtown Ridgefield was typically Saturday morning busy. There didn't seem to be a day that the town was void of walkers, with and without pets. Books on the Common had attracted a fair number of window shoppers, and Tazza, as usual, its handful of outdoor tables was filled. The Lantern was packed with people spilling out onto the sidewalk as they waited for one of the outdoor tables. I would have enjoyed sitting there watching the world go by, and I suspected, from the way Kip looked longingly at the restaurant, that he would too.

"I love this building," said Kip, nodding toward a replica of the charming Victorian that had burned to the ground in 2005. Owners recognized the landmark structure as key to the eclectic architecture of the downtown area and rebuilt so it looked exactly like its predecessor. Along with the restaurant, it also housed Ursula's, a cute little boutique. "I have a bead on one of the apartments on the upper floors."

I looked up at the inviting covered porches overlooking Main Street. "It would be a great place to watch the Memorial Day parade," I said.

* * *

Ten minutes later, as we pulled into the driveway of the lake house, that same black truck drove by. It disappeared too quickly for me to catch any more of the plate—just the *AV.*

"That's three times in two days," I told Kip, indicating the truck's taillights as it rounded the corner and disappeared from sight.

"Keep the doors and windows locked when you're here alone," said Kip. "Just in case it's not a neighbor."

* * *

Burton Hemlocker, 79, an antique car collector who could be seen around town driving his bright-red snub-nosed vintage Ford pickup, died peacefully at his home on Wednesday (date). He is survived by his wife of ten years, Marietta Hemlocker, who says his greatest moment in

Ridgefield was his cameo performance on the ACT stage, which he was awarded for his continued support.

Unlike some subjects of my obituaries, Burton Hemlocker had a lot of good local color, and I was going to enjoy doing this one. Apparently he'd had a great sense of humor. He'd taken advantage of the town senior center, Founders Hall; the library; the Men's Club—you name it, Burton Hemlocker was involved. He was a world traveler and a voracious reader. He came from a lineage that really did go back to the *Mayflower*, had gone to impressive colleges, and had made a fortune in hedge funds. As I made my list of things to include in Burton's obituary, I found myself wishing I had known the man, an emotion I try to evoke whenever I write an obit.

I was probably going to have a little pushback on this one, because Marietta had already insisted I include "died peacefully of natural causes." I didn't plan to include the *natural cause* bit without official determination, but *peacefully* was probably open to interpretation.

According to his wife, Burton had still been alive when she'd found him, and between tears, she'd explained how she'd run to the house to get the defibrillator they had purchased when Burton's heart problems got more serious. She also called 911 and then returned to the garden, where she found him dead. I wasn't sure how peaceful that kind of exit was, and I hated misleading obituaries where solace for the family overrode accuracy. Not knowing all the facts and because he'd died in the garden, a place he loved, I could swallow the compromise.

"Sorry, Burton," I said aloud. "You aren't paying my bill, at least not directly."

Burton. The name triggered something rolling around in my brain. I chased it for a few moments before I caught it. It reminded me of the name on the Great Dames Book Club list. Balkan—that was it. Balkan, like the sea. First name Barbara.

I put the obit aside and went to work searching for Barbara Balkan. I hoped that I was in lottery-winning mode when I searched Legacy.com for her; however, no one fitting the profile of a woman old enough to have been in Lottie's book club popped up. I then checked obituaries going back a few years, hoping to find a male relative in the New York area. And suddenly there he was. Andrew J. Balkan III had died three years ago in Chappaqua. Lots of info about his life, predeceased by his parents . . . blah . . . blah.

Survived by . . . that stopped me short. He was survived by his sister Barbara Wysocki (David) of Stamford, Connecticut.

Bitsy was none other than one of Lottie Arlington's fellow book club members. Why hadn't David told us that? His claim that he and Lottie weren't close wasn't completely truthful, was it?

It took several tries to reach Kip.

"Sorry, I didn't recognize the number. I forgot to add you to my address book," he said when he finally answered.

"You aren't going to believe this," I said, too excited to worry about the implications of him forgetting to add my number to his contacts. "I finally remembered one of the names on the Great Dames Book Club list."

I told him about Barbara "Bitsy" Balkan Wysocki.

"I think another visit to the Wysocki house is in order," said Kip. "And this time we'll make sure Bitsy is there."

"While you arrange that, I'm going to finish my work and take our four-legged Houdini for a walk," I said. "Call me as soon as you know something."

As I worked through Burton's obituary, I made a list of questions to ask Marietta and opted to text in case she too didn't recognize my number.

She texted back that it would be easier to meet with me later this afternoon. I agreed.

Then I texted my uncle that he should put my new number in his contacts. My thumbs were getting tired.

Uncle Richard called immediately. "Where is your phone?" he asked.

I gave him the rundown. He agreed to watch Diva so I could meet with Marietta.

"Okay if I cook at the cottage tonight?" he asked. "The power is back on, and Horace and I want to enjoy some of these late-August evenings on the porch before it gets too chilly. If you're busy, I'll just carry it over to Horace's deck."

"Actually, can you cook extra? I'm feeling a little badly about neglecting Scoop these days."

"I owe him a huge dinner for alerting the firefighters that you were trapped inside that house. I could make a butterfly lamb on the grill with roasted potatoes and some mint jelly," said Uncle Richard, warming to his menu.

"Scoop is a vegetarian," I reminded him.

"Oh, right, let's keep it simple. We'll have portobella mushroom burgers," he said, and then listed off a number of other things he planned to cook. So much for keeping it simple.

Before we hung up, he also gave me the name of a lawyer to call, just in case. I texted Scoop and explained about the burner phone. It rang almost immediately.

"What happened to your regular phone?" he asked.

I was getting tired of explaining, but I did owe it to him.

"You can still call my regular number because the calls are getting forwarded. I wanted you to be able to recognize me in case I called or texted you from the burner."

"Hey, did you check out the info I sent you on Roth Arlington and Henry Harmless?" he asked. "I left it on your email."

"Not yet, but I will."

"It's interesting, though probably not anything for your obituary."

"Well, that's done and gone, so even if it was something, I couldn't use it," I said, and told him about Sondra Milton.

"Sorry I haven't been any help. These pets take a lot of time."

"Tell me about it," I said, and looked at Diva, who was doing her big-eye thing at my feet. "By the way, tonight will be a good time to talk to Horace next door. He says he's interested in the kittens."

"Not to be insensitive," said Scoop, "but does Horace know how long a cat can live? Horace is how old?"

I hadn't thought of that. And then I wondered again about Mrs. Arlington adopting Diva. From my nosing around on the internet, I'd learned that a Great Pyrenees had an average life span of ten to twelve years. I couldn't see Mrs. Arlington adopting this adorable little pup if she thought she had only a short time to live. I was now more certain than ever that whatever had made her want an obituary had happened between the time she'd adopted Diva and the time she'd called me.

Before hanging up, I made Scoop swear that he wouldn't write anything for the paper until he had permission from Kip. I'd leave the kitten-adopting process to him.

Chapter
Twenty-Four

D iva and I were halfway down Mamanasco Road heading toward the high school when the black pickup slowed and passed. The side windows were tinted, and I couldn't make out the driver except to see that he wore a baseball cap with the bill pulled low. If scaring me was the intent of the driver, he was doing a good job.

As the tail of the truck disappeared around the corner, I was able to make out the entire plate, and I memorized it. I was undecided on what to do next. If I went forward to the high school, where I planned to run around the large field, I might find myself alone and completely vulnerable. School wasn't in session, and I had no idea if any of the sports teams were practicing yet.

No one was fishing or kayaking out on the tranquil lake. Mid-August was like that in Ridgefield. People were beginning to change gears. It was still hot enough for the beach, but no one was there. Maybe they were shopping for school, taking kids off to college, or squeezing in a last-minute vacation before autumn settled in. Wherever everyone was, I realized Diva and I were very much alone.

I reversed our direction. We were just even with Horace's cottage when I heard a vehicle coming up quickly behind me. I scooped

Diva up again and raced to his front door. I was about to pound on it when a car full of teens whizzed past.

By the time I got home, I was shaky and out of sorts. Diva sensed my distress and hovered close as I locked doors and checked windows.

Black pickup followed me on my walk! I texted Kip.

My cell rang seconds later.

"Where are you?" Kip asked.

"Home, all locked in with Diva, and I feel ridiculous," I said. "Whoever is following me doesn't want to hurt me. I'm just going to go about my business and hope the person gets up the nerve to confront me in person rather than stalk me with their truck."

"I don't think that's a good idea," he said. "You have no idea of their motives."

"If they wanted to hurt me, they could easily have done so numerous times. Oh, by the way, I did memorize the plate number."

Kip said he would run it and then asked if I wanted to go over the entire case again. He had some additional ideas he wanted to bounce off me. I told him about everyone coming for dinner and asked him to join us.

"You might as well get everyone's opinion," I said. "Because trust me, Scoop, Horace, and my uncle will have one."

After we hung up, I fed Diva and scrounged around for the last of the leftover chicken for myself, though I didn't have much of an appetite. An hour later, I was ready to take Diva for another short walk and then bring her to Uncle Richard. We headed up the steep hill of Rock Road, and when we returned, I stopped in my tracks. The black pickup was parked at the bottom of the street.

"Enough," I said, and with Diva in tow, I approached the driver's side door. I pushed through a tangle of shrubs that only a few days earlier had had wires pulsating from them. I felt the scrape of prickles against my jeans as I banged on the tinted window.

The window slid slowly down. I felt my breath catch. If there was someone with a gun, I was a sitting duck. I took a step backward into shrubs that blocked my retreat. Diva, dangerously close to the back wheel of the truck, stubbornly held her ground despite my efforts to pull her away.

"Miss Snow," came a timid voice from inside the truck. "I need help."

A frightened-looking Brittany Bennett blinked back tears. The first thing I noticed was how unkempt she looked. She removed the baseball cap, and her edgy haircut looked as if it hadn't been washed or styled in days. Her T-shirt looked as if she had slept in it, and her face was void of makeup. She looked like a child after a rough day in the sandbox.

"Where have you been?" I asked sternly. "We've been looking for you."

Diva was suddenly jumping against the door trying to reach her.

Brittany sniffled. "I didn't know where to go. Can we talk somewhere safe?"

I had her pull the truck into the second bay of the two-car garage so it was out of sight. Inside the house, I fixed her a plate of the remaining leftovers from the fridge and set it along with some chocolate chip cookies between us. She ate with obvious hunger. Diva curled against her feet, and while she gobbled her food, Brittany periodically reached down to pet the dog.

"I'm sorry," she said. "I didn't realize how hungry I was."

"Are you ready to explain why you've been stalking me?"

I poured water for both of us, carried the cookies into the living room, and opened the sliders to let in some air. Brittany didn't exactly smell fresh as a daisy.

As she wove her story, pieces of the puzzle began to knock into place.

"Over the last couple of weeks, Aunt Lottie got increasingly agitated," Brittany explained. "She'd already told me about her past and how she used information about people as leverage for . . . well . . . something she wanted."

"You can call it what it was—blackmail," I said. "Why don't you start from the beginning?"

Brittany shrugged and continued. "I was kind of a lost soul for a while. When my mom told me that my great-uncle had a sister, I decided to look for her. I'm a bit of a genealogy buff. I got in touch with her a year ago, and she invited me to come visit. At first, things were great. She hired me to help her put her things in order—files, photos, all that stuff. Recently, we started scanning photos into her new iPad. For her it was a walk down memory lane, and I think she liked having someone to share it with—besides Mark. She wanted to tell someone her secrets and had started writing her memoir. For me, it was fascinating. My grandma Alice was always so removed. She would be present in the room, but in her head, it was like she was living somewhere else. Aunt Lottie was more like the grandma I always wished for."

Brittany was proving to be insightful and articulate as she told her story. Somehow that persona didn't jibe with the one Mrs. Arlington had presented to me. And she certainly didn't seem like the bad guy that Kip and I had made her out to be. Could we be wrong, or was she just a very clever liar?

"The one worry my great-aunt always had was that someone from her past might come back and try to hurt her or someone she cared about. She kept a running list of everyone she had ever . . . uh . . . blackmailed. She knew where they were and what repercussions her actions might have had. By the time I showed up, she wasn't as worried anymore. Many of the people had died or moved on with their lives and never looked back."

"How so?" I asked.

"Like the guy she caught having an affair with one of her coworkers—he and his wife stayed married, raised their family, and now have grandchildren and great-grandchildren. I think he's about ninety now and appears to be a pillar in his community. The coworker who was so distraught when he broke it off went on to marry and have six kids. She now has tons of grandkids and recently moved in with one of her daughters when her husband died. Aunt Lottie got in touch with her, you know, as old coworkers, and the woman claimed she had a wonderful life and still does." Brittany paused in reflection. "I guess part of what I did for my aunt was keep tabs on all the players, as she liked to call them."

"What did your boyfriend do?" I asked. "And where is he?"

Brittany gave me a mischievous smile. "Aunt Lottie created a different identity for me. She thought if anyone ever did come after her, they would ignore the ditzy assistant who lived with her badass boyfriend elsewhere on the estate. I got so good at acting the part that I thought I should think about a stage career. Anyway, Aunt Lottie thought it created a good story. She thought people might actually feel sorry for her that I was all she had."

I felt my freckles erupting.

Brittany caught my look and smiled again. "It worked, right? Anyway, there was no boyfriend. My aunt was adamant that I live in the cottage instead of the house, because she said it made me appear less important to her. I didn't mind. I liked the solitude, and that big house is kind of creepy, if you know what I mean."

I did.

"Right after we got Diva, things changed," said Brittany.

At hearing her name, Diva put her front paws on Brittany's knees.

"I don't know how much longer I'll be able to do this," she said, and lifted Diva up onto her lap. "God, how I love this dog."

Brittany cuddled her ferociously, nuzzling her nose and whispering in her ear. Diva leaned in and gave me her *This is how you care for your pet* look.

"You were saying that things changed, right after you got Diva," I reminded her.

"Before that we were making plans with David—that's my great-uncle. We were going to get together—plan a family reunion of sorts. My parents and brothers were going to fly out for a big party at the house. Bitsy was one of Aunt Lottie's friends from the old days, and my aunt had cut off any relationship when she married Uncle David. Early on Aunt Lottie had gotten threats to her and her family, which is why she never wanted family around. Like I said, though, we determined that there really wasn't much risk these days. And then, all of the sudden, she hit pause on everything. She canceled our plans, and she told me to pack up and go home."

Brittany paused and swiped her eyes, then let out a long, slow breath before continuing. "I asked her why, and all she said was that she no longer thought it was safe for me to be here. She started keeping all the doors closed and didn't want me to answer the doorbell. That's why I was so startled when you showed up. I never heard the doorbell. All I could hear was that storm crashing around us. I thought you might be after her."

Brittany's story jibed with my suspicions. Mrs. Arlington had probably gotten Diva to keep Brittany company as well as herself and would never have done so if she'd felt threatened. As Brittany unraveled her tale, I began to get a different picture than the one David had painted of his sister. Mrs. A, as Mark had affectionately called her, had been protecting Brittany by sending her away. She was taking care of her sister's grandchild in the way she had never had a chance to do for her sister. She was acting out of love, not selfishness.

"Did your aunt tell you why she was suddenly worried again?" I asked.

Brittany cocked her head in thought.

"No," she said finally. "That's the thing—I pored over her list of players to see if there was anyone at all who might have made a threat. No one emerged. This had to be something new, because everyone else was either dead or accounted for."

"And you have no idea what it might be?"

"No. And neither did Mark."

The man who'd died keeping Mrs. A's secrets.

"Tell me about Mark," I said.

Brittany confirmed his story about deserting from the army and feeling overwhelmingly guilty about his friend, whose dog tags he'd exchanged to fake his own death. She also confirmed the rest of the story of how Lottie had gotten together with Roth and Henry.

"I never met Roth and Henry—they were long gone before I got here, but my aunt spoke very highly of both," said Brittany. "Mark and my aunt had a very special relationship. He loved her, and in her own way, she loved him. I left to go home because she insisted, and I also knew that Mark would take care of her. On Tuesday after the storm, I went to stay with David and Bitsy. When I spoke to my aunt, she promised to check in the next day. On Wednesday, David was going to take me to Westchester County Airport to fly home. When I couldn't reach my aunt, he loaned me his truck to check on her. Mark told me what happened, and I've been staying with him ever since. But now . . ."

So David had lied. Could Brittany also be lying to throw us off track? My instincts about her said no, this was a scared young woman who didn't know where to turn next.

"Now you wonder if you're in danger," I finished for her.

"Yes. And will David and Bitsy be in danger if I'm linked to them?" She looked suddenly like a deer caught in the headlights. Which way to turn?

"I can't leave," she continued. "I have to know who did this. Besides, there's no one for Max or Diva right now."

"Max, is he safe?" I asked.

"Yes. He's staying at the pool house. That's where Mark was hanging out to watch over Aunt Lottie and then to watch the house. Usually Max comes with me or Mark in case anyone's checking the premises. Today I left him there, and I have to go back and get him."

Brittany wrung her hands and put a balled-up fist to her lips. "I shouldn't have left my aunt alone."

"So why were you stalking me?" I asked, feeling a spike of anger.

If she heard my agitation over being followed, she didn't show it.

"I was trying to get up the nerve to tell you what was going on. My aunt trusted you, so I figured I could trust you too."

"Did you know Mark was going to meet with me?"

"We decided together that it was the best thing to do. That day I was following you to see if you were coming alone as agreed."

"Did you know Mark had locked me in your aunt's study? Did you realize that I almost died in the fire?" Anger prickled my voice.

Brittany heard it and held Diva tighter.

"Mark came back to the pool house where we were staying and told me he had locked you in. And then your phone rang—it has a weird ring, by the way. I was throwing things in my duffel, covering our tracks so no one would know we had been there, because Mark said we had to disappear fast. And then he ran out the door back towards the house. I didn't know what to do. I packed things up and just sat and waited. When I saw the smoke and heard the fire engines, I panicked. I just sat there praying he would return," she said, and now tears streaked her cheeks. "I'm sorry."

I studied her, wondering if she was using the very good acting skills she'd admitted to having or if there was at least a kernel of truth in her story.

Suddenly my phone rang, startling us both. It was Kip.

"He's okay," I told her. "He's a cop."

She rose quickly, and Diva slid to the floor with a thump.

"No police," Brittany said, alarmed. "When I asked if Aunt Lottie had been threatened and should we call the police, she was adamant. She didn't trust them. No cops."

I put my fingers to my lips and answered the call as Brittany slid back into her chair.

"The truck belongs to David Wysocki," said Kip without preamble. "He sure has some explaining to do. When I told him that I knew about the truck and Bitsy, he didn't make any excuse. All he said was, 'That didn't take long,' and then added that he and Bitsy would meet with us tomorrow. What I can't figure is who is driving his truck, because unless the guy has a clone, he couldn't be in Ridgefield following you and at home answering his landline just a half hour later."

I hurriedly explained that I had an appointment with Marietta Hemlocker, which got an eyebrow raise from Brittany. I promised to call him later.

After disconnecting, I told Brittany about tonight's dinner with my uncle, Scoop, and Horace. I didn't mention Kip for fear of scaring her away. She agreed to stay at the cottage to watch Diva until I returned.

"Maybe I can help your uncle cook," she said.

I thought about the spices, knives, messy mixing bowls, and other cooking accoutrements my uncle always had strewn around the countertops when he cooked. He was not a clean-as-you-go kind of guy. Brittany had no idea what she was getting into.

After alerting Richard to the plan change, I settled Brittany with some clean yoga pants, underwear, and a T. I added a bathrobe for good measure. She was smaller than me, but the clothes would do for now.

"How about a shower and a nap?" I suggested as I led her to the guest room. "Help yourself to products and whatever you need."

Brittany explained how to reach the cottage from a back service road and how to convince Max that I was his pal. She also asked me to grab her duffel that was stashed in one of the changing rooms.

"Max looks scarier than the devil," she said, "but he is really a big marshmallow."

* * *

A half hour later, I was about to ring the doorbell when the door flew open and an anxious-looking Marietta met me. She had obviously heard me coming.

Her pristine white jumpsuit and her carefully coiffed look from the other day had been replaced by a casual ponytail, blue jeans, and a crisp white blouse. Even without her makeup and with her face scarred by a deep frown, she was the kind of woman who made you want to sign up for a makeover.

"Is something wrong?" I asked as I tucked a few wayward strands behind my ear.

"Everything is wrong," she said as she led me into the opulent living room. "Burton's son from his first marriage has been badgering me for details about his death. And he's after me about the estate settlement. And on and on."

She waved her arms like a conductor not getting the results she was looking for.

"Didn't Burton have a will?" I asked.

"Of course," Marietta snapped, almost spitting out the words. "But that little brat wants to make sure all the conditions of the prenup have been met. He is the executor. Can you believe Burton actually put his son in charge?"

Well, actually, yes, I could imagine, though I didn't say so. I didn't think it wise to ask what conditions were in the prenup. Instead, I declined a beverage and got right to work. I handed Marietta a copy of the obituary I had drafted and sat, pen poised, ready to make changes and fill in blanks.

"You forgot to add that he died of natural causes," she said, and the frown line grew to a crevasse.

I explained to Marietta that there was no evidence yet about the cause of death and no death certificate had been issued. She took her fury out on my carefully written obituary by crumbling it up and tossing it aside.

"Oh, for God's sake. This is all just . . . just . . . too much," she said, her voice rising to soprano pitch.

"Mrs. Hemlocker," I started.

"Stop calling me that. The second I get through with this probate mess and funeral, I'm going to legally change my name. Call me Marietta!" Her high-pitched voice, close to a shout, sounded loud enough to shatter glass.

"Marietta, I can see you are very upset. Can I call someone to be with you?" I was trying to keep my voice soothing and quiet, hoping it would calm her.

"No, I don't want anyone," she spit out angrily. "I just want all this to be over with."

"Probate takes some time," I said, thinking that an estate the size of Burton's, depending on the assets, could take a year to probate properly. If Burton had done some preplanning, he might have put things into trust, which could bypass part of the process. Regardless, there was at least a three-month wait from the time the papers were filed just for creditors to have their chance to collect. Then came those relations who might contest the will, like Burton's son.

"You should have immediate assets if you are the beneficiary of the estate," I said. "And you will receive Burton's Social Security benefits."

"I've contacted the life insurance company," she said. "Turns out I wasn't the beneficiary of *that*."

Oh dear. Maybe this was where the wrath was coming from.

"Who was?" I asked, because I was having a hard time suppressing my curiosity.

Marietta pursed her lips into a snarl and said, "Some backstabbing tart named Brittany Bennett."

Chapter
Twenty-Five

B rittany Bennett! I wondered if Mrs. Arlington's grandniece knew
she was about to inherit some money.

"I can't believe Burton was so insistent that I sign a prenup," continued Marietta, her anger still bubbling. "I was the one who was to
stay married for at least ten years and remain faithful until he died,
or I would forfeit any inheritance. Can you believe that? Now I find
that he was the one fooling around—probably with some hussy he
met on one of his jaunts into the city. After all I put up with, taking
him to specialists and filling those stupid pill bottles every day to
keep him alive. You can't imagine my relief at making it to our ten-
year anniversary."

It struck me that it probably wasn't the idea of Burton's infidelity
alone that had gotten her so worked up. More likely it was the pos-
sibility that he was bestowing money on the woman she thought he
had cheated with.

"I seriously doubt that Brittany was having an affair with your
husband," I said gently. "She's only about twenty years old. She was
Mrs. Arlington's assistant."

Marietta went still, maybe listening for the first time.

"The little gal who disappeared? The one they think caused Lottie's fall and ransacked the house?"

Now why would she know about Brittany's disappearance? And no one had implicated Brittany in the fall, at least not publicly. The fact that someone had rummaged through the bedroom shouldn't have been on anyone's radar except mine, the cops', and the late Mark Goodman's. It wasn't a great leap to guess that Tom Bellini was feeding Marietta details. I wondered if she had heard yet about Mark and the fingers pointing in my direction.

"As far as I know, no one has accused Brittany of anything," I offered. "Did the insurance company say anything when he added her as his beneficiary? When did he do that?"

"Sometime this past year," said Marietta. "But why give money to her? Walking Burton home to make sure he got here safely after a visit with Lottie hardly seems like a good reason to fork over a small fortune."

I wasn't about to tell Marietta that Brittany was tucked away at a lake house less than five miles away and I would ask that question when I got home. And then I thought about her—alone and vulnerable.

A chill shot through me as another realization hit. Brittany had every right to be afraid. I was pretty sure Mark had died because the bad guy assumed he knew something that—how did he put it?—you wouldn't want on your résumé. Mark had sworn Mrs. A wouldn't tell him about whatever had her worried. That hadn't stopped someone from killing him. Brittany had also sworn that she knew nothing, but if you were tying up loose ends, you might consider her one. For that matter, you might consider me one too. I was the last one to have seen Mrs. Arlington alive. A killer might think she had given a deathbed confession.

I stared at Marietta and wondered vaguely if she could be the murderer. I shook it off and mentally admonished myself for my active imagination and suspicions that were all over the place.

"I'm so sorry you're going through all of this," I said, "especially now, when you have unanswered questions from your late husband."

"Husband, ha," Marietta spat. She grabbed the crumpled obituary and tossed it at the black-granite fireplace. "He was more like a zookeeper, always prancing me around on his arm and doting on me in public. In private he told me countless times that he married me for my looks and because he was lonely and that we really had nothing in common."

"Why did you stay with him if you weren't happy?" I asked.

"Why do you think?" She waved her hand around the glittery room. "What other job could I get that would pay this well over ten years?"

The bitter and greedy woman sitting before me was nothing like the apparently grieving widow I had originally met. Her true colors were a startling change. Was she telling me all this because she just needed a listening ear, or did she want the record set straight and somehow think I could do that?

I stood. "Marietta, I should leave you alone. Let me know what you want me to do about the obituary."

Marietta looked up in surprise—then grew anxious again.

"No, stay, Winter, please. I'm sorry I blew up." The mourning persona returned as quickly as if she'd flipped a switch. "If Burton thought that poor little thing who worked for Lottie deserved some money for her future, then so be it. Maybe you can help me track her down."

"I think it's up to Burton's executor or the lawyers and probate people to track her down," I said in a steely voice. "I don't think you need to bother with that."

Marietta looked at me curiously for a moment before grabbing my hand and pulling me back to the seat. Then she got up herself, retrieved the balled-up obituary, and smoothed it out on the glossy coffee table in front of us.

"It's very important that Burton's death be—how should I say this?—unchallenged," said Marietta. "Any hint of impropriety would send that nasty son of his on a mission to discredit me so I would inherit nothing."

"I don't think a heart attack or stroke would hint at impropriety," I replied. "Burton was elderly, with a heart condition verified by his doctors. That hardly points a finger at you. Why don't we give it a couple of days to see what the state of Connecticut has to say? They try very hard to be sensitive to timing."

Marietta sighed and stared for a moment at the obituary. Then, rallying, she said, "Thank you, Winter, I'm sure you're right. Of course. I'll follow your advice. The rest of the obituary is lovely; it really is. You will want to add that he was predeceased by his first wife and that his son is also his next of kin. It might appease his son a bit. Please send me a digital copy so I can send it to him for approval."

And then she did a head shake so violent that half her ponytail came out of its loose scrunchie and she emitted a sound like a horse snorting. "God, I thought I was done playing these kinds of games."

The way I saw it, I had two choices: walk away now—because this woman was a Jekyll and Hyde if I ever saw one—or finish the job, get paid, and more importantly, add Burton Hemlocker to my prestigious client list.

"I'll do all that for you right now," I said, and pulled my computer from my satchel. Clients could get squeamish about sharing internet connections, even if it was for their benefit, so I set up an internet hot spot with my cell phone. I was relieved to see this part of the mountain had cell service, so my equipment was good to go.

"All set and ready," I said. "I'd just like to use your bathroom first, if I may."

Between my adventures with Kip and Brittany, I hadn't eaten much, but I had been hydrating with plenty of water. I now found myself wiggling in discomfort.

"Of course," she said, and pointed me down a hallway.

* * *

I entered a small powder room with sink and toilet. An open door beyond revealed another room with a full shower. On the other end, yet another door opened to a second powder room, a twin to the one I had entered from. It reminded me of the Jack and Jill closet in Mrs. Arlington's house, and it wouldn't surprise me if that had once been a shared bathroom like this one.

After taking care of business, I stepped into the middle room. The shower had a handicap bar, a bench, and a handheld shower. I stepped through to the next room, confirming that it was identical to the one I had used. Beyond, I poked my head into a bedroom I surmised might have been Burton's. There were the usual accoutrements for someone who was failing in health. A cane and a walker were positioned close to the king bed. It was one of those expensive beds that could adjust for each occupant, though there was no evidence that Marietta shared this space. I recalled during our first visit that she had said the master was on the second floor.

I stepped inside onto cushy gray-and-navy carpet. The walls were also gray, with stark-white moldings. A wall of soft gray drapes, closed to the afternoon sunshine, suggested that the large window beneath faced the same view the living room offered. On an adjacent wall, photographs of famous places like the Taj Mahal and the Giza pyramids, presumably from Burton's travels, created a spectacular collage. The room was comfortable and looked well lived in, with more photographs on top of a desk, including one of a young couple with a little boy in front of a Christmas tree. Burton's first family. I saw no photographs of Marietta.

Alongside a chair and ottoman was a table holding the portable defibrillator Marietta had mentioned. I resisted the temptation to open the lid and see what it looked like because there was a sticker still sealing the lid in place. I guessed that Marietta had grabbed it and run but hadn't bothered to open it, given that she thought her husband was gone. Why resuscitate him if you had been waiting for this day for ten years?

The bedside table had numerous books piled on it, and it made me sad to think that Burton would never get to finish them. Two books caught my eye—one on the essentials of college admissions and another on how to write a college essay.

Feeling like a voyeur, I returned through Burton's bathroom to the powder room, groaning audibly when I glanced in the mirror. All this cloak-and-dagger stuff was taking its toll. I suddenly wanted to get Burton's obit done and get home to shower so I could wash away all this sadness. Nosy person that I was, however, I opened the medicine cabinet just to sneak a peek. Didn't everyone do that when they used someone else's bathroom?

Marietta was right: there were mountains of medicine bottles. I reached for one just as I heard the click of shoes on the marble hallway floor.

"Winter? Is all okay?" Marietta called.

I quickly turned on the water and hollered back that I'd be right there, but as I returned the bottle I was holding, I knocked the others, and they sounded like a martini shaker on steroids as they fell into the sink.

"Winter?" Marietta called again.

"Sorry, Marietta, I'm coming," I called back. "Just some tummy troubles."

I quickly shut off the water. Flushed the toilet again, as if I were having a gastrointestinal issue. For a moment all was silent, and I held my breath until I heard her shoes click on the marble stones heading back toward the living room.

Meanwhile, the bottles were now sopping wet, with labels beginning to peal. *Great, Winter.* How embarrassing was this? One by one, and as quietly as I could, I dried them and returned them to the shelf.

And then it struck me.

All the bottles were completely full.

I studied each of the labels. It appeared that the prescriptions were all renewed monthly and all for Burton. Some had been filled just a month ago in July, and here we were in mid-August, almost ready for a September refill, and none of those pills were even close to being used up. In fact, if I had to guess, Burton had just gone two months without the very meds that Marietta claimed were keeping him alive.

While I didn't know much about heart attacks or strokes, I was pretty sure that pills prescribed for high blood pressure, statins, beta blockers, and such were important to keep up with. I would've taken a picture if my phone weren't sitting in the living room on the coffee table acting as a hot spot for my laptop.

I opened one of the bottles, stuffed the space between the pills and the lid with toilet paper, and then capped it tight before slipping it into my pocket. It made an outline that would be hard to miss, so I undid my jeans, slipped it into my underwear, buttoned up again, and pulled my shirt down as far as it would go to cover the lump. Hopefully it wouldn't jiggle out, but with skinny jeans, I didn't think it was in any danger of falling onto the floor. To test it, I jumped up and down, and was happy that the toilet paper had done its job. No rattle. For good measure, I flushed again, ran more water, did a quick survey of the bathroom, and hurried back to Marietta.

"Are you okay?" she asked, studying me from head to toe. As I sat back down, I could feel the pill bottle press against my flesh. I prayed she hadn't seen it.

"I'm so sorry, just a bit of tummy trouble," I said, and felt as queasy as if this weren't a lie. "Let's get this done, and I'll get out of your hair."

Marietta frowned toward the bathroom, then shrugged and agreed. We got the necessary information included, and I reworked a few segments. I then forwarded the finished obituary to Marietta so she could get approval from Burton's son.

I let her know that I'd update the obituary as soon as the services were finalized and that I would follow through with all the places she wanted it published. She chose the *New York Times* along with the usual local newspapers because Burton was such a prominent New York City businessman. She also listed the son's hometown newspaper as well as Burton's college publication. I would have additional work making sure each version of the obit fit into the required format before this job was done.

Marietta watched me as I hurried out the door, and I could still see her face in my rearview as I pulled away. I was sure she was going to check Burton's room and bathroom to see what I had been doing in there. Once free of the driveway, I reached into my underwear, pulled the bottle away from where it had been pressing into my skin, and stuck it in the car pocket.

Chapter
Twenty-Six

First Mrs. Arlington's key, now Burton Hemlocker's medication bottle—these impulsive moves were not the actions you expect from your trustworthy obituary writer. And ignoring police warnings was not the kind of behavior that built a good reputation either. However, with Max alone at the Arlington pool house, I'd have to defy orders to stay clear of the estate in order to coax him to come home with me.

I parked in front of a forlorn-looking building. I was surprised that while I'd been busy filling water buckets the day I found Mrs. Arlington, I hadn't noticed how far into the woods the structure went.

It was easy to see how hidden a vehicle tucked away on the wooded service lane would be. I pulled up behind what I gathered was Mark's truck and could hear Max howling inside. I did as I was instructed by calling his name and telling him in a gentle but confident voice that all would be okay.

When I opened the door, a behemoth of a beast bounded past me and straight to the yard. Max was by far the largest German shepherd I had ever seen. All black and brown with huge pointy ears, he looked as if I could ride him like a pony.

Poor thing. I knew exactly how he felt as he took care of business. While he was busy sniffing and peeing, I entered the pool house. The segment where he had been held his bed, two bowls, and a chew bone. The rest of the room had a counter, sink, refrigerator, small cooktop—all things you might need as you lounged by the pool for the day. Adjoining this space was a hallway, and off it funneled several rooms, which turned out to be a bathroom with a shower as well as two changing rooms with hooks for clothing and shelves with stacks of towels, just as Brittany had described. Both rooms held blow-up beds. This was where Mark and Brittany had been hiding in plain sight. I retrieved Brittany's duffel from its hiding place behind a large laundry basket and unzipped it.

Inside were the usual types of things you might expect from someone planning to spend a night or two away. Extra underwear, jeans, and a couple of T-shirts. The boots she had on the first day I met her were on the floor tucked behind the blow-up. Before sticking them in the duffel with her other belongings, I noted the size—eight. The blue sneaker wasn't hers.

I carried the duffel along with Max's things to the car.

Now all I had to do was convince the dog I was friend, not foe.

Max was suddenly behind me, sniffing, and I resisted stiffening, remembering Brittany's instructions. "Put a smile on your face and speak to him happily. Offer your hand and give him a dog treat. He has excellent instincts about people."

Winter Snow, failed amateur sleuth, died when the dog she was trying to rescue chewed off her hand . . .

I followed directions. Max wagged his tail. I gave him a pet, and sure enough, this formidable shepherd with his inquisitive brown eyes leaned into my hands. Like Brittany said, he was a marshmallow with people he trusted. Still, his size was off-putting.

Max climbed into the back of the Subaru without protest. I cracked the window halfway, and he seemed to enjoy the breeze on his face as I hurried us away from that dreaded place and the police checks, which I was sure would now be more thorough.

When I arrived at the Mamanasco cottage, my uncle's car was already in the driveway. I inched past and put mine in the garage next to Brittany's truck and shut the door so it wouldn't be visible from the road. Inside, Uncle Richard and Brittany were chatting away as they prepared dinner, and Max beelined it for Brittany, suddenly making the kitchen feel small.

"Wow," my uncle said. "You didn't tell me he was a horse."

"Where is Diva?" I asked.

As if on cue, a puff of white peeked in from the open door to the living room. Max zeroed in on her. Diva wagged her tail and approached happily, but Max's instincts apparently didn't apply to dogs. All hell broke loose as Max charged. Brittany tackled the large dog before he got to Diva, who sauntered forward anyway, oblivious to the snapping jaws. Uncle Richard joined Brittany, who was having trouble holding Max back, and suddenly the two of them were on the floor with the shepherd. I tried to grab Diva as she skirted his jaws, chose a butt sniff, and then rested innocently at my feet.

"I think we're going to have to come up with plan B for Max," I said.

"Horace will take him next door," said Uncle Richard, out of breath as he tried to get off the floor while maintaining his hold. "Brittany and I already arranged it. I should have told you."

I picked up Diva, carried her upstairs, and locked her in the bedroom, which I was sure I would later regret, especially as I could already hear her frantic scratches. Brittany and Uncle Richard took Max next door.

I made sure the chocolate chip cookies that Brittany had been baking were out of the oven and placed on a tray. Through the open door to the living room, I could see that the table was set, and a robust Brunello was breathing on the sideboard. At some point I would have to tell Brittany that Kip was joining us.

My uncle and Brittany had just returned through the sliders and were updating me on Max and Horace when the doorbell rang.

"Too early for our dinner guests," said Richard, frowning.

I opened the Ring app I had loaded on my burner phone and stared.

"It's Tom, the police officer who wants to question me about the fire," I said.

Brittany looked like she wanted to run for cover.

"Go out the sliders and stay with Horace until he leaves," I instructed her. "Richard, take her—make sure she isn't seen."

"I don't want to leave you with this Tom fellow," my uncle protested.

"He's harmless," I said, wondering if that was true. After they were both through the sliders, I crossed the house and opened the front door.

"Why are you avoiding my calls?" Tom demanded, taking an aggressive step into the foyer.

Upstairs, Diva was barking and scratching like crazy.

I pulled my phone from my pocket, scrolled, and saw that he had called several times. It had probably been while I was at Marietta's house, when I'd turned off my ringer, something I always do so as not to be disturbed when I'm with clients. I explained that to him as I shoved the phone back in my back pocket.

Tom looked like he wanted to squeeze the life out of me, and his bare, beefy arms poking out of his red golf shirt looked like they could do the trick. He glanced over my shoulder toward the dining area, where the table was set.

"Having a party?"

"Just my uncle and a couple of his friends," I replied vaguely. "Tom, is this visit official? Because if not, I'm pretty busy right now. And, as you can hear, Diva wants out."

Tom bullied his way forward and sat down in one of the living room chairs. I followed but remained standing.

He ignored my question and said instead, "Looks like you're having quite a few friends."

I followed his gaze. I wanted to get him out of here before Kip arrived.

"What do you want?" I asked.

"It isn't looking good for you—what with Mark Goodwin dead and you stealing something from his pocket. You should wrap up any work you have, because you're going to be spending all your upcoming time trying to defend yourself."

"I already explained," I said. "I believe there is adequate proof that I was telling the truth about Mark locking me in the study and taking both my cell and the key. And speaking of keys, where is the key you took from Mrs. Arlington's house the other day?"

Tom looked momentarily surprised. "I left it in the bedroom lock. There was no need to take it, remember?"

I hadn't thought to look there, only in the bowl. I felt a little foolish and said nothing.

"What did Mark Goodwin tell you when you met him there at the house?" pressed Tom.

Despite the fact that this little dance we were doing wasn't in my favor, no way would I mention the lost file or any of the other details I had found out from David Wysocki, Brittany, and Mark.

"Nothing that would help solve the mystery of why Mrs. Arlington needed her obituary by yesterday." If Tom hadn't gotten any information from Kip, I wasn't going to tell him. "Mark hoped there might be some information in the files, but someone beat him to it. I don't suppose you know anything about that, do you?"

Tom frowned. "Why would I?"

I found that whenever there was a conversational lull at the cottage, the water became a refuge from any awkwardness. We had both turned our eyes in that direction, though Tom appeared calculating rather than at a loss for words.

"You're hiding something," he said finally. He abruptly stood and jabbed his finger toward my face. "I don't know who you think you're playing games with, but it isn't going to work. I know what's going on."

I wished that someone would tell me what was going on. Tom's thick finger continued wagging in my face, and he had grown red with anger. I thought the guy might have a stroke right here in my living room. I took another step back from his posturing and his coal-black manic eyes.

"Tom, I have absolutely no idea what you're talking about." I tried to coat my voice with calm. "Scoop told you about the phone calls from Mark Goodwin, and I think they prove I was telling the truth."

"I want to hear for myself," he said, dropping his eyes to the pocket where I had stuffed the burner. "Let me have that phone."

I was surprised that he didn't know that my personal phone, with my world of information stored inside, was now at the police station being tested for fingerprints. If his fellow police officer hadn't trusted him with that detail, I certainly wasn't going to share it. And I wasn't going to tell him about the shoe Diva had carried around for days before Kip took that away too. What had Brittany said? Mrs.

Arlington didn't trust the police. Maybe it was a particular police-man that she hadn't trusted.

"I need to check on Diva." The upstairs racket had grown omi-nously quiet. What was she up to?

I backed away toward the entryway and staircase.

"I want that phone," Tom said, closing the distance between us. He grabbed my wrist to hold me in place and pulled the phone from my pocket. It felt extremely personal and invasive, but this was no time to get my #MeToo ire up. The man had the upper hand.

"Give me the password," he demanded as he squeezed my wrist tighter.

My internal debate was short. Tom was going off the rails.

I recited the password.

And then he surprised me by letting my arm go, pushing past me, and almost running out the door.

Great. For the second time in two days, I no longer had a cell phone. And even more upsetting was the fact that Tom could see any recent calls or texts, because he now had access.

When I was sure he was gone, I ran next door and entered Hor-ace's house through the back door. Richard, Brittany, and Horace were huddled in the kitchen with a much-calmer Max at Brittany's feet.

"Quick, give me your phone," I said to Richard. My uncle com-plied, and I texted Kip: *This is Winter—Tom was at my house and took my phone. Don't call or text to the burner.* He texted Richard's phone back immediately: *Stay put—on my way.*

"Will there be any record of texts sent prior to your getting the throwaway phone?" asked Richard.

I was pretty sure the temporary phone recorded only the mes-sages I'd received since I'd acquired it. There wasn't much I could do about the calls to and from Kip. At least I'd never set it up for email. "I do want to warn David Wysocki—just in case."

"Warn him of what?" asked Brittany, who I could see was visibly shaken.

"Mrs. Arlington did not trust the police—maybe it was one policeman in particular," I said. "Tom doesn't know about David and Bitsy, and David has my number."

Though I doubted David would call me after our confrontational visit, I thought we should err on the side of caution.

"I'll warn him right now." Brittany pulled out her cell to make the call and fiddled. "The service here is pretty bad."

Uncle Richard led her to the deck, where she could get more bars, and I followed, Horace and Max at my heels. Max was suddenly yowling, his version of a bark, and I looked over to see Scoop lounging on my deck next door.

"Hope you don't mind," Scoop called as we all traipsed across the grass to join him. Feet up on an outdoor ottoman, he was relaxing in one of the chairs, a can of Heady Topper in his hand. Diva crouched in her usual spot near the open slider door.

"When I arrived and no one answered, I let myself in," he said. "Then I heard all the noise upstairs and got worried. Diva was going crazy, all drool and panting, so I let her out. She's okay—the bedroom, not so much."

By now we were all on the deck, including Max, who seemed to know that Diva wouldn't come out despite lingering by the sliders with her tail wagging like a fast-beat metronome.

I filled everyone in on as much as I knew and then plopped down into the chair next to Scoop. I could almost taste the chilled, hoppy, slightly bitter IPA, but since COVID, no one took a sip of anyone's drink anymore.

Scoop noticed my longing look. "I brought more."

I declined, and we all settled around on the deck to wait for Kip. It took some persuading to convince Brittany that Kip was a good guy. When he breezed onto the deck, she still looked ready to bolt.

"Are you okay? What did Tom do to you?" There was no hug from Kip this time, though I could feel his intensity as he searched my face.

I relayed the entire encounter.

"He's in this thing up to his eyeballs," said Kip. "I just can't figure out how."

"Tom knows Marietta well enough to be sharing information about the investigation," I said, explaining that Marietta knew about the ransacking. "She even knew about Brittany disappearing."

"Me? How would she know that?" Brittany asked. "Aunt Lottie told me not to tell a soul, and I didn't. Only David and Bitsy knew. And, of course, Mark and Burton . . ." Her voice choked as the loss of her friends hit her again.

"It wasn't public knowledge," said Kip. "Why would Tom confide in Marietta Hemlocker, and why would she even care?"

"Maybe Marietta is the owner of the blue sneaker," I said.

Kip looked at me and then cast a sideways glance at Brittany's feet. I shook my head no.

"There's something else," I said. "Brittany, is there some reason why you would be the beneficiary of Burton Hemlocker's life insurance?" I asked.

All eyes turned to her. To my surprise, she put her hands up to cover her face, as if she thought by doing this she couldn't be seen.

Scoop put down his Heady Topper and moved his chair close enough to reach over and pull her hands away. "We can still see you, you know," he said, and he gave her a comforting smile.

She turned her pale face toward him and said, "I can't do this."

Scoop kept one of her hands in his and gave it a squeeze.

"I'll help you," he said.

Scoop asked questions, the way a good reporter does. He didn't push or threaten, just became her friend, and in a low, quiet voice, Brittany began explaining.

"He was always talking about my future. I didn't understand it. He sounded like my parents—they wanted me to go to college like my brainiac brothers. But Burton said there were different kinds of smarts and that I just had to find mine."

Brittany turned pleading eyes toward Scoop.

"Burton was right," he said. "You just have to find a way to use the gifts you were given."

Such wisdom from such a young kid, I thought as Brittany continued. "It turns out that I have a knack for electronic devices. Burton said it was like I could speak French when no one else in the room could. He said I spoke computer. That's how he described it, and he wanted me to go to school for it."

I thought back to the day I'd first met her when she couldn't even figure out how to turn off Mrs. Arlington's driveway alarm. She hadn't seemed techie to me.

Brittany appeared to read my mind, because a small smile reached the corners of her mouth. "Only Burton, Aunt Lottie, and Mark knew about my so-called talents. I didn't even tell David, Bitsy, or my parents. Aunt Lottie was adamant that I act like a ditzy assistant. She didn't want anyone else to know that she had taken any special interest in me. I got so good at the acting, I was beginning to wonder if maybe I should ditch the IT idea and become an actor. Aunt Lottie and Burton quickly discouraged me from that, though. They said succeeding in that was like winning the lottery."

Could Brittany be acting now? She was so darn believable and appeared so vulnerable that it was hard not to want to reach out and wrap my arms around her and say, *You are safe.*

"So, the day I came to meet your aunt, you knew you could turn off the driveway alarm from the inside," I said.

"Sure, but Aunt Lottie was terrified that someone might sneak up on us, so I thought it might be better to see if I could fix it from the outside to make sure it would still be operational."

"What about the insurance policy? Did Burton tell you he was going to do that?" I asked.

"Yes, and my aunt told him not to do it. She said she would take care of my education, but he was insistent. He said this was for after I finished school because he planned to still be around for my graduation."

Brittany blinked away tears, and Scoop swiped at his own eyes. He was a softy when it came to bleeding-heart stories.

It occurred to me that all the answers to our questions might be revealed if only Diva could talk. She sat watching, her intelligent eyes traveling back and forth between speakers as if she were intent on a tennis match. Kip did pretty much the same thing. I wished I could read both their minds.

Scoop continued to prompt Brittany through her story, everything from the time she arrived at her aunt's estate until today.

"There must have been a trigger point that made your great-aunt want you to leave," said Scoop.

She hesitated before answering. "One minute we were all about planning a reunion, and the next minute she was like, 'You have to go home.'"

Brittany looked down at her hands, then picked at lint on her jeans. She was holding something back. I made a mental note to press her later about it.

I asked her about her walks with Lottie and Burton, and it was the first time she visibly relaxed. Her dark eyes sparkled as she described the path they'd created through the woods between the two houses.

"It was pretty messed up, although it was getting better, because Mark was weed whacking it and trying to even it out for them," she said. "It was still filled with stuff—protruding rocks and roots that might trip someone. So, I started walking with them. If Burton wanted to come over, he'd text, and I'd meet him at the edge of the path and walk with him. If Aunt Lottie wanted to go there, I'd walk with her. Burton always insisted on walking her home, and so I would again go back with him. I'd watch from the edge of the path until he got inside. At first it seemed silly to me, but then one day my aunt did trip, and I was there to help. It got so routine that both always wanted me with them."

"Did they visit each other a lot?" I asked.

"Enough. A couple of times a week, and some weeks almost every day. They were good friends."

"And what about Mrs. Hemlocker?" I asked. "Did you see her much?"

"I never met her," Brittany said. "Mostly, I would watch Burton from the edge of the path until he got inside, and then I would go back to my aunt's house. I did get to see Burton's library once or twice, but that's in his car barn. His wife was never around."

That explained why Marietta wasn't familiar with Brittany, though one would assume that Burton would have mentioned her. On the other hand, because Lottie wanted Brittany out of the limelight, Burton might have kept their interest in the girl a secret.

"Where was Mark on all this?" Kip asked.

"Mark kept his distance from people," said Brittany. "He was what you'd call a loner. He encouraged the friendship, though. Like I said, he was working to make the path safer. Why is any of this important?"

"Because something happened that made your great-aunt cancel all your family reunion plans and send you away. And it happened recently," said Kip.

Again, Brittany looked away. She studied her fingers, then the lake, and finally went back to lint picking on her jeans before saying, "I can't think of anything."

"How was Burton's health?" I asked, remembering the pill bottles.

Brittany shrugged. "He was old and frail. He was always saying that Marietta complained about his pill planner being so full that it was hard to close the little compartments."

Pill planner. I hadn't seen one of those in his room.

Kip studied me with that *What are you thinking?* look he had.

"Be right back," I said.

I went inside, gave Diva a little pet, retrieved the pill bottle from the car, and returned to the deck.

I held up the little plastic container of pills and relayed my story about the remaining bottles in the cabinet.

"There was no visible pill planner that I could see," I added.

"You actually stole medication from the Hemlockers' cabinet?" asked Kip, and predictably, along came the brow rub.

"I just borrowed it," I said. "It was an impulse."

Kip shook his head and sent his eyes skyward.

"So you think Marietta wasn't giving Burton his pills," said Uncle Richard, who appeared to see nothing unreasonable about my theft. Maybe this was a family compulsion and I came by it naturally.

Tears escaped Brittany's eyes, and she did nothing to wipe them away as the implications of the filled bottle hit home.

Kip looked resigned as he took the bottle from me and studied it. The one I had taken had a June expiration and was filled to the brim with little white pills. I explained about the July and August bottles also being full.

"I think it was Marietta, with the pill planner, in the bedroom," said Scoop.

Brittany smiled.

"Wait a minute," I said. "What if Marietta was filling the planner with vitamins or some other placebo? Could that be what Mrs. Arlington learned? Maybe Marietta pushed Mrs. Arlington down the stairs to shut her up and then killed Mark Goodwin because she assumed that he was in the know."

I then filled them in on the prenuptial agreement and the suspicions of Burton's son.

"There could be other clauses in that agreement, like giving Burton the best care and so forth," I said. "Marietta did say that any hint at impropriety would set Burton's son on the warpath."

"Did Marietta sound desperate enough to kill to protect her inheritance?" asked Kip.

"One minute she was lamenting her poor husband, the next railing about wasting ten years of her life," I said. "Grief does do strange things to people, so I couldn't tell you if she would murder for money."

"Why did she stay with someone she didn't love?" asked Brittany. "Burton was such a sweet man. How could anyone harm him?"

"She stayed because, as she put it, where else could you earn that much money in ten years?"

Brittany's face contorted as if she had just taken a shot of vinegar.

Kip was pacing now, lost in thought. Horace and Uncle Richard headed into the kitchen to see about dinner. Max made the rounds on the deck, receiving numerous pets, all the while keeping his eye on the door, where Diva solemnly watched.

"Whoa, Scoop, what are you doing?" Kip asked suddenly, noticing Scoop busy scribbling away on a pad of paper.

"This entire evening is off the record," I reminded him. "You can't write any of this."

"*Yet,*" he said. "I can't write any of this *yet.* For the moment, I'm just trying to create a timeline. Think about it. Marietta might have been holding back the meds for months—maybe even right after their ten-year anniversary last January."

"How do you know their anniversary was last January?" I asked.

"If you would read your emails, you would see that I researched the Hemlockers and that was the date of their ten-year celebration," said Scoop. "They had a huge party at their estate—lots of conversation in social media about vaccination requirements and so forth."

I sighed. I hadn't gotten to my emails yet.

"We should probably consult his doctor," I said. "Marietta might have killed him from neglect or duplicity."

"He was tired all the time," added Brittany. "Aunt Lottie wanted him to go for a complete checkup, but he always waved her off."

"Stop," said Kip, holding up his hands. "This is a lot of speculation. Full pill bottles prove nothing. For all you know, his docs might have changed his prescriptions and these are the old ones." And then Kip turned to me. "You have the most vivid imagination for doomsday scenarios of anyone I've ever met."

"You sure got that right," injected Scoop. "She thought I was in danger and kept warning me to watch my back because of the note with a box of kittens left on my doorstep. I was living in fear, locking doors and windows, and looking over my shoulder."

"When someone tells you to *mind your own business*, you should look over your shoulder," I said.

"Turns out that the kittens were strays found at Village Square," said Scoop, ignoring me. "The guy who dumped them on my doorstep grabbed a box from the recycling bin. The note was already in there."

"How do you know all that?" I asked.

"If you read the *Press*, you'd know that I wrote a story about the kittens and needed more information to suitably place them. The guy got in touch."

"And he didn't write the note?" I asked.

"No, it was a note written to the Nosy Parkers, and they had tossed it out with their other recycling, including the box."

"How can you be sure it was their box that the guy grabbed?"

I was feeling all eyes on me, and my cheeks flamed with embarrassment. And yet I felt justified in worrying about my friend. That note had been in all caps, like it was shouting at him.

"There was still an address label on the box," he said with a shrug. "I called them, and they said they get those kinds of notes all the time. They just toss them."

"Well, thanks for keeping me informed. Here I was worrying about you, and you had the mystery already solved. Did the Nosy Parkers know who was telling them to mind their own business?" I asked.

Scoop gave a head shake and said, "Narrowing that down would be akin to finding Waldo."

"Well, you could have told me," I said.

"It's not my fault that you're paranoid or that trouble seems to follow you," said Scoop, blowing me off.

Kip ignored our squabble and turned to Brittany. "I want to ask you a couple of questions, and I want you to think long and hard about the answers."

Brittany visibly shrank away as she reached for Scoop's hand.

"He's a good guy," Scoop said quietly. "Your great-aunt trusted Winter, right?"

Brittany nodded.

"Winter and I both trust Kip," he reassured her.

Brittany nodded and waited with wary eyes.

Kip edged closer to her and leaned forward, hands on his knees, as if talking to a child.

"Tell me exactly what you remember about your great-aunt's conversations with Burton," he said. I felt a twinge of jealousy at realizing that this quiet, gentle tone wasn't the one he used with me.

Brittany turned her eyes to the water as she reviewed things in her mind. Then she slowly began.

"Burton was proud of the fact that he only needed a cane to walk the path," she said. "It was as if he was trying to convince us and himself that he was feeling better. But we all knew it was because Mark had made the path smooth enough to navigate. Aunt Lottie humored him and brought her own cane with her, though she didn't really need it. She told him that they both had to take care of themselves and that they would both start with blood workups. I remember because she said he looked pale, like he wasn't getting enough oxygen. It stuck with me, because if you got COVID, oxygen levels were the major thing everyone talked about during the pandemic."

"Good," said Kip, smiling at her. She gave a timid smile back.

"Do you think your aunt suspected that Burton wasn't getting his medication?"

"Maybe," she said slowly, and then nodded. "Now that I look back, yes."

"Would she have confronted Marietta?" I asked.

"I'm not sure, but it was around that time when she told me she was worried about Burton that she weirded out. She made me cancel the reunion and told me to start packing my bags."

"Marietta and Burton are the official key holders for the Arlington house," I said. "Maybe she snuck over last Tuesday night, when she thought Mrs. Arlington was asleep, so she could retrieve whatever proof there might be of her neglect. She might not have known yet about the super-smart Great Pyrenees puppy who might alert her owner to danger."

"It would be good if we had Mrs. Arlington's day planner or calendar," said Scoop, warming to my theory.

"Her calendar is digital and not in her cloud. She was paranoid about things rolling around in heaven, as she put it," said Brittany. "Anyway, she was old school and kept her calendar on one device only—her iPad."

"So where is that iPad?" asked Kip.

"She usually kept her iPad in the sunroom next to her chair. Was that room destroyed in the fire?" Brittany asked.

"Most of the downstairs damage was confined to the living room, entry and staircase," said Kip. "Whoever ransacked the house probably did a pretty good job of searching the whole place before they started the fire. I personally did a run-through and didn't see any electronics."

"Winter, you're looking a little flushed. Are you okay?" asked Uncle Richard, who had returned to call us to dinner.

My lie detector was apparently in full bloom. At some point I was going to have to admit my sunroom subterfuge—yet another example of my tenuous relationship with the law. Not yet, however.

"Just hungry," I murmured.

* * *

Richard poured a Lewis pinot noir that had been breathing on the high-gloss sideboard. He was known for his wine collection, and this one apparently didn't disappoint. I stuck to a glass of Rombauer from an open bottle in the fridge, and Brittany opted for sparkling water.

Scoop ate like he hadn't seen food in days, gave an apologetic smile, and dug in for seconds. After helping to clear the dishes, he yawned, stretched, and begged off for the night. Brittany walked him to the door and rapidly retreated upstairs. Max, who was Mr. Confident after establishing himself as alpha dog, trotted home after Horace. Richard hovered for a few minutes, asking what I would do about my phone. I promised to call him tomorrow after my visit to Verizon for yet another burner. That left Kip and me to wrap up.

"I think Diva is toying with Max," Kip said as he loaded the last of the dishes into the dishwasher.

"What do you mean?" I asked as I poured hot water into two cups and dropped a chamomile-with-lavender tea bag into each.

"She's just biding her time, letting him think he's in charge, and then, boom. Next thing you know, he'll be following her around, trying to please her," he said.

I handed him his mug, and he followed me outside, where we settled into lounge chairs. The Sturgeon Moon was a few days into the wane but still bright enough to illuminate the contours of the lake—the Cliffs, the craggy shoreline, the pale strip of beach between splashes of light from the houses. The windless night left the water itself smooth as glass, and the moonbeams were like camera flashes on a dark mirror.

"Interesting," I said, just as Diva showed up next to the door.

I patted my lap and said softly, "Come on. Don't be afraid."

She stayed put.

"What were you trying to tell me about the shoe?" asked Kip.

"Brittany is a size eight. It would be like one of Cinderella's stepsisters trying to squeeze into the glass slipper." It triggered a thought. "We should get Marietta to try the shoe on."

Kip sipped his tea and looked out at the lake in thought.

"I mean, if the shoe fits—" I added.

"It would be more like Cruella, or Ursula from the *Little Mermaid*," he finished.

"You know your Disney," I said, amused.

"I like movies with happy endings," he said, and looked away shyly.

* * *

After Kip left, Diva and I climbed the stairs for the night. She opted to slip into Brittany's room—or, I should say, I opted for her to sleep there. My room was sufficiently torn up from her earlier frustrated escape efforts, and I was not in a happy-with-my-dog mood. By the time I cleaned up and crawled into bed, though, I was already missing her.

An hour later, alone, tormented by a million thoughts that kept me from sleep, I knew there was one more thing I had to do and do it soon. The question was, should I tell Kip that I planned to sneak back into the house to get Mrs. Arlington's iPad?

It would jeopardize his job if he knew and didn't report it. And if I told him, he'd have to go through channels and convince someone that it was important. All of that. And then Tom might find out. He might tell Marietta. And if Marietta had some part in this, she had a key to the house and might get to the iPad first, assuming there was something she was searching for.

When six AM came, Diva was making noises in the next room, so I dragged myself from bed and I stuck my head in. Brittany was leaning against a pile of rainbow-colored pillows, a matching comforter tucked up to her chin. She looked reluctant to move.

"This is so much better than those blow-ups," she said with a bright smile. She looked so childlike that it was hard not to see why Mrs. Arlington, Burton, and Mark had risked their lives to protect her.

"Stay in bed," I said. "I'll take Diva out."

"I don't mind taking her," she said as she pulled herself up and stretched. "I like our early-morning walks. That was the thing about

Diva my aunt hated. She didn't like to have to get out of bed until half the morning was over."

"Let's go together." I didn't want to chance that Tom might be watching the house. If he and Marietta were the bad guys, which I was beginning to believe, they might think Brittany was also a threat. That prenup could be the motive for everything that had happened, including Mark Goodwin's murder. Which could put Brittany next in line.

Brittany wanted to pick up Max for the walk. I thought it was too early to tap on Horace's door, and besides, I wasn't sure I wanted to deal with dueling dogs. As we walked by, however, a groggy Horace opened the door, and Max came bounding out.

"I've got this," hollered Brittany.

"We don't have a leash," I said as the dog beelined happily toward her.

She gave Max lots of hugs and pets while I stood by uneasily, shielding Diva.

"He won't need one," she said confidently.

"What if he tries to snack on her again?" I asked, indicating the small furball now pressed between my legs.

"He won't; he has established himself as superior," she said. "It's that organic thing that dogs do."

And she was right. Diva was content to be on the leash while Max trotted ahead, checked things out, and then retreated next to Brittany as if he were a scout reporting back. If Kip was right about Diva, however, Max's reign would be short-lived.

"Do you have a key to Mrs. Arlington's house?" I asked as we walked.

By this point I had no idea if the doors to the mansion were locked or not, but I knew without a doubt that I had to get that iPad.

Brittany stopped, and both dogs sat at attention, picking up on her body language as she eyed me suspiciously.

"You aren't going back there, are you?"

I felt the color rising in my cheeks. "I hid her iPad under the cushions of one of the chairs in the sunroom. If I could get it, we might find whatever secret your great-aunt had. It might tell us what happened to her and who killed Mark."

At the mention of her friend, Brittany gave Max an extra massage behind those pointy ears.

"He was trying to help me," she said thoughtfully. "He knew Aunt Lottie was sending me away to protect me, and when I came back to check on her, he insisted that I return to David and Bitsy's house and wait there until he found out what was going on. But I had to stay to be there in case Aunt Lottie needed me. Plus I was worried about Diva, and I knew I could help him with Max. After she died, we talked a lot about whether he should bring you into his plan to go back inside and search. He decided we needed someone on the outside we could trust, and we decided it was you."

"Why me?" I asked.

"Simple," said Brittany, "Aunt Lottie trusted you."

I digested this. The two of them held Leocadia Arlington in such high regard that they were willing to risk everything based on her trust level.

"Did he tell you what he was searching for?" I asked.

"Proof that she was up to her old tricks and that she knew something about someone," said Brittany. "He was convinced that there was something in her files. I told him to look in the book club folder. My aunt never let me see those files, which made me wonder what was so important about them, but her memoirs had details about her past, and I figured they must have something to do with what happened to her."

"I'll go over there this morning and get the iPad. I'll then go to the Verizon store and get another phone and get back here as soon as I can. You can get into the iPad, right?" I asked.

Brittany shielded her eyes from the rising sun before answering. It was going to be another sizzler, from the feel of things. "Her iPad and her iPhone were rarely out of her sight, and while I had access to her computer, I didn't have passwords to those. I do know the way her mind worked. We'll just have to hope she used the same types of passwords on those devices that she did for her computer and house alarm."

"With the power now restored, will the alarm be on?" I asked.

"Not unless someone set it," she said. Brittany gave me the password and instructions on how to turn it off, just in case. "I'm pretty sure the driveway alarm will be working."

* * *

An hour later, I was on my way back to the Arlington house with Brittany's key in my pocket. I opted for the service entrance and parked out of sight, snuggling my car into the woods behind the pool house. For good measure, I turned the Subaru around so it would be facing in the exit direction in case I needed a quick getaway.

I left the keys on the dashboard and hugged the wooded landscape as I made my way to the house just in case there were still investigators inside.

It was another picturesque morning, with a clear blue sky, and I could already feel the heat rising off the grassy carpet—it was going to be a steamy one. There was still enough dew to dampen my sneakers, and I debated taking them off before entering the house. With all the damage from the fire and so many people traipsing through, I doubted anyone would notice my footprints, so I left them on.

I crept across the stone patio, peeked through the windows to make sure the crime teams were cleared out by now, and unlocked the back French doors—the same doors where I'd watched Diva skirt the pool to avoid water on the day I discovered Mrs. Arlington at the bottom of the staircase.

At least the patio doors didn't squeak, although the noise from the lock was significant enough to rattle my edgy nerves. I had fingers crossed that no one was inside the house, because this was not the quiet entry I had planned.

The smell permeating the house made me gag. The odor was akin to what you might find in a dumpster filled with rotting food. Inside the wide front-to-back hallway, I stood still and listened as I took in the scene. Charred furniture was piled atop what had once been a lush carpet. Everything was smoke stained and water damaged. Surprisingly, the structure was still in place, a testament to the FD's expertise in knocking the fire down before it could get inside the walls. An old house like this wouldn't have fire stops between floors.

I heard nothing and as I hurried toward the sunroom, I glanced into the living room where most of the damage had been confined. With much of the fabric disintegrated, there were now only skeletal remains, all charred black and sooty. Oddly, the curtains, though limp and streaked gray, were still hanging. The sooner I got out of this creepy house, the better.

Just as Kip had said, the sunroom had escaped fairly unscathed, except for the overpowering odor now settling in. It made me sad to think Mrs. Arlington's beloved home would probably be torn down and the land sold off in parcels for development. I wondered again who the beneficiary of her estate was. I hadn't heard a word from Sondra Milton, Mrs. Arlington's lawyer.

The iPad mini with its black magnetic cover was right where I'd left it under the cushion of Mrs. Arlington's chair—the one where she'd sat when I interviewed her. I opened the cover, and surprisingly, there was still a charge, though not much. I quickly abandoned the idea of trying a few passwords, because the tomblike setting of the empty mansion was giving me the willies.

Somewhere in the distance of the house, I heard the now-familiar ding-dong of the driveway alarm. I grabbed the iPad, and as I was replacing the seat cushion, I bumped the side table. Before I could grab hold of the wobbling piece, it toppled over, shattering a vase as it went. In my efforts to save the table and what I hoped was not a Ming, the iPad slid out of my hand to the floor. In a flash I was down on hands and knees, frantically picking away the glass, sliding it discreetly under the chair and out of sight as I reached for the iPad. Finally, tablet in hand, I rose, hurried across the room, paused, and listened. Nothing.

And then, just as I crossed into the hallway to exit through the patio doors, I heard the unmistakable click of a key turning in the front door. There was no time for anything but to rush into the living room, the closest room adjacent to the hallway.

As the front door opened with its familiar squeak, I cast about for a place to hide. I zeroed in on the fireplace. No, I thought. I'd had enough of fires.

As the door shut, I tiptoed across the room and slid behind the panel of drapes that pooled onto the floor, old-style. They smelled so bad that I thought I might begin coughing or sneezing, so I held my breath. Whoever had entered went straight into the sunroom, and I debated slipping back into the hallway and out the doors. Then I remembered the noisy clicks the lock made when it opened and the mess of debris from destroyed furnishings I would have to navigate. I cursed myself for not leaving the door ajar. Whoever was in the sunroom would have plenty of time to chase me down the lawn if they heard me exit.

So I waited, frozen behind the drapes, terrified that my gagging might erupt into vomiting. I closed my eyes and practiced the techniques I had learned over the years to manage a panic attack. I couldn't exactly imagine myself on a sandy beach with a balmy breeze. Instead, I managed a quiet room with a dead-bolted door.

A few moments later, when the heavy-footed intruder crossed the hallway and entered the living room, I had my breathing under control, though not so much my racing heart. He stayed only long enough to recognize that there was nothing left in this room to salvage. If he headed toward the curtains, I would leave the iPad on the windowsill and emerge empty-handed to confront him.

My plan proved unnecessary, because he moved on down the hallway, and judging by the sounds of rattling crystal, the search was now in the dining room.

I slipped out from behind the curtains, quietly exited into the hallway, where I picked around anything my feet might crunch, and with my hand on the doorknob of the French doors, waited. Sure enough, more noisy rattling as the perpetrator investigated another cabinet. I opened the door, raced down two steps, and sprinted toward the pool house.

Once there, I glanced back and was shocked to see a man barreling in my direction. And that man looked a lot like Tom. I wasn't about to wait around to find out for sure. Instead, I used my significant head start to get out of there and fast. Thank goodness I'd left the car pointed in the right direction, because a quick getaway was exactly what I needed.

As I fishtailed it away, I could see my pursuer rounding the corner to the pool house and heading straight for Mark Goodwin's truck, which was still parked on the service road. I said a silent prayer that Mark hadn't left the keys inside.

Chapter
Twenty-Seven

The smartest thing would be to drive to the firehouse or even the police station so as not to risk a confrontation without a witness. Tom's aggressive behavior yesterday and his physical act of taking my phone had left me rattled. Instead, I took the fastest route home. Brittany was alone and vulnerable at the cottage, and I had no other way to warn her.

I'd cut my driving teeth on the snarl of country roads I was now winding through. I was sure Tom, as a Ridgefield police officer, also knew the roads well, though he probably wasn't as seasoned at driving them at a breakneck pace. I was counting on my head start and the fact that as a teen I had tested every speed limit on these back roads. But the urgency of teenage angst didn't compare to the urgency I felt now as I pressed the pedal closer to the floor.

Finally, on Mamanasco Road, with no one in my rearview, I felt the tension in my shoulders ebb. My grip had been so tight on the wheel that my knuckles were white. I had worried with every corner that I might come upon some early riser out for a walk. I was finally home, safe, and relieved that I hadn't taken any casualties along the way.

And then, as the garage door slid down behind me, I heard a vehicle racing toward the house. My heart picked up its pace when it screeched to a stop. As I launched myself inside, I called out to Brittany.

She emerged, looking sheepish. In one hand was one of the locomotives from the train room, in the other something small that must have broken off.

"I'm sorry," she said. "I was admiring the trains, and when I picked this up . . ."

She didn't finish, just held up a small metal rod.

This was no time to let her know that she had invaded my private place.

"It can be fixed." I cut her off and pushed past her to make sure the front door was locked.

"I'm terribly sorry." She stared at it mournfully as she laid the engine tenderly on a side table. A distant memory flicked through my brain as I set the alarm. Me standing in front of Richard with the remnants of his prize caboose, wheels dangling like broken limbs. Summer had done the damage, and I had been elected to tell our uncle.

"I'll have it fixed," said Brittany, as she registered the look on my face.

I cleared my head. "It's not that. The train can be fixed," I said. "Someone might be after us. Help me lock all the downstairs doors and windows."

After last night's conversation about my doomsday imagination, I wondered if she might think I was crying wolf. Before I could explain, both dogs came bounding out of the study to greet me. I was relieved that they were now getting along and marveled that Brittany had predicted it happening—how had she put it?—organically.

"We have to call for help," I said, even as I heard the front door-knob jiggle and the doorbell blast as someone pushed and didn't let up.

Pale yet efficient, Brittany didn't question me. She clamored behind me as we hurried to the second floor to get her phone. I thought both dogs would follow, but Max stayed at the bottom step, alert to the sounds of the would-be intruder, and let out a thunderous growl.

Upstairs, I dialed 911, thinking how ironic it would be if Tom himself responded to Tom trying to break in. I blurted the address, the break-in attempt, and then called Kip. No answer. I realized he might not recognize Brittany's phone. I texted him, Scoop, and Uncle Richard. *It's me, Winter. Someone trying to break into cottage. Maybe Tom.*

The room where Brittany was staying had a small Juliet balcony that was the joy of the cozy space. It didn't face the lake directly, but if you stepped out, you could crane your neck around and get a partial view of the water and also the deck below. I did that now. Sure enough, Tom was there, testing the sliders. I ducked back inside before he noticed me.

There was no way for him to see the inside of the garage, where my car was parked, so I'd hoped he would assume I'd gone elsewhere. What was on that iPad that he didn't want me to see? Because, right now, I was sure he'd been searching for it.

"Brittany, see if you can open this thing," I said, handing her the iPad.

She flipped open the magnetic cover and murmured something about a low battery. I was already heading to my room in search of my iPhone charger. No luck. It was downstairs, and I didn't want to risk being seen through the wall of deckside windows.

Brittany's phone pinged. Scoop and Kip were both on their way.

Richard texted. He'd also called the police. *Keep doors locked. I'll call Horace.*

Great, that's what we needed—a frail octogenarian confronting a workout buff who was also a cop.

"Have you gotten into that yet?" I asked Brittany.

Still tapping frantically, she shook her head. "None of the usual passwords work."

"What have you tried?"

"Alarm code, her birthday, my birthday—her usual."

"How about Roth or Henry's birthday?"

"Tried them. I even reversed them all—something she was fond of doing," she said, her face scrunched up in thought as she studied the iPad.

"Keep at it."

Suddenly the loud, earsplitting blare of a vehicle alarm overpowered the persistent banging on the door. The sound was coming from the house next door. Horace, alerting the neighbors that he needed help. Horace's own personal SOS.

Oh, how I loved that guy.

A moment later, all door pounding ceased. Brittany and I stayed frozen in place until we heard the doorbell blast again. Of course, I couldn't check my Ring app to see who was there, because I had no phone. Talk about frustrating. I hadn't been kidding when I said my phone was my life.

I told Brittany to stay upstairs while I crept down. Max was howling his version of barking. The insistent doorbell had been replaced with banging and calling out, voices I recognized.

Through the side windows of the front door, I could see Scoop pounding away. Horace, our key holder, had a huge chain with about a hundred keys jingling as he tried various ones. At the sliders in the back, Kip was knocking loudly on the hurricane glass. Diva, still upstairs with Brittany, was yapping, and I couldn't decide who to respond to first.

The front door was closest, and while wrenching it open, I forgot to turn off the alarm, so the loud, steady blare competed with the rest of the noise. Max howled frantically at the high pitch, which no doubt hurt his sensitive ears. I yelled to Brittany to come downstairs. I shut off the alarm feeling some of the tension release from my shoulders as Horace and Scoop barreled through the front door. I then headed to the back sliders to let Kip inside.

Everyone crowded into the living room, including Brittany and the dogs, and for a brief moment I felt relief at the relative quiet.

"You have some explaining to do," said Kip, breaking the calm. I could see the storm brewing in the slate sky of his eyes.

Brittany sank into one of the chairs, as did Scoop. Horace sat on the couch, and Max settled near his feet. That left Kip and me facing off.

"Well?" he said in a frigid tone.

"Well, what?"

"Do you want to explain why you ran away from a cop while you were trespassing? Why did you go back there? And what did you steal this time?"

I took a deep breath and felt all eyes on me. My scarlet face with prominent freckles wouldn't allow for a lie. Just as I was about to explain, Uncle Richard rushed in the front door. The dogs went yapping and howling again, and my uncle almost tripped over them as he rushed into the room.

"Are you okay?" he asked, hurrying toward me.

"Fine, everything is fine," I said, waving him off.

He looked around the room and registered the scene. Plenty of people had come to the rescue, and I could see him calculating. He got the tension. Attempting to disguise his relief, he held up a rumpled paper bag. "Bagels and cream cheese from Steve's. I got smoked salmon too." He then retreated to the kitchen.

Richard's way of buying time until he figured out what was going on.

"I'll help," said Brittany, leaping up to follow.

Scoop looked back and forth between us, apparently trying to decide which way to go. The kitchen won out. Horace and the dogs quickly trailed behind him.

Kip stared at me with seamed lips.

"I went back to the house to get Mrs. Arlington's iPad," I confessed. "I thought it might have the information we were looking for."

"I scoured that house and found no electronics," Kip said with a frown.

I explained how I had slipped it under the seat cushion in the sunroom while he and Tom were upstairs checking the house on the day Mrs. Arlington fell down the stairs.

"Why didn't you just tell us you thought it was important?" he asked incredulously.

"Because I didn't trust either of you that day. And as time went on, I didn't trust Tom. If I told you, you would have had to make it official or risk your job keeping it a secret."

Kip paused, considering. "Tom says he was checking the house today when he saw you running across the lawn. He said he called after you, but you didn't stop, so he came here to see what you were up to."

I now registered that Kip was clean shaven and in uniform. It occurred to me that he might be here to arrest me. He pulled my burner phone from his pocket and handed it to me.

"Tom turned it in to the station last night. He said he originally thought it might hold vital information regarding the case on it. He's returning it because there was nothing of interest."

"He's very good at covering his tracks, isn't he?" I said angrily. "Did he tell you that he nearly broke my arm taking it from me? And bullied me into giving him the password?"

"I believe you, Winter," said Kip, relenting slightly. "But that doesn't explain you breaking and entering."

"She didn't break into the house," said a voice behind me.

Brittany emerged from the doorway, carrying a tray with bagels and lox. A slab of cream cheese and a bowl of capers were also balanced on the tray. She placed it on the dining table and continued. "I gave Winter the key so she could get the iPad. Technically, I still live on the property and take care of the place, so I think I'm entitled to send someone there on my behalf."

Kip did his brow rub. "There was a murder there. It's a crime scene."

"No one informed me that I wasn't allowed to return," Brittany said coolly, turning back toward the kitchen.

"If you hadn't disappeared, we would have notified you," Kip said loudly, to catch her on the retreat. He then turned to me. "Why did you run? Tom says several of the rooms downstairs were a mess and that you were searching the place."

"Tom is lying," I replied.

I explained what had happened from start to finish, leaving out nothing. "I had no need to ransack the house," I added, "because I already knew where the iPad was hidden. When I heard an intruder tearing things apart, I took the first opportunity to run."

* * *

Everyone was back in the living room, hovering around the dining table. Along with the bagels, smoked salmon, cream cheese, and capers, there was a fruit salad and a large platter of chocolate chip cookies. Forgoing Keurig cups, Richard had brewed a pot of fresh coffee, which sent an enticing aroma throughout the house. I stuck to chamomile—if ever there was a time for a stomach-soothing tea, it was now.

Kip spent some time on the phone, talking to his chief and the detectives assigned to the Goodwin murder investigation. When he hung up, he said he'd be back shortly and hurried out the door.

As we all ate, the dogs patrolled the perimeter, hoping one of us would drop a morsel. They needn't have worried. On various occasions I saw Brittany, Scoop, Horace, and Richard sneak them bagel bites. Despite my hollow stomach, I had little appetite. The dogs would have a field day with my plate.

After cleanup, Horace and Richard took the dogs for a walk. Scoop lingered, seemingly in any area of the house where Brittany happened to be. She appeared to enjoy leading him around, so I gathered there was a huge mutual crush going on.

I retrieved the iPad from upstairs where we had left it, plugged it into the charger I kept in the kitchen, and watched in relief to see that it was working. As I listened to the telltale charging sound, Kip returned.

"Are you back to arrest me?" I asked. I was trying for levity, but I think part of me worried it might be the truth.

"No," he said seriously. "But about that lawyer we talked about . . ."

I put my fingers to my lips and led Kip to the study for privacy. He began speaking the moment I closed the door.

"Winter, I have to ask you something."

Whatever he was about to ask sent his hand darting back and forth between rubbing his brow and drumming on the arm of the chair he had slid into. His fidgeting made me nervous. I waited. Finally, he dove in.

"Is there anything you told me about Tom that might have been, well, exaggerated? Or assumed? Something open to interpretation?

What I'm saying is, are all your memories of your interactions with him crystal clear?"

I knew these were questions he had to ask as a cop—even as a human being trying to understand a bizarre set of circumstances where people kept ending up dead. However, the idea that he thought I was lying cut deeply, and my natural defense mechanisms kicked in.

"I don't lie," I replied coldly. "Maybe I lie by omission on occasion, as with most people, but I am not a liar. Are you sure you're not here to arrest me?"

Before meeting my eyes, he looked away, considering. "He's building a convincing case against you."

The wall I'd carefully built to protect myself from this type of feeling, the wall Kip had slowly been chipping away, suddenly felt as unbreachable as the Cliffs across the lake.

"It sounds like *you're* the one building a case against me."

"No," he said sharply. "I just asked you a question . . . to see how you would react."

He leaned toward me and reached for my hand. I pulled away and couldn't meet his eyes.

"Look, Scoop told me that whenever you try to twist the truth, your freckles get more pronounced and give you away. I thought, well . . . Right now, though, your face just looks . . . sad."

Scoop. Leave it to him to tell all my secrets.

Kip reached out, this time grabbing my shoulders.

"Full disclosure," he said. "I wanted confirmation that you weren't letting your imagination distort the truth. I'm sorry."

I felt the punch of his words. He hadn't believed me after all.

"I'll call that lawyer now," I said.

"Before you do that, can we try to figure out why Tom might be lying?" asked Kip. "He had to be looking for something when he tossed the cushions at the Arlington house. He also had to be looking for something on your phone, and I doubt this has anything to do with pill bottles."

I could hold a grudge with the best of them, but right now, I swallowed my anger. Once we figured this out and I cleared my name, I could fast-track it to New York and erase Kip Michaels from my life.

"Please make sure Tom doesn't have access to my phone at the police station," I said.

"He doesn't," said Kip, and he pulled my iPhone from his pocket. "You'll have to get Verizon to stop forwarding your calls to the burner. And before you ask, there were no identifiable prints besides yours. Now, let's see if we can't open that iPad before I have to confiscate that too."

Shoulders sagging and distracted, I took stock. In that moment, I noticed I was no longer hearing chatter from Scoop and Brittany.

I went into the other room and immediately saw why. A note was taped to the slider door where I couldn't miss it.

Heading down to talk to David and Bitsy. Scoop is coming. Dogs with Horace.

Brit

With the iPad sufficiently charged, I returned to the study to find Kip eyeing the train room from the open doorway. I felt my temper rise. He had no right to invade my space, especially after his lie-detector test. Why should I trust him if he didn't trust me?

He turned to me with an unexpected smile. "It's amazing. When we have more time, I'd like a tour."

"Sure," I said, though both of us knew I didn't mean it.

I handed him the note from Brittany. He read and frowned.

"Dammit, I told her to stay put. It's not safe for her to be running around." He looked at his watch and sighed. "I'm sure David and Bitsy will be relieved to have Brittany there to hold their hands when I question them. I should get going."

"Is it official this time?" I asked, nodding at his uniform.

"Not really, though appearing official might shake some answers out of them."

"So, you're lying by omission?"

He ignored the jab. "What did Brittany say about passwords?" he asked, glancing toward the iPad I still held.

"Apparently Lottie liked to use birthdays. She would sometimes reverse them, like if you were born in 2001, she'd use 1002. Brittany tried all the scenarios she could think of, including Grandma Alice's birthday."

Kip's sigh came out more like a groan. "Maybe the station will have ideas, though I don't have a lot of hope that we can get any fast answers. In fact, you and Brittany are as good a bet as any at the moment. Why don't you ride with me to Stamford and keep trying?"

My anger at Kip paled in comparison to my desire to solve this riddle.

I raced upstairs while Kip made some calls and changed into the same outfit I'd worn for the last visit, this time replacing the white jeans that had been lost in the fire with black ones. I checked the mirror and stopped short. My hair was flying all over the place. I had no makeup on, and I'd never even doused myself in the shower after my sweaty run from Tom Bellini. I quickly stripped, tied my hair atop my head, and rinsed off in the shower. After redressing, I applied eyeliner, mascara, and lip gloss and combed my hair. I looked better, though the ends of my hair were damp from the spray and steam. At least I smelled clean.

* * *

As Kip drove the unmarked car, I opened the iPad cover and stared.

"This looks fairly new," he said, reaching over to tap the black magnetic cover.

"It is. Brittany mentioned that Mrs. Arlington had recently updated her electronics."

We traveled in silence, him navigating the roads, me trying to navigate the iPad.

"New iPad, new pet—it's too bad we don't know Diva's birthday," he said.

"But I do," I said, suddenly excited. "Names I forget. Numbers I remember. It was in her file."

I entered the four digits of Diva's birthday. The screen did its little dance, followed by its pop-out window: *Incorrect password*. I reversed the numbers.

And suddenly I was in.

"Wahoo! Photos or email first?"

"Start with photos. And also check to see if there's a copy of her memoir on that thing."

Mrs. Arlington had organized the photos into albums. I opened *Home* and scrolled through a picture of Brittany with Diva, probably taken when they'd first adopted the dog. The look of pure joy on Brittany's face made me smile. The date stamp said it had been taken three weeks ago. I couldn't believe how much bigger Diva had grown in that short time. How big was this dog going to get? I skipped the older pictures and jumped to *Recents*. Just more of Brittany, Diva, and one with Mrs. Arlington and Mark Goodwin. A video of Burton petting the puppy made it obvious why Mrs. Arlington had been so worried. His face was pasty, his body all bones, his voice barely audible.

As I flipped through the memories, I scanned the albums listed along the sidebar: *Fundraisers*, *Art Collection*, *New Year's*, a rather

OCD compilation titled *Home Repairs* . . . and then jumping out at me, *Great Dames Book Club*. Subcategories of that album read *Members* and *Players*. Under *Players*, I found the photos that had no doubt led to Mrs. Arlington's fears and Mark Goodwin's death.

The first was of two people kissing in the shade of the gazebo. The angle of the picture made it clear it had been taken unbeknownst to the subjects: Marietta and Tom. In the next photo, they were locked in an embrace, Marietta pressed against a tree. Tom had one hand placed on her butt like he owned it. The date stamps on the photos showed they had all been taken within the last two months. Mrs. Arlington had probably tried to blackmail Marietta—"Get Burton help, or else." Something had happened in the last three weeks that had shifted the tide and made Marietta the alpha dog.

If Burton's son found out about Marietta's infidelity, the prenuptial agreement would allow him to cut her out of the will. Tom must have been searching for any evidence that would void the prenuptial. He must have assumed that Mark also had photos, and because I'd met with Mark, he might have assumed that Mark had sent the photos to me. Was that why he'd taken my cell phone?

"Maybe Tom and Marietta plotted to make sure Burton didn't get his medications," I said. "They could be in this together and that's why Tom was tearing the house apart. He was looking for whatever photo evidence there might be that the two were having an affair. Maybe they stole her computer and her iPhone. Tom was probably searching for her remaining device—the iPad."

"How would Tom know Mrs. Arlington had an iPad??

"I told you both, remember? The day we met?"

I reminded Kip that we had been sitting at Gallo discussing the messed-up file drawers when I mentioned that she might have had some information on her computer, iPhone, or iPad. It was at the mention of her electronics that Tom had perked up.

"You might not remember because it wouldn't be on your radar to worry about what kind of electronics Mrs. Arlington had. Even in his inebriated state, however, Tom was paying attention."

Kip nodded. "Tom and Marietta might have been getting paranoid, and their judgment might have been tainted."

"The stakes were getting higher. If they were plotting to get rid of Burton by holding back his pills and Mrs. Arlington suspected, Marietta could be charged with caretaker neglect. In some states that's a felony," said Kip.

"Who knows? Lottie might have opened the cabinet in the Jack and Jill bathroom, just as I did. If she used the information against Marietta, maybe Marietta threatened her and that's why she became afraid enough to request an obituary."

"But why kill Goodwin?" asked Kip. "He told you he didn't know anything, and you believed him."

I had wondered about that, and then I remembered that Brittany had said Mark was clearing the path for Burton and Lottie to take their walks. Mark could have seen Tom on the property. He might not have registered why Tom was there and might not have been aware of the prenuptial, but Tom wouldn't have known that. And in their paranoid state, Tom and Marietta might have thought of Mark as a threat. I relayed all of that to Kip, whose head was now bobbing up and down like a Texas oil drill.

"They might have thought he was sent by Mrs. Arlington to take photos," he said, following the thread. "We need more information. Right after we talk to Bitsy and David, let's go through Mrs. Arlington's email."

While he drove, I opened the photos titled *Family*. Feeling like a peeping Tom, I scanned through pictures that recorded Mrs. Arlington's life with Roth and Henry. I was surprised at how many showed her laughing. That didn't sync with the stern woman I had met, and I suddenly realized just how troubled she must have been.

I recognized David Wysocki in what was obviously a holiday photo card that had been scanned. Across the front read *Happy 2022 from Sunny Florida*. It was hard to make out a lot behind the writing that ran diagonally across the card, though I could see he was with a pretty woman about his own age with a gray-streaked bob. She was posing for the camera with her arms around his neck and one foot bent back in a swooning position. They were both in summer garb, and as I took in the details, my breath caught.

"Oh no!" I said, so loudly that Kip hit the brakes and we jolted to a stop.

"What's wrong?"

"How far are we from the Wysocki house?"

He stared at the device in my hand, eyes widening as I spread-eagled my fingers to expand the photo.

"Cinderella's shoe," we both said in unison.

Kip slammed the gas, hurtling us toward a far more unsettling version of the dreaded truth.

In the photo, Bitsy Wysocki was wearing the same kind of blue sneaker with sparkles that Diva had carried around for days.

And that was where Brittany and Scoop had been headed.

Chapter
Twenty-Eight

"We're about two minutes out," said Kip, whose white-knuckled grip clenched the steering wheel like it was a life-line. "I want you to stay in the car while I go in."

"No way. You might need help."

"I have help," said Kip, patting the gun he wore on his belt. "Look, I don't know what the situation might be. Bitsy's shoe choice could be a coincidence. I'd rather go in, check things out, and then have you come inside if it's safe. Meanwhile, keep texting Scoop, but don't tell him about Bitsy and the shoe. If he gives it away, that could place them in more danger."

We pulled up to the pretty little home, which suddenly looked ominous. Had Bitsy been the one ransacking Mrs. Arlington's study drawers while Diva and I sat innocently downstairs? What had Bitsy been looking for, and had she now asked Brittany to come to the house so she could get it from her? I stared down at the iPad on my lap. This was, in essence, Mrs. Arlington's little black book. I hadn't found a copy of her memoirs on it, but there was enough damaging evidence to point fingers at Bitsy, not to mention Tom and Marietta. I shoved it deep under the seat.

"Shouldn't you call for backup?" I asked as I pushed the car door open, and Kip frowned as I leapt to join him on the front walkway to the house.

Before Kip could protest, the front door flew open and David Wysocki emerged with palms up, looking contrite. He then moved aside as a small, timid-looking woman I recognized from the postcard stepped from behind him. She was very attractive, petite, and while more gray than black had taken over her bob, she looked younger than her seventy-something years.

"I killed Lottie," she blurted out, and then burst into tears.

"Where are Scoop and Brittany?"

No one replied to my question, because David was busy comforting Bitsy and Kip was assessing the safety of approaching.

Both Bitsy and David were dressed in shorts and golf tops. David had on Top-Siders, and Bitsy wore slip-on sandals with thick white soles. They looked like they were about to lunch on their yacht.

"Brittany? She's not here," said David, looking confused. "I thought she was with you."

Bitsy said nothing as she wiped a steady stream of tears from her cheeks.

David ushered us inside, and we sat in the same room with the drop-dead view where we had been only days earlier. Today's sunshine was a stark contrast to the gloomy rain we'd had on Friday, and I could see what David had meant when he'd said we should see the view when the weather was clear.

Bitsy sat close to her husband, wringing her hands, wiping her eyes, and blowing her nose, but so far had added nothing.

"I think you have some explaining to do," said Kip as I sent Scoop a text: *Where are you?*

"It's my fault," said Bitsy in a small, quiet voice that I had to lean in to hear.

For the next fifteen minutes we listened as Bitsy, between sobs, relayed her story. She'd first met David when he came to visit his sister in the city. It was a chance meeting, and neither had been aware that the other knew Lottie. When Bitsy realized that David knew nothing about the Great Dames Book Club, she had distanced herself from Lottie and the club.

"When Lottie saw that David and I were attracted to each other, she stayed clear of us," said Bitsy. "I knew why. She wanted to disband the Great Dames. We all agreed. It was getting too . . . I'm not sure of the word, though *big-time* comes to mind. The stakes for the people we researched were getting higher. By then she had gone after Roth, and what she was asking of him was almost more than he was willing to give."

"She wanted Roth to know that his nephew, Andrew Arlington, had been the soldier killed during training and that he did not desert," I said. "She wanted the family to agree not to go after Mark Goodwin for changing places with his dead buddy."

Kip whirled his head around so fast I thought he might get whiplash. He stared at me with a question on his face.

"How did you know?" asked Bitsy.

"Mark mentioned that Lottie suspected he wasn't who he claimed to be and that he might have asked too many questions about her boss. I put two and two together, and Mark confirmed it. Mark said he could hardly live with himself, knowing what he had done to that family and the damage he'd done to Andrew's character. I'm guessing that he came east to work in Roth's company so he could find a way to atone. That was Lottie's leverage: 'You get to know the truth about your nephew and Mark gets to walk.'"

"When he came to work for us, doing research and all, he was always so sad. Lottie promised him that she would fix things, and she did," said Bitsy.

She took another swipe at her eyes with a tissue she pulled from her pocket and looked at David, who just stared down at his hands. I suddenly realized that he too was probably hearing much of this for the first time.

"Can you backtrack?" asked Kip. "You met David, got out of the book club business, then what?"

"Lottie told me she had been getting threats. She insisted that I pretend I barely knew her. She didn't even come to our wedding, and I never told David any of this until yesterday. I couldn't. David is just so . . . honorable. The things we did to people were . . ." She let that trail, put her head in her hands, and wept.

David put his arm around her, though when she lifted her head, he didn't meet her probing eyes. Still, she forged forward, and I envied her courage. She had been holding all this in for so many years, it must have been a relief to finally get it out. I also admired her trust that he would forgive.

"I'm not that honorable," said David, finally looking into his wife's red-rimmed eyes, and then he turned to us. "I'm sorry. I lied when I said we didn't know Brittany or keep in touch with the family. Brittany had been giving her parents problems for years. She hung with the wrong crowd and was a tough kid, always skirting the edge of trouble. We—that is, Lottie and I—decided to help her. We brought her to Connecticut. She thinks it was her idea to come, but you know my sister—she could manipulate anyone."

By now I was beginning to understand Mrs. Arlington better than ever. I wished I could rewrite that obituary. *Leocadia Wysocki Arlington, modern-day Robin Hood turned superhero . . .*

David and Bitsy continued to weave their story of living a simple life in Connecticut, raising their son, and eventually trying to help Brittany restore family relations by making plans for a reunion.

"Something pivotal must have happened a few weeks ago," I said. "After Mrs. Arlington got Diva."

Bitsy nodded, looking miserable. It was suddenly as if the volcano had erupted, and the lava spewed.

"I visited Brittany often. I would meet her here or in Ridgefield for lunch to catch up . . . you know, keep an eye on how things were going and report back to her parents. On a visit about a month ago, Brit mentioned that her aunt was writing her memoirs and that she was shocked at the details she was learning." Bitsy reached to grab her husband's hand. He squeezed back.

"Shocked as in upset, or shocked as in awe?" I asked, because I was now pretty sure Mrs. Arlington's motivations were more altruistic than evil.

"I think a little of both. She didn't like that the book club squeezed money out of some people. We only did that so we could keep Mark Goodwin on the payroll," she said, and she jutted her chin forward in defense. "When Brittany shared some of the things in Lottie's memoirs, I pointed out that what the club was really doing was righting wrongs."

"She didn't know you were part of the book club?" asked Kip.

Bitsy shook her head no. "Brittany said that Mrs. Arlington referred only to the book club and never mentioned any names. Brittany is smart, and she figured that I knew more than I was letting on. I'm not a very good liar. That's one of the reasons I didn't want to be here when David met with you. You have to understand, David didn't know any of this. It was me, although I think Brittany thought otherwise."

"*You have to pay to play,*" I said, and again Bitsy looked at me in surprise before continuing.

"I got worried. I'd never told David about my involvement. And oh God, imagine what our son and his wife might say. She's one of those—what do they call them?—helicopter moms. She might not let me see the grandchildren anymore," said Bitsy, looking so stricken I thought I might march over to her son's house myself and plead her case. "Lottie was getting older, and I worried she might tell all because she wanted the record set straight. I panicked."

The night of the storm, Brittany had come to stay with Bitsy and David.

"When she couldn't reach Lottie, she was almost frantic with worry. We thought it must just be because of the storm and all. Not Brittany. The poor thing paced well into the night until we convinced her to sleep," said David. "She slept to almost noon the next day."

Bitsy told us how she'd left before anyone awoke. The note she'd left saying she would be gone for a couple of hours for her meditation session wasn't unusual, because that was something she often did. Instead, she drove to Ridgefield, parked her little blue VW convertible out of sight in the garage of the guest house where Brittany lived, and hiked the muddy driveway to the house.

"And that's why I didn't see your car, even though you were still there," I said.

The corners of Bitsy's mouth curved, and I got a glimpse of her prettier side. She was cheerleader cute, and that little impish grin made her charismatic.

"I got very good at hiding the car so no one would see that I was visiting. Lottie or Mark didn't need to know how closely I kept tabs on Brit. Anyway, that morning I lifted the key from Brittany's backpack. I'm not sure what my intention was initially. I knew Lottie was a late and very sound sleeper. I'd been to the house. Brittany had told me a lot about her habits, including how she used birthdays for her codes and reversed them. Brittany and I once played a game where I tried to guess Lottie's codes from what I remembered about her, so I knew how to shut off the alarm."

Bitsy paused to dab at her eyes before continuing. "I figured that the alarm might not even work without power, but if it did, no problem. Brittany said the upstairs of the house had never been updated, so I convinced myself that there'd be no alarm panel there to hear any telltale beeps when I snuck inside. You have to understand, I was frantic to find out what was in those memoirs, and I wasn't really thinking straight," she said, almost pleading now.

David continued fiddling with anything in reach of his fingers, and I imagined what his wife's duplicity might be doing to a fifty-year marriage.

Bitsy described how she tiptoed across the kitchen. She was about to sneak up the back staircase when she realized she had left a trail of mud with her shoes. She quickly took them off, grabbed a paper towel from the sink area, and then backtracked to clean the floor.

"Brittany hadn't told me about Diva yet. I couldn't believe it when this little ball of fur dashed in and grabbed one of my shoes and then dumped it in another part of the house. I was trying to quietly coerce her to come, but she started to bark.

"All I could think about was getting out of the house. I would go home, confess everything to David, and Lottie would never know I had been there," said Bitsy. "That's when I heard noise, picked up my other shoe, and I ran into the pantry to hide," she said.

Diva kept barking, and after a while, when no one came into the kitchen, Bitsy decided she could sneak out the door, run up the driveway to retrieve her car, and go home to face the music.

"Just as I was about to leave from the kitchen door, I heard a car in the driveway. They have this alarm thing that rings," she said.

I knew all about that alarm thing. That's what had alerted me that someone was coming the day I snuck back to the house to retrieve the iPad. Brittany had found a way to reset it after the first day I visited when the downed branches caused it to keep ringing. It obviously had battery backup. *Smart girl*, I thought.

Bitsy was no longer clinging to her husband, though their bodies still looked glued together. Confession must be doing wonders for her soul.

"I didn't know what to do, so I ran upstairs and locked myself in the study. By then I was shaking so hard my teeth were chattering. How would I ever explain this to Lottie?"

Through the commotion, Bitsy had heard the barking dog, a loud thump, and then a short time after that, the persistent ringing of the doorbell.

It was probably my car that she'd heard pull into the driveway, which would mean that I arrived just moments after Mrs. Arlington had fallen down the stairs. And she had probably either tripped over Diva or caught her slipper, or maybe she'd even stumbled on the blue sneaker Diva deposited at her feet. Either way, it was an accident, though Bitsy wouldn't see it that way. She would see that her actions had set everything in motion.

Bitsy began crying hard again, and between sobs, she said, "I killed her. If I hadn't snuck into her house, she wouldn't have been checking to see why her dog was barking and she wouldn't have tripped on the stairs. You have to believe me. If I had known that was the sound I heard, I would have called for help."

David patted her hand. "It was an accident. She could have tripped anytime."

Bitsy shook her head. "When I finally got the courage to run, I raced from the house so fast, the devil of a dog couldn't have caught me."

So it was Bitsy I'd heard clambering down the stairs and slamming the creaky front door while I sat with Diva in the kitchen.

"No," she moaned into her tissue. "I killed her."

* * *

None of Bitsy's confession explained who'd trashed Mrs. Arlington's bedroom later, scattered her files all over her study, and stolen her electronics. For now, though, part of the mystery was solved.

David rose from his seat and went to the kitchen to get Bitsy some water. A few minutes later he returned carrying a full glass pitcher with lemon slices floating at the top. He then walked to a cabinet and pulled out four crystal glasses.

"Water?" he offered to us as he filled each tumbler.

We all accepted his offering and drank. Bitsy had composed herself by now and dabbed at her eyes before excusing herself to "put my face back on," as she put it.

We waited in silence until David left to fetch his wife. When she returned, her eyes were still red rimmed, though she looked more pulled together as she picked up her story.

"I couldn't open that damn computer that was sitting on her desk. I've never been good at that stuff." Bitsy looked at David for confirmation.

"It's true," he said, with a gentle smile directed at his wife. "I'm the one who does all the online bill paying."

After her failed efforts with the computer, she used her time in hiding to rifle through the file cabinet.

"I felt dizzy when I saw that *Great Dames Book Club* file. When I opened it, I could have cried in relief. My name wasn't listed with the other club members. And Roth's name was also missing from the players list. It was then that I realized Lottie would never have betrayed us—she was all about protecting her family. I feel so ashamed that I didn't trust that from the start."

I didn't tell Bitsy about the unedited file that had been hidden in the faux bookcase, the one that had led me to her—the file that was now missing and could potentially be in the hands of a murderer. The one with her name at the top of the list.

"I felt like a fool," said Bitsy. "Here I had snuck into my sister-in-law's home, locked myself in her study, and invaded her privacy. Still, I stuffed the lists into my pocket. Most of the book club members are gone now, but I wanted to protect the few that are left, especially if they have kids and grandkids. Who knows what kinds of questions a file like that might raise? Then I just sat and waited until I had to face Lottie."

Bitsy had heard the sirens and thought Lottie had called to report an intruder, and when the study door handle rattled, she knew the jig was up.

"And then all was quiet. By some miracle, no one had found me. I did some soul searching. I would just have to face Lottie. And I'd tell David everything. These secrets had been tearing me up for years. You should see my therapy bills."

David winced. He was probably thinking that maybe a man who had been living with a woman with so many secrets for five decades might have noticed. I suspected he would have his own guilt to deal with.

"If she was the Lottie I had always admired, I hoped she would take it in stride," continued Bitsy. "Hey, we might even laugh about it."

I doubted Lottie would have found it funny that Bitsy had broken into her home because she didn't trust her sister-in-law not to betray her. I kept my thoughts to myself.

"So, what happened?" asked Kip. "What made you change your mind?"

245

"I was planning to go down the back staircase when I heard sounds in the kitchen. I saw an opportunity to go out the front door and maybe avoid confrontation. I wasn't exactly quiet and I could hear that little dog, so I just ran out and down the driveway to my car. The whole time I thought Lottie would call after me, but she never did."

Once home, Bitsy showered, bandaged her foot, which had gotten torn up on the driveway jog, and decided to shut the door on the entire episode. Later, when Brittany couldn't reach Lottie and began to worry, the Wysockis loaned Brittany their truck to go back and check.

"That's another reason why we wanted to talk to you," interrupted David. "Bitsy and I are worried sick about Brittany, especially now that we've heard Mark Goodwin was murdered. Brittany hasn't called us since yesterday."

"She said she was coming down to see you this morning," I said. "She wrote us a note."

David and Bitsy exchanged worried glances.

"She hasn't been here, and she hasn't returned our calls," said Bitsy.

Kip rose abruptly. I felt a wave of fear that landed in the pit of my stomach. If Brittany and Scoop had never gotten here, where had they gone?

"Find her," pleaded Bitsy. "Please."

And then the tears came again.

Chapter
Twenty-Nine

We were making it to Ridgefield in record time, though it wasn't fast enough for me.

"We got distracted with Bitsy and David and that shoe," Kip said as we hit the stomach-lurching hill to Pound Ridge. "I think we missed that there are two separate things going on here."

"I'm listening," I said, clenching the arm of the door.

"Bitsy thought she needed to destroy the memoirs. She never got that far because she realized Lottie wasn't going to betray her. It's Marietta Hemlocker who has the real motive."

Kip was driving like a maniac, looking so defeated that I wanted to do something to help. He wasn't the only one who had been distracted.

"The prenup," I said, gathering my thoughts. "Marietta and Tom have a relationship that threatens her inheritance. Mrs. Arlington was trying to blackmail Marietta into taking better care of Burton. So how did it backfire?"

"I don't know," said Kip, slowing the car as he rounded one of the sharp curves. "If they were tying up loose ends, they might have taken advantage of a situation that would rid them of Mark, who probably saw them together, even if he hadn't added it up."

"Other loose ends might include Brittany, and now Scoop," I said, feeling my breath catch.

Kip accelerated again, and we were suddenly hitting the curves like we were driving in the Indy 500.

* * *

By the time we reached Mamanasco, the frost between Kip and me had completely thawed. This was bigger than my bruised psyche. It was bigger than Kip's lack of trust. Both of us instinctively knew Scoop and Brittany were in danger.

We screeched to a stop in front of my cottage, and I threw open the door.

"Check the house and garage," he said. "I'm heading to the Hemlocker place."

"If what we just pieced together is true," I said, "those two have probably already murdered once—twice, if you count Burton. You can't go alone."

"To Hemlock Hill?" he asked with a smirk.

"It's not Hemlock Hill—it's Hill Manor."

"No, Winter," he said. "It is definitely Hemlock Hill."

"My last visit to Marietta—she was a Jekyll and Hyde. She could be a psychopath who tried to burn me to death! My friends could be burning now. I'll stay out of sight, and we'll work out a signal if you need me and—"

"Stream of consciousness," he cut in.

I blinked, chasing his meaning. "Non sequitur much?"

"Exactly," he replied. "You're like a run-on sentence—endless thought without punctuation. Isn't that what stream of conscious-ness is?"

It was a fairly artful assessment for a self-described "uncreative guy." And one any writer could appreciate.

"This time you really should call for backup," I said, ignoring his question.

"I will. First I'll check out the scene. We might have this wrong, just as we were wrong about Bitsy. Besides, I don't want to tip off Tom if he's listening on the radio."

"Be careful," I said, meeting his eyes. It was the best I could do for now.

I shut the car door, and Kip rolled down the window. "Let me know if the kids are home."

Another one of his silly comments that left no room for response, because he pulled away and all I was looking at was the dust he left behind.

* * *

I knew the scooter Scoop had left in the driveway meant nothing. He never would have taken it all the way to Stamford, especially with a passenger. Once inside the garage, I was relieved to see David's black truck nestled beside the Subaru.

I pushed through the kitchen door and called out.

No response. And then like a smack in the face, I realized that Scoop and Brittany hadn't left in one of their own vehicles. I kept calling out, though the house was as empty as a theater during COVID. How had they left without a car?

Racing next door, I could hear the dogs barking even before I started pounding on Horace's door. He answered with a smile that fell fast when he saw my face.

"What is it?" he asked, opening wide for me to enter.

"When Brittany and Scoop left the dogs, did you see where they went?"

Horace looked puzzled.

Diva and Max were bumping me for attention. I batted them away until Diva finally crawled between my legs and Max stood on his hind legs to lick my face. Impatience wouldn't do anyone any good, I realized, so I took a moment to scratch their ears. It appeased them and calmed me enough to explain.

"We have a problem," I said.

Horace waved me in, and I followed his shuffle to a small kitchen stuck in the 1960s: wood-paneled walls, hickory cabinets, even an avocado-green fridge and pink-swirled Formica countertops. He reached into a jar on the counter and tossed out two Sizzlers—bacon-laced twists from Blue Buffalo. The dogs pounced on them and paraded away. Horace led me to a small table by the window that unveiled the same soothing view I stared at every day. For some reason, though, looking at it through his eyes made it appear different.

"This is where I do my best everything," he said as he noticed me taking it in. "There's no problem I can't solve when I sit here. And do you know why?"

I shook my head no, though impatient for answers.

"Because it reminds me that I'm not in control of the universe. See those ducks on the lake? Not a care in the world. Why? Because they aren't in charge and don't think they need to be. Do you get what I'm saying?"

"You want me to let it go and accept the big picture?" I asked.

"Sounds more succinct when you say it," he said. "Probably why you're the writer."

"Okay then, here's the smaller picture," I said. "When Brittany and Scoop brought the dogs over earlier, what exactly did they tell you?"

Horace rubbed his stubble and looked toward the pups, who were now lounging in makeshift dog beds and chewing pork treats.

He took his time, trying to relive the moment exactly as it had happened. Finally, he brightened.

"They said they were driving down to Stamford and didn't want to take the dogs because they didn't know how long they would be. They said they called your uncle to come this afternoon and give me a break. I don't need a break—Diva and Max are already family."

At the sound of their names, both dogs looked up, tails thumping.

"Did they say they were actually driving? As in, driving themselves?"

Horace squinted out at the lake again as he mentally reviewed his conversation. The clock ticked agonizingly before he started nodding.

"Brittany said, 'We're taking the truck.' Those were her exact words."

"Did they go out the back door, across the deck, or out the front door?"

Now he looked at me curiously. "Why do you ask?"

I explained about the growing commuter lot with the scooter and truck parked next door.

"Now that I think of it, I was almost laughing, because we were all in the kitchen and I was opening more treats for the dogs, and suddenly they were gone. They'd snuck out the front door, the way parents do when a new babysitter takes over."

"I remember," I said, tamping down a bittersweet memory from childhood. "Did you hear or see any vehicles—maybe stopping to pick them up?"

"Sorry," he replied. "I stayed in the kitchen with my dogs. Well, your dogs."

I patted his hand, because I could see he was trying so hard to help.

"Where are they, then?" he asked somberly.

It was tough to see Horace's eye twinkle extinguish, but I would not sugarcoat this. People often treated the elderly like children, shielding them from pain and discounting their ability to help. If working in the obit biz had taught me anything, it was to never underestimate a senior.

"I don't know, and I'm worried. Kip and I found photos proving that Marietta Hemlocker broke her prenuptial agreement by having an affair. She stands to lose her inheritance if her stepson finds out, and it's likely that Marietta thinks Brittany has the photos to prove it."

I relayed the details we'd learned that morning from the Shippan Point interlude, including our assumption that it was Marietta and maybe Tom who'd killed Mark Goodwin.

Horace remained quiet for a moment. Then he stood abruptly, his chair stuttering backward. "Let's roll," he said.

"Roll?"

"To the Hemlockers'. That's where you're going, right?"

I was stunned that he knew my plan before I'd fully formulated it.

"You'll need help."

I nodded and stood as well. "Actually, it would help me more if you would—"

He raised his hand in a gnarled high five. "Man the phones?" he finished. "I know, I would only slow you down." He sighed. "I'll let Richard know what's happening."

"Thank you, Horace."

"Just don't park at the Hemlockers'," he instructed as I hurried out. "You'll be a sitting duck."

* * *

Today felt like the day that wouldn't end: dawn-patrol with the dogs, my break and enter at Mrs. A's, a narrow escape from a someone who was coming unraveled, the Stamford distraction, and now what felt like my final act in the play. I'd texted Kip that indeed, the kids had broken curfew, and he hadn't replied.

Ridgefield Police Officer Kip Michaels, partner to a corrupt cop with a gold-digging girlfriend, died by murder because he refused to listen to reason and call for some damn backup like certain smart people told him to . . .

So once again, it was just me climbing into a cranky car, tempting fate on the back-road curves that I was careening around. This was a different kind of storm than the recent one I'd navigated, but a storm nonetheless.

Up on the mountain, I pulled onto the now-familiar service road and parked behind the pool house in my lucky spot, nose out like last time. I hiked up to the wooded side of the yard out of view of Mrs. Arlington's house, then headed west. Mark Goodwin had done an excellent job of making the path to the Hemlocker estate not only passable but nearly four feet wide through every stretch, and smooth enough for someone to bring along a cane or walker if needed. The precision of the work brought a stab of regret for his wasted talents.

The temperature was pushing eighty, and I felt uncomfortably warm in long jeans and a three-quarter-sleeve top I had worn to Stamford. I was, however, grateful for the hiding place the outfit provided for my cell phone. I turned off the ringer and slipped it into my jeans, very much the way I had done with Burton's pill bottle. I pulled my top over to cover the bulge. I left the burner phone in the small cross-body bag I wore.

Stopping at the end of the path to study the house, I saw Kip's unmarked car parked in front on the circular driveway. The house looked different from this angle. The imposing structure had an L-shaped wing housing a three-car garage protruding off the back. An additional detached two-story barn stood to the left of that. This was where I presumed Burton had kept his antique cars. While Kip was inside distracting Marietta and Tom, I would start searching there for Scoop and Brittany.

Still hugging the tree line, I hurried toward the barn, keeping my eye on the house in case someone exited. I crossed a small open area to get to the unlocked side door and slipped inside. Just as I expected, four tarps roughly shaped like cars lined the large space. I lifted each as I passed—an antique Mustang, a Rolls-Royce so polished I could see my reflection, a very old Porsche 911, and a vintage red snub-nosed truck—the one Burton had driven around town. I made my way toward a door that I assumed would open to Burton's office.

The room was larger than I expected, paneled in dark wood and lined on two sides with shelves where rows and rows of books were crammed. The fourth side held French doors that led out to a patio with the same postcard view as the main house. A fireplace on the opposite wall was also surrounded by bookshelves. Three burgundy leather chairs occupied an Oriental carpet.

As inviting as it was, I didn't have time to enjoy the room I assumed was Burton's library. From the fireplace, I grabbed a poker leaning against the fieldstone. Weapon in hand, I crossed and began looking behind closed doors. One led to a bathroom with a full shower and the other to a small bedroom. Back in the garage, a staircase led to a second floor. I ascended.

Reaching the top step, I held my breath, listened, and heard nothing. I peeked my head around the corner to find a large bare-bones storage space, finished with flooring, paneled walls, and large windows. And completely empty.

Back on the ground floor, I exited the barn and moved toward the attached garage, an appendage to the main house. The side door on this one was locked. Through the window, I could see a large black SUV. Now what?

I couldn't risk creeping around to the main patio, because I'd be visible from the large windows in the living room. If I snuck around the front, I figured, I'd have less of a chance of being seen. I headed in that direction, and just as I was making my way to peer into one of the windows, the front door swung open. I leaped behind one of the weak shrubs framing the stark home before Tom and Marietta walked out. Thank goodness they didn't even glance toward my sparsely covered hideout as they strode to Kip's car. As Tom opened the car door, they were so close I was afraid they would hear me breathe.

"Where will you hide it?" Marietta asked.

"I'll leave it at the Arlington place," Tom said. "That should buy us enough time to get out of here."

"I don't like being alone with them," she said, tossing her head back toward the house.

"I'll be back in a few minutes. Put the stuff you need in the car. We have to be downtown when this all comes down."

I crouched low as Tom pulled away and Marietta hurried back inside. That settled it. Kip, Scoop, and Brittany were being held inside. I couldn't call 911 yet—not with Tom still in the unmarked. He would hear the radio and be back before help could arrive. He could even respond that it was a false alarm.

With Tom out of sight, I took a breath and, with the poker still in hand, crept to the front door and pushed it open.

Thank God there was no squeak. And no Marietta either, although I could hear her upstairs. I assessed my options. I ruled out the large living and dining rooms on the first floor, which were doorless open spaces unsuitable for holding hostages. Two smaller rooms on the front of the house, acting as a study and sitting room, were equally implausible for prisoners because of their view from the road. Besides, both doors were wide open.

Off to the right was the long hallway that housed the bathroom I'd raided and Burton's bedroom. To the left would be the large kitchen and family room I'd seen on my first visit, and while I hadn't noticed a back staircase, I was sure there would be one. Because that would be the closest stairway to the garage, I had to assume Marietta would use it to put her "stuff" in the car.

How much time did I have to search this house before Tom got back?

And then I had a terrible thought. Kip had been in uniform, complete with weapons and radio. Would Tom now have those in his possession in addition to his own?

Focus on what you can control, I reminded myself.

I listened for sounds and heard Marietta crossing the upstairs hallway, away from the main staircase. I crept up the stairs, stopped at the top, and stole a glance in the direction of the noise. It sounded like she was indeed heading down a back staircase.

Unlike Mrs. Arlington's house, this upstairs hallway was light and bright, with windows looking out at the view on one side and all the rooms on the opposite. I didn't bother with what I was sure was the master suite at the end of the hallway. The massive double doors, yawning wide as if to display the sleek king bed and contemporary tones, left literally nothing to the imagination.

At the other end of the hall, where Marietta had disappeared down the back stairs, another staircase climbed to a third floor. I hurried toward it, passing numerous doors open to handsomely decorated bedrooms. Just as I was about to climb, I heard Marietta returning.

I retreated into one of the bedrooms and positioned myself behind the open door. I held my breath, waiting for her to pass. It felt like an eternity, and then she paused outside the door. I was sure she could smell my perspiring body or hear my thundering heart.

To my momentarily relief, she muttered aloud, "Now where did I leave that phone?"

The first inclination of people who lose their cell phone in the house is to call it from a landline if they have one. I gazed around the room, and sure enough, on the opposite end was a small table with a cordless. I willed Marietta to keep walking.

And then she entered the room, passing so close to the open door that her perfume teased my nose. I could see her reflection in a mirror on the opposite side of the room as she picked up the handset and tapped in her number. At the same time, she peeked through the blind slats to look outside, presumably for Tom. If I could see her, couldn't she see me? I prayed I didn't cough or sneeze.

Distantly but unmistakably, a shrill ringtone echoed. Without looking around, Marietta hurried from the room in that direction. I breathed a sigh and was about to step out when she returned through the doorway, dropped the cordless in its cradle, and took another look through the slats. Then she hurried out again, to my relief never glancing toward the mirror on the opposite wall. A few seconds later, I heard footfalls back down the stairs.

I emerged from my hiding spot, wiping sweat from my forehead, and attacked the third floor. Tiptoeing up the stairs, I found a far less cheery environment. No furniture, no carpeting, no sense of use. Even the walls had been left bare and unpainted—chalky Sheetrock held in place by skeletal wood studs. I opened one creaky door after another, praying the sound wouldn't carry.

Suddenly I heard Marietta back on the second floor, and something had changed. Her steps were hurried and purposeful as she spoke urgently into her phone. I couldn't hear what she was saying, and a minute later the door to her room slammed shut.

I crept down two sets of stairs, landing in the kitchen. Through the kitchen window, I saw Tom jogging from the path toward the house. *They know I'm here* was the last thought I had before I heard the breath of movement behind me and felt a hard whack at the back of my knees. I hit the floor with whiplash pain in my limbs and back.

Tom burst into the kitchen, panting hard, and took in the scene.

"I have her phone," said Marietta triumphantly, holding up the bag she had wrestled from my shaking body with the burner phone inside.

As I slowly sat up, I could still feel my iPhone in my jeans. My top had slid up in the fall, so I maneuvered awkwardly to pull it down. My arms and shoulders burned, and pain shot through one knee. A fireplace poker, a twin to the one now sitting uselessly at my side, lay across the countertop where Marietta had dropped it.

"Breaking and entering seems to be your modus operandi," said Tom, sweat dripping down his forehead.

"I didn't break anything. All I did was open the door," I said. "Where's Kip?"

Marietta shoved her phone in front of my face. I watched as she pushed "history" on her Ring app, and there I was, sneaking around the garage and then entering the front door.

So much for my supersleuthing skills.

"You just can't keep your nose out of things, can you?" said Tom. "And what makes you think Kip is here? I haven't seen him since he asked for a new partner."

"You don't have partners," I shot back. The second it was out of my mouth, I regretted it. Why remind him that I was a former reporter for the *Ridgefield Press* and that I knew very well how the town police department operated?

"True," he said thoughtfully. "Kip was assigned to me to get him through that rookie stage. Can you believe he requested a new mentor?"

I'd have been surprised if he hadn't. Kip had never told Tom about David or Bitsy or even taking my phone to the station to check for prints. He might have had reservations about my truthfulness, but his actions spoke loud and clear about his lack of trust in his "mentor."

"Can you blame him?" I asked. I knew I should zip it, but it was hard not to respond to this sleaze.

Up until this point, I'd been hoping Tom and Marietta might send the nosy obituary writer away, but I now saw that Tom was reassessing.

"Kip said he was coming here to see you, though I guess he's not here," I said, trying to backpedal.

Tom ignored me and asked Marietta for her phone. She punched in the code, and he opened it to the Ring app. From the time stamp, he could see how long I'd been on the property. He would know I'd seen him leave with Kip's car.

"Where's your ride?" he asked.

I didn't answer.

"Who knows you're here?"

"A number of people." Technically, it was true—there were two of them right in front of me.

"You're lying," he said.

"What do we do with her?" Marietta asked.

"The same thing we do with everyone else," Tom replied, "unless you have a better idea."

"Brittany and Scoop are no threat to you," I said.

"That tramp is not getting Burton's life insurance policy," Marietta snarled, and for a moment she looked like a child whose sibling had just gotten the bigger slice of cake. "If she's out of the picture, the money reverts to me."

"Is that all this is about, money?"

"I told you, it's been ten long years, and I am not walking away empty-handed."

"Tom," I said, "what about you? Why would you get involved with all of this?" I gestured toward Marietta.

I knew my fate was cast when he pulled a gun from the back of his waistband.

"I'm sick of this rat race," he said, aiming everywhere as he talked with his hands. "I'm sick of goody-goodies like your boyfriend. He's the one the chief is looking to promote, and he's brand-new. We're getting the money and getting out of Dodge. Now, enough—let's get this thing done."

He indicated that I should move into the living room.

My legs were shaking, and my knee ached from my fall. No way would I let them see that, so I managed to put one foot in front of the other.

"I have the photos of you two," I blurted out. "They're on Mrs. Arlington's iPad."

At this, Marietta, who had been trailing behind, came around to face me, halting us all in our tracks.

"Prove it," she demanded, and a spray of spittle hit my cheek.

I swiped it away in disgust before answering.

"It's safe for now. But if something happens to me . . . well, I made a backup plan."

"If your plan was with your friends, that isn't going to work," she said smugly. "We have your nosy reporter friend, and those old men you hang with can be handled."

I forced a yawn, which made Marietta's eyes turn to daggers.

"So, *prove* it," she said again, jabbing at my chest.

I stepped backward and felt the gun graze my back. "Who killed Mark Goodwin?" I countered.

Tom moved around to face me. "That was a mistake," he said. "Marietta was trying to burn the house to get rid of any evidence when Mark trapped her, so she clobbered him. It was self-defense."

"I grabbed one of those iron statues that Lottie had all over the house. I didn't think the hit would kill him," she said.

"But you were going to leave him in there to burn," I pointed out.

"Not a great loss," Marietta huffed. "He wasn't a man you could trust. Now, where are the damn photos?"

"Just so you know, Mark had no idea that Mrs. Arlington was troubled by your affair," I continued, ignoring her question. "And he certainly knew nothing about your prenup."

"He must have told Lottie," Marietta insisted. "She sent me the photo, obviously taken from that shortcut he had been working on. He saw us; I know he did."

"It was Lottie who took the photos, not Mark. She wanted something in return for not showing them to anyone. What was it? Better care for Burton? Did she find out you were sitting on his meds?"

"So you *were* snooping in my bathroom."

Tom whirled his head toward Marietta. "You did that?"

She looked wistful for a moment before shrugging. "He was old and sick. Pills or no pills, he would've died soon."

I was trying as hard as I could to appear calm, but my insides were starting to catch up. I could feel the panic rising, from the tips of my shaking fingers to my rapid breathing. I closed my eyes and tried to calm myself while the two of them went at it.

"God, Marietta, I thought he died of a heart attack!"

"First Burton, then Mark," I pushed. "So far, I don't see a good future in front of you, Tom."

"Don't listen to her, sweetie," said Marietta. "She's trying to turn us against each other."

Tom's mouth twitched, and his charcoal eyes deadened even more.

"I gotta hand it to you, Marietta," I said. "You really did spook Mrs. Arlington. I thought she was made of Teflon. What did you say to make her so frightened?"

Marietta smirked. "She wasn't the only one who could play that game. I told her that I knew about her book club." Her lips curled. She was enjoying the shock she saw on my face, and I hoped Tom would see her real colors.

"What book club?" asked Tom.

"My mother was one of Lottie's famed book club members," she said. "Her 'club,' as she called it, used to dig up dirty secrets and blackmail people."

"Seriously?" he asked. "Mrs. Arlington did that? Your mother did that?"

"And more," said Marietta.

Was that why Marietta and Burton had moved to Ridgefield? Had Marietta been protecting her own mother's reputation by keeping an eye on Lottie?

"We changed our identities when my mother started getting death threats over things Lottie had cooked up. My mother got sucked into it and couldn't get out, because she was as guilty as anyone."

Marietta was wrapped up in her trip down memory lane, so I played up to her, trying to look rapt with her every word. Anything to give me time to think of a way out of this mess.

"Who were the threats from?" I asked.

"Some guy they caught with his hand in the company coffers. He worked for Roth Arlington and suspected it was Lottie and her crew who destroyed his career. He's long gone now, and once we changed our names, no one ever came after us again. But that didn't stop my mother from uprooting us every year or two. She was always looking over her shoulder. Before she died, she told me to keep an eye on Lottie."

"How did the guy who threatened your mother die?" I asked.

Marietta's face twisted into her Cruella de Vil look.

"Unfortunate accident," she said.

"Fatal house fire," I prompted, and Marietta smiled.

With pieces of the puzzle falling into place, I now understood why Scoop had never been able to find Marietta's backstory—there wasn't one. She had been reinvented when her mother changed their identities. I also understood why Mrs. Arlington was suddenly afraid that her days might be numbered. She would have known about the "player" dying in a fire way back when because she kept track of everyone she had leveraged. She'd probably suspected that Marietta's mom had killed him.

"Did Lottie know you'd learned about the book club?" I asked.

Now Marietta laughed and confirmed my theory. "I told her who I was. Seeing her squirm after all the squirming she made my mom do was such poetic justice."

"I'm guessing your mother crossed the line and Lottie found out she had started the fire that killed the threatening player. Your mother wasn't looking over her shoulder because she was worried about retribution from other players. It was because she knew Lottie didn't approve of what she had done, and now she was watching."

Tom, who had been silent during the entire exchange, was looking at Marietta as if seeing her for the first time.

"Lottie turned on my mother!" Marietta erupted. "She thought my mom was going off the rails—into arson and all, I get that. But she wasn't crazy. She just wanted certain people out of our lives. And I got back at that crazy old coot Lottie. She thought she was so smart until I told her that her days were numbered. You should see her emails."

If I ever got out of this, I would definitely track down the digital record. My guess was it would have started right about the time Diva arrived. The emails must have been what convinced Mrs. Arlington that the psychopath next door might come after her.

It was then that Tom shifted his feet, loudly, as if to punctuate a remark. Marietta looked at him like she had forgotten he was there. Her vindictive smile shifted effortlessly to something more angelic.

"You do realize," I said to Tom carefully, "she's a nutjob?"

"She's at it again," said Marietta.

In a wounded voice, Tom asked, "Did you kill Mark on purpose?"

"I told you it was an accident," she replied, eyes blazing with challenge. "I was afraid of getting caught starting the fire. When I realized he was dead, I thought it would be convenient if he were blamed for it."

Then she all but fluttered her lashes at him and added, "Really, what's the difference?"

I wondered if, while they were distracted, I might be able to knock the gun from Tom's hand. It was a desperate and fleeting thought, because Marietta turned to me.

"You're trouble," she stated coldly. "I knew it the first time I met you—all your questions."

"It's my job to ask questions, and by the way, you called me," I said, and suddenly thought of something else. "Was it you who trashed Mrs. Arlington's bedroom and study?"

Marietta looked at me in surprise. "It was a mess when I got there. But I found the photos under her mattress, of all places. My plan was to take my time, go through the whole house for more prints and any electronics, and then I heard the driveway alarm. I had to hide downstairs in the powder room until I heard that Goodwin guy leave. That's when I decided to torch the place."

Marietta described how she'd run out to the landscaper's shed, confirming my assumption that she'd found a gas can there. She then hauled it into the house, doused some major furnishings, and barely escaped without injury before retreating. The can had run out of gasoline, so she hurried back to the shed in search of more. That's when she saw Mark run back into the house.

"By then there was so much smoke. But I had to stop him. He probably knew where Lottie had hidden everything and was returning to get all the dirt. Next thing you know, he'd be the one doing the blackmailing."

"I thought you said he trapped you and it was an accident when you tried to defend yourself," interrupted Tom.

"Grow up!" snapped Marietta. "I was defending us both!"

"So you followed him, clocked him, and left him for dead," I finished. "Did you know I was locked in the study?"

Marietta looked back at me slowly, as if coming back to earth.

"I had no idea," she said, and I thought those were the first honest words to come out of her mouth.

Tom stared at Marietta for a few moments. Whatever inner debate he was having was decided when he jabbed the gun into my back, steered me toward Burton's room, and said coldly, "Move."

Marietta opened the door and, with a spine-chilling smile, called inside, "You have company."

Three distraught faces turned my way as I was led into the room. Brittany and Scoop were tied to separate bedposts. Tape had been wrapped around their ankles and chests, immobilizing their legs and pinning their arms behind them. Kip was in a chair that had been brought in from the dining room. The tape was wound around him so many times that he looked like a mummy from the neck down. All three had duct tape over their mouths.

Kip's angry eyes followed Tom as he stuffed the gun into his waistband.

"We have to find out what her backup plan is for those pictures," insisted Marietta.

Tom patted the gun and said, "As soon as one of her friends gets their head blown off, she'll talk," he said. "Now, quick, go get the other roll of duct tape from the garage, because this is almost empty."

As Marietta hurried out of the room, Tom picked up the nearly empty roll from a nearby table. Could I run into the bathroom before he could get the gun back out of his waistband? I might have time to dial 911.

And then I thought about his threat to kill one of my friends. He just might do that to control me. Was I selfish enough to sacrifice three others just to stay alive?

Tom appeared to know what I was thinking, because he said, "I *will* hurt them."

Logic said he would kill us all anyway, but if there was a chance, any chance, I wanted us all alive to take it.

He roughly grabbed my hands, pulled them behind me, and went round them once with tape. He shoved me onto the desk chair and began binding my feet together. I kicked and he ducked, but not before I got off a good foot to his lip. He pulled the gun from his waist and pointed it at Brittany's temple. She was visibly shaking as she closed her eyes, and tears streamed down her cheeks.

"Okay, I'll cooperate," I said.

"Good," he said, and laid the gun down next to him as he started to tape my ankles, but the tape ran out before he could get more than one wrap.

"Marietta," he called out, and just at that moment the doorbell rang. Commotion, dog howls, and puppy barks followed.

Tom cursed and said to me, "If you call out, I will kill whoever's there—and the dogs."

He ran through the Jack and Jill and paused in front of the mirror to check his lip. And then he was gone.

I immediately got to my feet and hopped over to Kip. I could see that he had been working the tape on his mouth and a small edge at the corner had come undone. I slid onto his lap and said, "This is going to hurt."

I leaned my mouth over his, grabbed the end of the tape with my teeth, and began to pull. This was definitely not the way I had hoped our first kiss might happen.

The tape slipped out of my teeth several times. Kip moved his head in the opposite direction, and I was finally able to rip it off. I then stood up and turned my back so he could reach my hands with his mouth. It wasn't easy, because Kip was so secured to the chair that he didn't have much flexibility. My arms throbbed, bringing tears to my eyes as I tried to keep them within the reach of his teeth.

Tom had done a lousy job of wrapping me, because he had been trying to contain me only while he waited for more tape. Kip was able to bite through and tear enough for me to free one of my hands.

"Lock the doors," he ordered when my hands came free.

I hopped over to the door, not bothering to take the time to undo my feet. Once they were locked, I hopped into the Jack and Jill and did the same with the two outer doors and then unwrapped the tape on my ankles. I pulled the cell from my jeans and raced back into the room.

"Nine-one-one?" I asked as I pulled open the desk drawer to find scissors.

"No, Tom has my radio," he said, and instead recited another number, which I plugged in. I held the cell in one hand toward him to speak while I worked the scissors with the other.

The dogs were making quite a ruckus, and I was relieved that Horace, Richard, Max, and Diva were enough of a distraction to allow Kip to complete his call to his captain at the precinct.

When he was done, he said, "Undo Scoop first. He and Brittany aren't bound as tight."

The scissors were sharp, and Scoop was free in no time. He scrunched his face in pain as he pulled the tape off his own mouth and then went straight toward a bronze statue of a golfer, grabbed it, and positioned himself near the door. I gathered he'd had a lot of time to think about weapons.

The moment Brittany was free, she ran for a lamp. She too had been thinking of self-defense.

All the while, Kip had been calmly giving instructions: The door was locked, but Tom might shoot the gun through it, so steer clear. Cut through the tape on his right side so he could use at least one hand if they returned before he was completely free. Hand him Burton's cane. I was to use the scissors as my weapon, and even if someone was shot, I was to ignore the distraction and drive the blades into Tom.

"The same goes for everyone else," he said. "All we're doing is buying time. The police are on their way."

I got through the tape binding Kip's right side and his feet before I heard the dogs retreating. There were greater gaps between barks until finally there were none. By then, Kip was out of his tape prison, and by the time we heard someone approaching, we were positioned. The doorknob turned, followed by a pounding sound, as if someone was throwing themselves against the door. We heard the same sound against the Jack and Jill.

And then there was silence as whoever it was, presumably Tom, retreated.

I hurried to the window and opened the curtain. It was the window I had assumed gave Burton the outstanding view of the landscape beyond, and I hoped we could escape that way. Better to exit into the yard, where we could spread out and diminish the effectiveness of the gun Tom wielded.

As predicted, the view from the window was spectacular, with distant rolling hills and a lake beyond. The late afternoon brought a halo of light over the valleys. Unfortunately, the windows had decorative bars—the kind designed to look nice but also to protect from unwanted ground-floor entry. The windows essentially imprisoned us.

And suddenly I knew why they had chosen Burton's room to secure us. If we got free, we would still be jailed. I got a glimpse of Burton's life with Marietta. If she had chosen fire like her mother instead of withholding Burton's pills, the poor man would have been trapped.

And then, as if the fog in my brain had finally lifted, I knew Marietta's plan.

"Let's go," I screeched. When the three of them looked at me in confusion, I added, "They're going to trap us with fire."

That got Kip moving, and he led us through the Jack and Jill bathroom, giving us the *shhh* sign as he leaned his head against the door and listened.

"Is everything in the car?" yelled Tom to Marietta.

I didn't hear her reply, but Tom must have been okay with it, because we heard him hurry past the Jack and Jill door toward the bedroom.

Kip didn't waste a second thinking things through. He threw the bathroom door open and raced behind Tom with the cane. Tom swung the gasoline can he held toward Kip and caught him in the side of the head. Gasoline sprayed everywhere, including on Kip, who stood in stunned silence as a gash on the side of his head gushed.

Tom yelled to Marietta for help. Scoop jumped in and came down hard with the statue. As Tom crumbled, we heard a door slamming. A moment later, a car peeled from the driveway.

I heard Brittany weeping behind me, though she clung to her lamp in the ready-to-swing position. Kip, now holding his head and still dazed, reached for the wall to steady himself. He was wobbly and made no move to take control. In spite of his gushing head wound, Tom was getting up from the floor while gasoline still flowed from the overturned can.

Tom stared at me for a moment, sadly, I thought, and then he looked so resigned that I knew we were in trouble. He reached his hand into his pocket, pulled a lighter, and tried to flick. The flame didn't respond. He was about to try again when I yelled at the top of my lungs, "Fire," and then leaped at him, slamming the scissors down on his hand as hard as I could.

Chapter Thirty

"What I don't understand is why Tom would try to light the fire." Brittany said, looking a little worse for wear. Her edgy haircut was due for a trim. Her temporary wardrobe, designed for a day or two away, now needed a reboot. But it was the way she stared into space and had to be reeled back in that worried me.

"He would have burned along with everyone else," she said, and I knew she couldn't reconcile what had happened yet.

Uncle Richard and Horace were in the kitchen, preparing a light dinner of pasta and salad. Kip, Scoop, Brittany, and I were on the deck, sipping drinks and nibbling on flatbreads from 109 Cheese and Wine. The sun had retreated for the day, and even the mosquitoes feasting on my fair skin couldn't chase me inside. The lake shimmered in the dusk as lights along the opposite shore began to blink on.

I watched Brittany knead Max's fur as if working a stress ball. The dog hadn't moved his head from her lap since we sat down. Good.

Next to them, Scoop sipped a Heady Topper, occasionally sharing in the petting. Diva, our reluctant lifeguard, observed us from the door. Sitting in one of the lounge chairs, Kip looked like a different man in his T-shirt and a pair of Richard's sweats that barely reached his ankles. His gasoline-splashed uniform was also coated with blood from his wound and was now stuffed into a plastic bag destined for the trash. I pulled close to him and applied ice to his swollen cheek.

"He had no way out," said Kip.

"Suicide by cop," Scoop added.

Brittany rose from her seat and said she was going to help in the kitchen. It was probably as much as she could handle, and I knew Richard would work his magic, engaging her in the food prep, soothing her with kitchen jobs. Max followed her in, Diva followed Max, and a moment later Scoop trailed after with a shrug, leaving Kip and me alone.

"I'm not sure I properly thanked you for saving my life," he said. "And the lives of those two." He nodded his head toward the house.

"We wouldn't have made it if Horace and my uncle hadn't arrived to provide all that distraction."

"True, but they wouldn't have even thought to do that if they didn't know where you were going."

Horace, Richard, and the dogs hadn't waited for my SOS. They were already on the way while I was sneaking around the Hemlocker house. According to them, they were hovering at the bottom of the driveway, and when they didn't receive a text from me for over half an hour, they decided to check things out on their own.

"Horace had suggested I park on the Arlington's service road, so they went there first and confirmed where I was. Then they drove over to the Hemlockers' house and rang. When Marietta and Tom insisted we had not been at the house, my uncle and Horace wavered. Fortunately, Diva and Max had our scent. They went crazy and tried to push inside. The ruckus is what gave us enough time to get free."

"I'm surprised they didn't call 911," said Kip.

"They wouldn't have," I said. "Before I left, I told Horace that Tom might be monitoring the police radio."

Kip started to move the ice pack toward his brow and then stopped when he realized what he was doing.

"I screwed up big-time," he said. "I wanted to get a look at the Hemlockers' house before alerting anyone. We had already called it wrong once with David and Bitsy—I just thought if I had a look . . . and I never got your text telling me that Brittany and Scoop were still missing. By then I was wrapped in duct tape."

Kip had already described the thumping he'd heard while talking with Marietta in her foyer. When he asked about it, she feigned worry and asked him to take a look. As he reached Burton's room, Tom slipped up behind and tased him. The noise, of course, had been Scoop and Brittany, trying to attract attention by lifting and dropping the bedpost they were tied to.

"Next thing I knew, I was duct taped to the chair." Kip rubbed his hand across his mouth.

"Sorry about that," I said, gesturing toward the angry red marks circling his mouth.

"Couldn't be helped," he said.

After my uncle and Horace left the Hemlockers', they'd called the police and parked at the bottom of the driveway, blocking anyone who tried to exit. Marietta probably would have rammed them with her Land Rover, but by then the first cruiser had arrived. As Richard told it, there were a few tense moments until he flashed his CERT volunteer ID.

"So, what's going to happen to Tom and Marietta?" I asked.

"She's all lawyered up," said Kip. "And Tom, well, he's a mess. He realizes she's leaving him high and dry, so according to our chief, he's trying to cut a deal."

"I don't think Tom knew how ruthless Marietta was. He also seemed to think Mark had been killed by accident. And when I asked her about Burton's pills, he was truly stupefied."

"He might have been duped," Kip admitted, "but I had a bad feeling about Tom from the start. I had the sense he wasn't being totally honest. He always had a hidden agenda."

"Well, if he was so into Marietta, I'd like to know what agenda he was following by hitting on me."

"Oh, Tom was into Marietta all right. He was also a guy about town. I think he has some kind of complex. Besides, when he found out you were Mrs. Arlington's obituary writer, he and Marietta would have wanted to find out what she might have told you. You said yourself he perked up when you talked about her electronics. Maybe he was hoping to sweep you off your feet and find information that way."

Diva yapped lightly, and I turned to see that she had two feet out on the deck.

"You can do it," I urged her gently. Just then Max bounded out of the kitchen, followed by Richard.

"Dinner!" my uncle announced.

To my chagrin, Diva reversed her steps.

*　*　*

Inside, the dogs positioned themselves nearest those they thought most likely to drop nibbles as we dug into pasta coated in a veggie version of marinara, warm ciabatta, and an authentic Caesar salad, salmonella be damned. Generous glasses of wine kept everyone talking over each other as we relived our roles in the rescue and capture.

"I made the mistake of not remembering that Marietta had a Ring system with security cameras," I admitted.

"We all made mistakes," said Kip. Then he looked at Scoop and Brittany. "For example"—he wagged his finger—"you two were supposed to stay safe and stay put."

Scoop held up a defensive hand. "I know, I know. We let our guard down, but in our defense, all we did was go next door. When we left Horace's house, Tom was waiting for us with a gun, which he promptly pointed at Brittany's head. What were we supposed to do?"

The only one not trying to get a word in was Brittany. She stared at the untouched pasta on her plate.

"Do you want to explain why you trashed the bedroom and study?" I asked her.

The room fell silent, and Kip sent a questioning look my way. Brittany flushed as she realized the question was for her. It had been one of the loose ends bothering me. If Bitsy or Marietta hadn't done it, then who?

"I thought you saw Tom trashing the house," said Uncle Richard, eyeing me.

"True. Tom was looking for the iPad and anything else with the photos," I explained. "Marietta had already found prints in Lottie's bedroom, which was why she was starting a fire—in case the digitals or any other copies were there. The room had already been up-sided before that. And so had the study. If it wasn't Bitsy, Marietta, Tom, or Mark who ransacked the rooms, then it had to be the only other person with access."

Brittany's eyes remained on her plate. Poised next to her, Scoop reached over and touched her just under the chin. She looked up at him. Her eyes were two cups, brimming, just before the surface tension breaks.

"The truth shall set you free," Scoop said. On his face was the same tender smile I imagined he'd worn when he'd coaxed the abandoned kittens to food for the first time.

275

She breathed in sharply and said in a voice surprisingly loud, "It was me who messed things up."

Kip killed the idea with a shake of his head. Horace huffed. Richard appeared pensive. Diva and Max sensed the change and stopped scavenging. The afterglow of the sunset still streaked across the lake, and a reflective sliver caught my uncle's face, one that had seen its fair share of rays. Films of dust danced in the retreating light. It was as if time stood still.

"You started looking for Bitsy's shoe, right?" I asked, breaking the silence.

Brittany nodded again. Scoop squeezed her hand. She relented.

"Bitsy told me what she had done, and I wanted to protect her."

She then recounted the room-by-room search she'd been conducting methodically earlier in the day before Mark and I had met. By the time she reached the second floor, she had begun to panic.

"I knew I was out of time when I got upstairs. Mark told me he was going to meet you and he wanted me to follow you so you didn't bring anyone. I panicked and tossed the bedroom before I had to trail you. I didn't realize Diva had already found what I was looking for."

At the sound of her name, Diva dive-bombed Brittany's feet, receiving a generous head scratch in return. The gesture seemed to give Brittany the courage to continue.

"When I couldn't find the shoe, I decided to search for the iPad and any manuscript copies she might have had. I pulled everything out of the file cabinet."

"Why?" I asked. "You already knew Bitsy wasn't mentioned in the memoirs."

Brittany swatted away a tear and looked hopefully at the ceiling. We waited.

"She was writing the day of the storm," she replied. "She told me she was making the memoirs more accurate by including details about the book club members. By then I knew all about Bitsy's part. Aunt Lottie also said she was adding new information, and I worried it would include references to Bitsy."

Brittany weighed her next words carefully before saying quietly, "I also wanted to keep the memoir."

The room fell quiet before the most cantankerous in the party weighed judgment.

"*Keep* it?" Horace exclaimed.

Brittany nodded.

"But why?" he asked, swerving into a subplot of his own. "There's no reason to keep such things."

I saw Richard catch his eye and nod with a commiserating smile.

"Because I thought it might make a good book someday," Brittany said.

That stopped traffic.

Scoop finally broke the silence. "It probably would," he said, squinting his eyes as if reading the synopsis of the book she'd imagined.

"When I got to her study," Brittany said, "I tore through the files to make sure there were no other copies. After the fire—when everyone had gone—I snuck back to the house to see if anything was left. That's when I saw the *Great Dames Book Club* file on the desk. I knew it wasn't the one from the file drawers, because Bitsy had already taken the papers from that. This file was one I had never seen before."

"Where is it now?" I asked.

She flashed a look at Scoop to see how all this was sitting with him, and his face was even more encouraging now. For him, mild deception took a back seat to a good story.

"Under the seat of the truck."

"And the computer and iPhone?"

She looked resigned.

"How did you know I took them?" she asked.

"You were the only one who could have taken them. Bitsy didn't know a thing about opening a computer, and all she wanted to do was get out of there. She left the electronics where they were. Marietta and Tom wanted the photos, and by the time they searched the house, the electronics were gone. Marietta worried that they were hidden, which is why she was trying to burn the place down."

Brittany nodded. "Same place."

Horace cleared his throat. "Is there anything else you'd care to tell us?" he asked.

Brittany's tears were coming down like a mountain stream after a spring thaw, but she shook her head no.

"Well, if that's it, I'm having seconds," he said, sliding his chair away from the table with a screech.

"Hold on," I said. "Because Brittany has one more thing to add."

I could feel all inquiring eyes on me, but mine were on Brittany. I saw a spark of anger before she blinked and then sighed.

Horace slid back into his chair, not wanting to miss the next layer of this story. Richard continued staring, and I knew his quick mind was probably putting things together. Kip, on the other hand, looked like he was running behind a fast-moving bus. Maybe that knock on the head and taser experience had been worse than the ER docs thought.

"Do you want to tell us the rest?"

She shifted and looked again at Scoop, as if he could give her a way out. Finally, she took a breath and continued.

"I lied about Bitsy not being in the memoirs. And it was me who deleted all references to her in the files," Brittany said. "Aunt Lottie really was going to tell all."

"Did your great-aunt know that you erased things from the files?" I asked.

"I thought she might, and at first I thought that was why she was sending me away."

And there it was. The one thing Brittany was having a hard time reconciling. Had she not tampered with the files and told Bitsy about the memoirs, her great-aunt, the woman she admired and loved, might still be alive. Brittany's head fell back into her hands, and Scoop gently cupped her chin up again. He gave her a kind smile and took her hand.

"She sent you away because she was in danger," I said, gently. "She suspected Marietta's mother had started the fire that killed the threatening coworker and thought Marietta might try something similar on her or someone she loved. If Scoop did his deep dive into Marietta's family history, there were probably other fires that solved sticky problems."

Brittany just shook her head.

"Was Mark Goodwin mentioned in the memoir?" I was now curious as to why Mrs. Arlington would reveal his and Bitsy's secrets if she was all about protecting her family.

Coming clean was doing wonders for Brittany, because she wiped her tears and sat up straighter, ready to answer my question.

"Yes, and he knew it. He wanted me to delete the portions about him, but that would have been a lot harder than just eliminating one book club member. His story was woven into how Aunt Lottie and Roth got together and then all the stuff about Roth's nephew. It would have been way too obvious if I tried wiping him out."

"And did you find the hard copy of the memoir?" I asked.

Brittany nodded. "It's under the seat of the truck along with everything else." She turned toward Kip. "Am I in trouble?"

"That depends," he replied. "Did you push your aunt down the stairs?"

Brittany looked like someone was about to shove *her* off a cliff.

"No," she said, alarmed. "I would never hurt Aunt Lottie. She was good to me. On the day of the storm, I was about to admit to her what I had done, and then the darn driveway alert kept going off. That's when you—Winter—showed up. Later, when I talked with her on the phone from Bitsy and David's house, she told me that she knew what I had done, and she understood why. She also said that she was putting it all back in. She said she wanted it accurate and that I shouldn't worry, because her lawyer had explicit instructions on how and when it would be released. She said she would never throw Bitsy or Mark under the bus."

I suspected that there was a provision in her will that wouldn't allow her memoir to be released until after Mark and Bitsy were gone. And probably David too, for that matter. By then, I wasn't sure who would be interested in reading her memoirs. Unless . . .

"Scoop," I interjected, "remember that *Notable Ridgefielders* that Jack Sanders wrote? Do you think Mrs. Arlington is listed in that?"

I was asking about the compilation of names and vignettes of influential and well-known people that the former managing editor of the *Press* had compiled in order to preserve the town's history on such folks. If Mrs. Arlington was listed, she shared the distinction with such people as famed architect Cass Gilbert, pop star David Cassidy, *New Yorker* cartoonist Roz Chast, actor, producer, and comedian Harvey Fierstein, Judy Collins, Cornelius Ryan, Robert Vaughn, Alice Paul, Eugene O'Neill, Frederic Remington, Maurice Sendak . . . good grief, there were hundreds of notable people, some better known than others, who had called Ridgefield home at one time.

"Not sure if she's listed, but with her interesting history, she probably will be now," Scoop said.

"Wait, you think she wrote her memoirs so there would be an accurate history for the *Who's Who*?" asked Kip, finally catching up.

"Yes, I think she wanted a truthful record of the book club and especially about her relationship with Roth and Henry. That info you sent to my email, Scoop. I finally read through it. Roth had a passion for history."

Scoop's research had provided numerous quotes from Roth expressing the need for accurate historical records. Roth praised the stories the Ridgefield Historical Society kept on town history. It was too bad the man hadn't lived long enough to find out whose remains had been found buried under the Main Street house. The Battle of Ridgefield skeletons dating back to the Revolutionary War might have been right up his alley.

I had also finally read through Mrs. Arlington's thumb drive. The story of Roth and Henry was there.

"That reminds me," said Richard, turning to Brittany. "You told us about how Mark changed places with Roth's nephew. But you didn't say how Roth and Lottie ended up together."

Brittany's lips almost made it into a smile.

"Aunt Lottie was one of Roth's protégés," Brittany replied. "He was good to her and had taught her everything about the company. It was because of Roth that she became an early adopter of computers. I think I get my tech side from her." And now she did smile. "When she tried to blackmail Roth, he was shocked and deeply hurt. But when he finally understood that she was protecting Mark, he struck a deal. She would be his 'lady friend,' as he called her, so he could keep any rumors about him being gay quiet. Eventually, Roth realized what a gift Lottie had given his family. They became very close, and when my aunt moved to Ridgefield, the three of them became a family. Mark came shortly thereafter and lived close by."

"It's only recently that people have been willing to include same-sex marriage partners in obituaries," I added.

"You should watch the old Robin Williams movie *The Birdcage*," said Kip. "It's a funny movie, and you can see the extremes people felt forced to go to hide their homosexuality."

Brittany's disinterested shrug said it didn't matter. "Anyway, together they got to work trying to clear Andrew Arlington's name. They couldn't make it public that Mark had switched identities, so they concocted a story that said Andrew had been misidentified as another soldier and that soldier had disappeared."

"The army didn't want to know how Roth found out it was his nephew who had died?" asked Scoop incredulously.

"That part was easy," she said. "With DNA these days, Roth was able to demand proof that the dead soldier wasn't his nephew."

"Once the army found out that it was Andrew who died and not Mark, wouldn't they list Mark as a deserter?" asked Scoop.

Brittany shrugged again. These were details that didn't matter to her. "Roth had money, power, and connections. And even if the records did show a deserter, the name wouldn't be Mark Goodwin."

It seemed odd that a man who was so hell-bent on accurate historical records would be okay with not telling the entire story about Mark.

And then I got it.

"The memoirs were part of the deal Mrs. Arlington made with Roth," I said. "The record would eventually be set straight after Mark had died. The Ridgefield Historical Society would have the accurate account, including Mark's real name—all part of the memoirs."

"The records for Andrew Arlington were changed," said Brittany. "I don't know about the rest."

It was at that moment that my phone rang. I fished it from my pocket and stared at the screen. Attorney Sondra Milton was calling.

* * *

Sondra was able to tie up more loose ends for us. Yes, there was a letter signed and notarized explaining how Mark Goodwin had changed identities. It was to be released after Mark Goodwin's death, and Sondra was letting me know that she was in the process of sending it to army officials as well as any long-lost next of kin. How the army would rectify the history was up to them.

She confirmed that Lottie's memoirs—sent to Sondra as each chapter was completed—would be released to the Ridgefield Historical Society after anyone who might be harmed by them had either died or given consent to divulge the information.

"I wondered if you could write up the portion about her death. You would be handsomely compensated," said Sondra.

"I'm already being handsomely compensated," I pointed out. "No need for anything additional. Have Bitsy and David signed off?"

"Yes, and all of the other principles are gone or have signed off," she said. "Lottie didn't extend the provision to children, so the Wysockis' son does not have to be notified, although I'm sure Bitsy and David will tell him. Marietta Hemlocker or any of the other progeny from book club members don't have to be told, though I am trying to track them down as a courtesy. Imagine finding out about your mom's past from a book!"

I chewed on that for a moment.

"Who owns the intellectual property rights for the memoir?" I asked.

"You are quick," said Sondra. "Her great-niece, Brittany Bennett. Her will stipulates that Brittany can sell the memoir as is, or she could rewrite it into a salable format, but she cannot alter any of the facts. It also stipulates that she doesn't have to do either but that she must release the original to the Ridgefield Historical Society within a certain period of time regardless. Bottom line, Brittany can do what she wants for profit as long as the historical record is set straight and the Ridgefield Historical Society receives both the published version and the original unedited version."

"It's sad to think that in the end, Mark will be listed forever as a deserter," I said. "He was good to Mrs. Arlington."

"In a way, the day Mark shed his former identity was the day he was born," said Sondra. "Mark Goodwin's adopted name won't be mentioned as the deserter—it will be his birth name."

* * *

After dinner was cleared, Horace and Richard retreated to Horace's deck for a nightcap. By now, stars twinkled overhead and the brightly lit beacon of a moon spotlighted the Cliffs across the lake. Scoop and Brittany thought it an ideal evening for a dog walk and no doubt a good time to discuss the pros and cons of her next steps.

That left Kip and me alone, sitting in the empty living room with only the buzz of crickets, frogs, and quiet chatter from the deck next door filtering through the sliders.

I wondered aloud if Brittany knew how close to death she had come, not once but twice, and what affect that would have on her future. If Marietta had stumbled upon her while the girl was searching the house, she might have met the same fate as Mark.

Dead Brittany would have set a different set of wheels in motion. She and Scoop would not have been kidnapped, which would mean that Kip never would have gone searching for them at the Hemlocker house. Marietta would have burned down the Arlington estate— goodbye iPad photos, and the only loose end would have been Mark, who would have disappeared. Tom and Marietta would have ridden off in the sunset with an ample fortune.

"I don't think everything has completely registered with Brittany yet," said Kip. "Now that her own deception is out in the open, she might start reliving it all."

"At least she will have Bitsy and David for support."

"And don't forget Scoop. He is Velcroed to her, in case you haven't noticed."

"Oh, I noticed, and I'm not sure who I'm more worried about: Scoop breaking Brittany's heart or Brittany breaking his."

"Did you finish reading through Mrs. Arlington's emails?" Kip asked. "I really do have to turn that iPad over to the detectives."

"Yes. I've forwarded those I might want for a future story to myself and left everything as it was on the iPad. You won't get in trouble for that, will you?"

"We solved a murder. I think they'll give us some leeway."

"We were right, by the way," I said. "Marietta started threatening Mrs. Arlington right after Diva arrived. And she was nasty, saying things like she had proof of all the blackmails and that she was going to take Mrs. Arlington and her family down. I think most was bluster."

The back-and-forth emails confirmed that Mrs. Arlington had suspected Marietta of holding back Burton's medications and she'd used the photos of Marietta and Tom as leverage—*take care of Burton or your affair will be revealed to Burton's son*. At first Marietta was compliant, saying she would make the appropriate doctor's appointments immediately. When she didn't follow through, Lottie had given her a deadline, which was now three weeks ago. That's when Marietta told her that if she even hinted at her affair to Burton's son or anyone else, Marietta would tell everyone about all the illegal blackmailing that Lottie had done.

"If Lottie was already writing her memoir, why worry over the blackmail schemes being revealed?" asked Kip. "The statute of limitations for blackmail would have run out by now."

"Marietta's email said, *If you don't play, both you and Burton will pay*. In the end, Lottie was afraid for Burton's life. And if Marietta was willing to harm him, she was also willing to harm her—and, for that matter, anyone else she cared about."

"Which is why she was sending Brittany away," Kip said.

I reached for the iPad on the side table. No cloud, no emails on her computer, and Brittany would have had no idea about the threats because she hadn't had access to the iPad, the only place Mrs. Arlington had her email account listed.

"Something specific must have triggered Mrs. Arlington's need for an obituary by Friday," said Kip.

"Oh, something did. The last email that Marietta sent was dated the same day Mrs. Arlington called me." I opened the iPad, logged in, and went to Mrs. Arlington's Gmail account to read aloud. "*Someday very soon you will awaken in the night and think you died and are burning in hell—where you belong. It won't be hell yet, but you will wish it was. And you will be joined shortly thereafter by your friend Burton. Sweet dreams, Lottie. M.*"

"I guess that would be enough to make you think the woman was a nutjob who wanted you dead," said Kip.

"Lottie already suspected Marietta's mother of murder. It wouldn't be much of a leap to think her daughter would follow through on her threats. It would also make her scramble to finish her memoir and put her affairs in order, just in case. She sent the memoir to Sondra Milton, one chapter at a time, because she was afraid she would never get to finish it. And she made plans to send Brittany away."

"I wonder if the memoir talks about Marietta at all," said Kip. "Wouldn't she want that record set straight too?"

"I think Mrs. Arlington had one singular goal, and that was to live up to her promise to Roth by documenting the truth about the book club and his nephew. I think her gripe with Marietta was just Mrs. Arlington using the only tool she felt she had to protect her friend. If Burton died first, she would probably have revealed the affair out of revenge. Marietta would have known that."

"The moment Mrs. Arlington went after Marietta, she placed herself in danger," said Kip.

"Agreed," I said. "The irony is it wasn't Marietta who caused her death. It was simple bad luck, and like David said, she could have tripped down those stairs at any time."

"Bad luck and bad timing," said Kip.

Kip removed the iPad from my lap and rose. "I should go."

And then, unexpectedly, he reached for my hand and pulled me to my feet. The iPad still in hand, he wrapped his arms around me and pulled me close. I closed my eyes. It felt so safe.

"I was so angry when Tom and Marietta stuck you in that room," he whispered into my neck. "I thought you were our only hope of survival and that you would send help. And then I realized that my failure to call my chief before I went to the Hemlockers' house might get you killed too, and I felt sick."

"You're the one who said Tom was probably listening in on all the police transmissions," I said. "I didn't think 911 was a good idea."

"You do know you have a tendency to think you can fix things without help," he said, pulling back enough to look into my eyes. "Asking for help is something you might want to work on."

"That's like the pot calling the kettle black," I said as I pushed away farther.

Kip released me with a grin, took my face in his free hand, and studied me. "Like I said, I'm not good with jokes. Whew, that's a pretty bad bruise on your chin."

"Yours isn't anything to write home about either," I said, and we both laughed.

"How did you know that Brittany had edited Bitsy out of the memoirs?" he asked, growing serious again.

"I guessed. Mrs. Arlington was all about setting the record straight. If Brittany had been frantic looking for the shoe and any references to Bitsy in the files, it didn't take much of a leap to think that Brittany would go the extra mile to protect Bitsy."

"So, if Mrs. Arlington was all about accurate records, then why were Bitsy and Roth still removed from the original file in her drawer—the one Bitsy stole?" he asked.

Every part of my body was aware that Kip still had his hands circling my waist. When he brushed a stray lock from my face, I thought I might forget all the promises I had made to myself about avoiding commitment and drag him upstairs to the bedroom. Instead, I turned away from his steely eyes and concentrated on the question.

"When Brittany made the changes like she said, Mrs. Arlington probably left them that way so the girl would stop tampering with her memoirs. Sondra Milton confirmed that the version sent to her named everyone—including Bitsy and Mark."

"The Nosy Parkers are going to have a field day with this story," said Kip.

"There won't be much left for them to distort," I said. "Scoop will see to that. He's probably already got the story half written."

"From what you've told me, that hasn't ever stopped them before," said Kip, and then, releasing his grip, he moved toward the front door.

When he was parallel to the study, he paused and looked through the open door toward the train room, where I could just make out the shadows of the mountain pass. "If you're not too tired, I was wondering if you might show me," he said, and waved his hand in the direction of the beckoning space.

I glanced toward my refuge—the private place I shared only with my uncle. Showing Kip would be opening up a part of myself that I wasn't sure I was ready to expose. He would want to know about the cars loaded with happy families, the little cemetery beside the lake.

Every scene in that room was weighted down with a part of my history, a history I wasn't sure I wanted to share.

Before I could answer, he said, "Ah, looks like you might prefer that I leave."

The house, still quiet, held the lingering aroma of the enticing vegetarian sauce from Richard's comfort food dinner. We had turned on only a few lamps, and the ambient light reflecting off the lake was as soft as candlelight. Through the open sliders I could hear the low murmur of Horace and Richard chatting, an occasional outburst of laughter echoing off the lake as they sipped bourbon on the deck next door. Everything seemed so normal, and yet it was not. Horrific memories from our near miss today still bubbled close to the surface.

I moved in front of the door, blocking his exit. "I could make some tea, and I still have chocolate chip cookies we could bring out to the deck."

I looked at him hopefully. Would that be enough for now?

Kip grinned widely. And then he pulled me close.

"That sounds great," he whispered, and followed it with a kiss filled with such longing that I wished it would never end.

When we pulled away, Kip was smiling again.

"What was that for?" I asked, determined that this time he would give me an answer.

"That was for me." And he cupped my chin and kissed me again.

And then I suddenly knew.

I took his hand and led him through the study and into the train room.

I lifted the small remote from the train table and began pushing buttons. Kip smiled like a little kid, delighted as the room lit up with chugging trains meandering over hills, illuminating the tracks as they went.

"And this," I said as I met his eyes, "is for me."

Acknowledgments

From my first wobbly steps into the world of fiction, you might have thought that I just woke up one day and said, "hey, I think I'll write a book." Nothing could be further from the truth. My early story-telling memories are of my older brother and me hiding under a tent of blankets in our adjoining cribs and telling stories. Thank you to Rick Karwoski for being the inspiration for my first Uncle Richard. Six renditions later, Richard barely resembles my brother except to say that *good cook and messy kitchen* still resonate.

There is no question in my mind that this book would still be in its fledgling stages if my son Christian Lewis had not taught me how to knock some energy into my story. Christian is an amazing writer and editor himself and I'd like to say he got his talent from me, but in reality, it's turning out to be the other way around.

I applaud my sister Michele Karwoski who shares my love of mysteries, waded through all six versions of my book, met three different protagonists, and read through multiple characters and plots. And to my sister Leigh Karwoski, what would I do without your willingness to use your incredible eye for detail to do a last-minute read?

Acknowledgments

My very first readers—and this still makes me cringe to think of how awful that first version was—were my dear friends Sally and Jack Sanders to whom I am forever grateful. Sally was my former editor during my first newspaper writing days. She offered no nonsense advice, and when it comes to editing, the girl has a gift! Jack Sanders spent 47 years covering Ridgefield as a reporter and editor before retiring. He now focuses on keeping Ridgefield's history alive through books, social media, talks and the work he and Sally do at the Ridgefield Historical Society. It is Jack who keeps me on the straight historical track.

Adam Chromy of Moveable Type Management, nicknamed in our household as Agent Adam . . . gets a big shout out. I met Adam at a small New York City Conference and after I pitched my first book, he asked if I could turn my secondary character into my primary. Despite the fact that I had buried the lede, had a character that he promised no-one would like, and had a lot to learn about writing fiction, this no-nonsense guy never quit on me—even after how many rewrites?

Thrilled is how I felt when Tara Gavin, an acquisition editor for Crooked Lane Books said she loved my story. Tara, thank you and the entire team for all you have done to help me realize a dream that started in the cradle—oops, I mean the crib. And a special thanks to Rebecca Nelson for always answering all my questions so patiently and for keeping the production world running smoothly.

Many people helped me tweak to finalize this book, not just for accuracy but for content, punctuation, and to beta read. Ridgefield's Emergency Management Director Dick Aarons, an avid mystery reader himself, spent hours on numerous topics including teaching me how smoke travels. Thank you my friend for your continued willingness to share your bottomless pit of knowledge. Thank you Ridgefield's Police Chief Jeffrey Kreitz for his willingness to talk procedure

Acknowledgments

and to Captain Jeffrey Raines for his crash course in tasers. Thank you to my beta readers like Jan Elliot who would not let me submit my first three chapters without her critical grammatical eye. Also, I'm grateful to Mark Elliot, Dianne and George Russell, Dick Sanderson, Dave Goldenberg, and especially my sister-in-law Linda Drake who read my book in a hurry when I needed input.

In my thirty plus years as a writer, I've met many deadlines as three little faces pressed against my closed study door. Thank you to our children, Tyson and Christian Lewis and Gillian Sheerin for not rolling their eyes as I talked plots and process—and for cooking and cleaning up after family events so I could get back to the computer. To Shelby and Miles Lewis—your enthusiasm for my *Mirabelle* stories gave me courage to start this quest. And I thank our grandchildren Holden and Hunter Lewis and Lylah and Dylan Sheerin who were so excited about my mystery that they have started one of their own. I can't wait until it is finished. A most important thanks goes to Bob, my husband, who never stops believing in me, is always supportive with great ideas and who is already packing for a book tour!

And last but never least, I'm grateful to my readers and to my fellow mystery writers who offer support and share my passion.